FRENCH PASTRY MURDER

Books by Leslie Meier

MISTLETOE MURDER

TIPPY TOE MURDER

TRICK OR TREAT MURDER

BACK TO SCHOOL MURDER

VALENTINE MURDER

CHRISTMAS COOKIE MURDER

TURKEY DAY MURDER

WEDDING DAY MURDER

BIRTHDAY PARTY MURDER

FATHER'S DAY MURDER

STAR SPANGLED MURDER

NEW YEAR'S EVE MURDER

BAKE SALE MURDER

CANDY CANE MURDER

ST. PATRICK'S DAY MURDER

MOTHER'S DAY MURDER

WICKED WITCH MURDER

GINGERBREAD COOKIE MURDER

ENGLISH TEA MURDER

CHOCOLATE COVERED MURDER

EASTER BUNNY MURDER

CHRISTMAS CAROL MURDER

FRENCH PASTRY MURDER

Published by Kensington Publishing Corporation

A Lucy Stone Mystery

FRENCH PASTRY MURDER

LESLIE MEIER

KENSINGTON BOOKS
www.kensingtonbooks.com

KENSINGTON BOOKS are published by

Kensington Publishing Corp.
119 West 40th Street
New York, NY 10018

All Kensington titles, imprints, and distributed lines are available at special quantity discounts for bulk purchases for sales promotion, premiums, fund-raising, educational, or institutional use. Special book excerpts or customized printings can also be created to fit specific needs. For details, write or phone the office of the Kensington Special Sales Manager: Attn. Special Sales Department. Kensington Publishing Corp., 119 West 40th Street, New York, NY 10018. Phone: 1-800-221-2647.

Library of Congress Card Catalogue Number: 2014943592

ISBN-13: 978-0-7582-7704-6
ISBN-10: 0-7582-7704-0
First Kensington Hardcover Edition: October 2014

eISBN-13: 978-0-7582-7706-0
eISBN-10: 0-7582-7706-7
First Kensington Electronic Edition: October 2014

10 9 8 7 6 5 4 3 2 1

Printed in the United States of America

For Anne Toole

Chapter One

Lucy Stone shut her eyes tight and rolled over, trying to ignore the ringing phone on her bedside table. When that didn't work, she wrapped a pillow over her ears and held it tight, but the ringing continued. She knew who was calling, and it was beginning to be a nuisance, these phone calls at five and six in the morning. Sighing, she glanced at the clock, which read 6:30, noting a small improvement in timing. She picked up the handset and pressed it to her ear, bracing for the coming verbal onslaught.

"Mom! It rang and rang. I thought you'd never answer. I thought something had happened. . . ."

If only, thought Lucy, imagining herself someplace far away. A desert island, perhaps. "No. I'm fine. I'm right here, in bed. You woke me up."

"I'm sorry. I can't get the hang of this time difference. France doesn't switch to daylight savings for a couple more weeks. . . ."

Lucy wasn't up to making complicated time zone calculations, but she knew the clock had sprung forward last week. "It's six thirty here, in the morning, and I was asleep."

"I'll try to remember . . . but it's just . . . well, I . . . I . . ."

Lucy gritted her teeth, wishing she could avoid hearing the sobs of her oldest daughter, Elizabeth. "There, there," she murmured. "It's not so bad. . . ."

"It is! It's h-o-o-orrible!" exclaimed Elizabeth, her voice wobbling through her sobs. "I ha-a-ate Paris!"

Despite her affection for her oldest daughter, Lucy was finding it hard to sympathize with her constant complaints about her new situation. After working in Palm Beach for the luxurious Cavendish Hotel chain, Elizabeth had recently been promoted to assistant concierge in the Paris hotel. To Lucy, it seemed like a fantastic opportunity, especially since she herself had always dreamed of going to Paris but had never managed to make the trip.

"I know change is never easy," admitted Lucy, in a consoling tone.

"Everything they say about the French is true," declared Elizabeth. "They're rude and bossy, and they talk too fast, and when you ask them politely to '*Répétez, s'il vous plaît*,' they give you a condescending little smile and switch to English. How am I supposed to improve my French if they always speak to me in English, huh?"

"They probably think they're being helpful," said Lucy.

"No, that's the last thing on their minds. They're putting me down. That's what they're doing."

"It's easy to feel a bit paranoid when you don't quite understand what people are saying," suggested Lucy.

"Paranoia? Is that what you think? That I'm paranoid?" She paused. "You know what they say about paranoia. You're not paranoid when they're really out to get you."

"Who's out to get you?" asked Lucy.

"They all are, especially my coworkers. I know

they're just aching to get rid of me and take my job, they don't think I deserve it."

"Maybe you're the one who doesn't think she deserves it," said Lucy, hastening to add, "But you do. You did a super job in Palm Beach."

"That's yesterday's news," muttered Elizabeth. "Nobody here knows, or cares, about Palm Beach." She sighed. "I really miss my cute little apartment with all my nice stuff."

Lucy was busy listening between the lines, suspecting Elizabeth didn't actually miss her West Palm Beach apartment all that much but did miss her boyfriend, Chris Kennedy. Elizabeth hadn't been talking about Chris much lately, and Lucy suspected the relationship hadn't survived the long-distance separation.

"The place I've got here is tiny and grotty," continued Elizabeth, "and I really do have the roommate from hell. Sylvie has taken the bedroom all for herself, and I have to sleep on a fusty old futon. I think I'm allergic to it. And she smokes!"

"It's a big adjustment, but you'll manage," said Lucy, yawning and thinking longingly of her morning cup of coffee. "And you'll be a better, stronger person for rising to the challenge."

"Mom, that doesn't sound like you," said Elizabeth, finally lightening up. "What have you been smoking?"

"Nothing," insisted Lucy, "nothing at all. But I did watch Norah on TV yesterday. She had one of those motivational people on. 'If you dream it, you can do it.' "

"It's not that easy," said Elizabeth. "Sometimes your dreams turn into nightmares. Or *cauchemars*. That's what the French call them."

Lucy found herself smiling, satisfied that once again she'd talked her daughter off the ledge. "Hang in there, sweetie. Mommy loves you. And Daddy, too."

"I know," replied Elizabeth. "Thanks for listening."

"Anytime," said Lucy. "But preferably after lunch. Call me after you've had lunch. I should just about be finishing my shower then."

"I promise, Mom. Bye."

Lucy replaced the handset in its holder and flipped back the covers, getting out of bed. Winter tended to linger well into spring in the coastal Maine town of Tinker's Cove, and it was chilly in the upstairs bedroom on this mid-March morning, so she quickly put on her robe and slippers and hurried downstairs to join her husband, Bill, in the toasty warm, bacon-scented kitchen.

Bill was a much-sought-after restoration carpenter who fixed up vacation homes for old-time Yankee families from Boston and Wall Street hotshots. He was already dressed for the day in a plaid flannel shirt, jeans, and work boots. His still sported a healthy head of hair and a full beard, but the brown was now mixed with gray. "Elizabeth again?" he asked, filling a mug with coffee and handing it to her.

Lucy cradled the mug in both hands and took the first, life-giving sip. "Yes. She hates everything in Paris—the people, her roommate, her job."

The toaster popped, and Bill buttered a couple of pieces of toast, arranged them on a plate, and added the eggs and bacon he'd been frying. He sat down at the table and took a bite of bacon. "An improvement," he said philosophically. "Yesterday it was the entire country, all forty million Frenchmen, or however many there are now."

Lucy joined him at the table. "You are an optimist," she said with a sigh. "I'm disappointed in Elizabeth. I really am. This is a wonderful opportunity, and I don't think she's taking advantage of it." She paused, taking another sip of coffee. "You know, I took French in high school. I bet I could get along just fine in Paris."

That thought remained in Lucy's mind as she got herself ready for the day and saw her two younger daughters, who were still living at home, off to school. Zoe usually caught a ride with her friend Renée, shunning the school bus now that she was a junior at Tinker's Cove High School. Sara drove herself to nearby Winchester College in an aged, secondhand Civic. Lucy's oldest child and only son, Toby, lived on nearby Prudence Path with his wife, Molly, and their just-turned-four-year-old son, Patrick.

Since it was Thursday Lucy didn't have to get to work early; the deadline for the *Pennysaver* newspaper, where she was a part-time reporter and feature writer, was noon Wednesday, and the paper came out on Thursday, giving the staff of three a brief reprieve before they started work on the next week's edition. For years now she'd met three longtime friends for breakfast on Thursday mornings at Jake's Donut Shack; they all considered this weekly get-together a top priority.

This morning she was eager to share her anxiety about Elizabeth with the group and get their input, as they were all mothers and had plenty of experience guiding their children through young adulthood. When Lucy arrived, she found Rachel Goodman and Pam Stillings already seated at their usual table. She gave a wave to Norine, the waitress, and joined them.

"Another phone call," she began as Norine set a mug of coffee in front of her. "At six thirty this morning. Elizabeth is driving me crazy."

"She's all alone in a strange country," said Rachel, who was a psych major in college and had never gotten over it. "She feels alienated," she said, twisting a lock of long, dark hair. "She needs lots of support."

Lucy took a swallow of coffee, then shook her head.

"I can't believe she's not rising to the occasion. I mean, what I wouldn't give to be in her shoes."

"I know," agreed Pam Stillings, who was married to Lucy's boss at the *Pennysaver,* Ted Stillings. "Imagine being young and beautiful and in Paris!" Pam was a free spirit; she still clipped her hair into a ponytail and often wore the poncho she'd picked up during her junior year in Mexico.

"It's not that simple," insisted Rachel, adjusting the horn-rimmed glasses that covered her huge brown eyes. "Life isn't like perfume ads. Elizabeth is in a completely foreign culture. They even speak a different language. It's no wonder she's struggling to find her footing."

"I guess so," grumbled Lucy, looking up as Sue Finch arrived.

Sue was the glamorous member of the group, and this morning was no exception. Her glossy black hair was styled in a flawless pageboy, and she was wearing skinny black jeans and a bright color-blocked tunic. "What do you guess?" she asked, slipping into her seat.

"That it's entirely normal for Elizabeth to be miserable in Paris," answered Lucy.

"*C'est dommage,*" cooed Sue, adding a translation for the others. "It's too bad. I love Paris. I love everything about Paris. . . ." She curved her scarlet lips into a smile, seeing Norine approaching with a coffeepot. "Except the coffee cups are too small and everyone smokes."

"Regulars for everyone?" asked Norine. Receiving nods all round, she left the pot on the table and trotted off, scribbling on her order pad.

"That's one of Elizabeth's major complaints," said Lucy, picking up the conversation. "She says her roommate smokes all the time and stinks up their apartment, which is tiny."

"I can't seem to work up much sympathy," said Sue.

"You are hard-hearted," teased Pam as Norine arrived with a sunshine muffin for Rachel, yogurt topped with granola for Pam, and hash and eggs for Lucy. Sue never had anything more than black coffee and lots of it.

"No, I'm not," insisted Sue. "In fact, I have some amazing news. Norah is doing a show about women who make a difference. . . ."

They all knew that Sue's daughter, Sidra, was a producer for Norah Hemmings's Emmy-winning daytime TV show. "And you're one of those women?" asked Lucy, jumping to a conclusion.

"No. At least I don't think so. But Sidra says Norah wants to tape the show right here in Tinker's Cove."

"Here? Why here?" asked Rachel.

"Sidra says she thinks it's because Norah has that fabulous vacation house here and she's exhausted and wants a bit of a break. So she's going to tape the last show of the season here, and then she's going to turn off the phone and lock herself in her twenty-two-room mansion by the sea for a period of silent rest and recuperation."

"She's got millions of dollars and dozens of assistants who do everything for her, including walking the dog and running her bath. How can she be exhausted?" asked Pam.

"It's the constant pressure to perform. I'm sure it's terribly stressful," said Rachel. "She needs time and space to get in touch with her authentic self."

"Just turning off the phone sounds wonderful," said Lucy. "With twenty-two rooms, do you think she'd have one little room for me?"

"I doubt it," said Sue, grinning wickedly. "But Sidra says we can all have free tickets to the taping."

"Aren't they always free?" asked Pam.

"Don't quibble," admonished Sue. "Just think, you

get to see the show live without having the expense and trouble of traveling to New York."

"Wow," Pam said cynically. "Can't wait."

As it happened, Pam didn't have long to wait. In a matter of days a crew of workmen arrived and began constructing a temporary enclosure on the Queen Victoria Inn's spacious outside deck overlooking the cove. A stage with a seating area for guests was placed in front of large glass windows that provided a fabulous view of pine trees and a scattering of houses with steeply pitched roofs, and a glimpse of the harbor, where a few boats bobbed in the choppy waves, newly freed from the ice, which had melted only a few weeks ago. Heavy-duty power lines were installed for cameras and lights, and propane heaters and theater seats were added for the comfort of the audience.

Lucy covered the entire process for the *Pennysaver,* which got only a few letters demanding to know why Norah hadn't used local workmen instead of sending her own crew of carpenters. Most Tinker's Cove residents were caught up in the excitement, eagerly awaiting the glamorous TV star's arrival and looking forward to seeing the show live in their very own hometown. The free tickets quickly became a hot commodity, and those lucky enough to hold them got cash offers from people who wanted to see the show, but few gave in to the temptation to sell, refusing even fifty and a hundred dollars per ticket.

When the big day finally came, Lucy and her friends were seated in the very first row.

"It pays to have connections," said Sue. "I'm sure Sidra got these seats for us."

She pointed to her daughter, who was holding a clipboard and conferring with a lighting technician. Tall and New York City thin, she looked terribly professional in tailored black slacks, a gray cashmere sweater topped with a chunky necklace, and leopard-print ballerina flats.

"The lighting is always beautiful on the Norah show," said Rachel. "I don't know how they do it, but the people in Norah's audience always look terrific."

"Norah always looks amazing," said Lucy. "She's no spring chicken, that's for sure."

"I bet she's had plastic surgery," snorted Pam. "It's easy to look good when you can afford face-lifts and facials and professional makeup."

"I think it's the hair," said Sue. "When your hair looks good, you look younger. Frizz makes you look older."

"Really?" asked Lucy, who was suddenly painfully aware that she hadn't bothered to style her hair that morning but had given it only a good brushing.

Sue nodded. "Lucy, you should blow-dry every morning."

Lucy was about to protest that, what with breakfast and getting the girls and Bill out the door, she didn't have much time for herself, but she was distracted when Sidra came over, kissed her mother, and asked if they were all comfortable.

"Front row seats. We feel very special," said Pam. "I suspect you had something to do with it?"

"Nothing's too good for Mom's friends," said Sidra. "Geoff and I really appreciate everything you did for us—all the cards and flowers and food you sent."

Sidra's husband, Geoff, had needed a kidney transplant at Christmas, and the surgery was made possible through a chain of donors and recipients that included the Cunningham family in Tinker's Cove.

"How is Geoff doing?" asked Lucy. "He's been through a lot."

"It's amazing. He's doing great."

"It must be quite an adjustment, psychologically, I mean," speculated Rachel, "and not just for Geoff. You both had to face the possibility that his life would be cut short at a young age. . . ."

Before she could continue in this morbid vein, the music started, a lighted sign blinked on, signaling, AP-PLAUSE, and there was Norah herself, in the flesh. Sidra beat a hasty retreat, while the audience clapped enthusiastically. Norah was a local hero, and there was no need for the sign. They were welcoming her home.

"Thank you," said Norah. "Thank you. Thank you." The queen of daytime TV was gorgeous in a shocking pink dress and matching lipstick, her hair a perfectly smooth helmet, her skin aglow, and her teeth dazzling white. She waited while the clapping subsided, then began introducing the theme of her show: women who make a difference. "I'm happy to tell you that right here in Tinker's Cove you have an amazing group of women who have worked together for more than twenty years to make a difference for local children."

Lucy began to have a slight inkling of where Norah was going with this, and nudged Sue. "Could she possibly be talking about us?"

"No." Sue shook her head. "Don't be silly. The Hat and Mitten Fund is tiny. I bet she's talking about the Hospital Auxiliary."

"Twenty years ago these four moms, all with young children of their own, began collecting hats and mittens for less fortunate children," continued Norah.

Lucy's jaw dropped, and she noticed Pam and Rachel were equally stunned. Sue turned and grasped Lucy's hand. "I was wrong," she whispered.

"Dubbed the Hat and Mitten Fund, the four moms went from simply collecting donated hats and mittens to actively raising funds to make sure that every child in Tinker's Cove is ready for school with warm winter clothing, a nourishing breakfast, and a backpack full of school supplies." Norah paused, adding one of those impromptu asides that made everyone watching the show believe that she was right there in their living room, talking directly to them. "Over the years we've added this up. These four women have raised over five hundred thousand dollars. . . ."

Here the audience erupted into enthusiastic applause.

Norah nodded sagely. "I know. Five hundred thousand dollars. It's a lot of money, and it's all gone for the benefit of local kids. So now I ask you to welcome these women who make a difference. Sue Finch, Rachel Goodman, Pam Stillings, and Lucy Stone. Come on up, ladies."

Lucy found herself unable to move, but Sidra was at her elbow, guiding her, and she joined the others, all equally dazed as they made their way up the steps to the stage. It was terribly bright under the stage lights, Lucy was blinking, and the applause was a roar in her ears. Then they were all sitting down on a long couch, and a screen dropped behind them and a video was shown. Lucy recognized Lexie Cunningham and her daughter Angie, and Lexie was saying how the Hat and Mitten Fund had helped her family when Angie was in the hospital, waiting for a kidney transplant. Then a smiling and healthy Angie was shown, sporting her backpack and climbing onto the school bus. The picture faded, the screen slid out of sight, and the audience was once again clapping enthusiastically.

Lucy wanted to get up and tell them to stop, tell them that they hadn't done anything special, that they'd just seen a need and tried to fill it. She felt like a fraud, un-worthy of all this attention. Wouldn't anybody do the same thing?

"I'm sure these women would all say that they didn't do anything extraordinary," said Norah. "But the truth is that just by being good neighbors, by helping others in their town, they have made a real difference. They have made Tinker's Cove a better place for children and families and . . ." Here she paused dramatically, appealing to the audience. "Don't you think they deserve a reward?"

From the roar of approval that followed, it seemed that the audience did think they deserved a reward. What would it be?

"An all-expense-paid trip to Paris!" announced Norah as the lilting notes of "La Vie en Rose" began to play and the screen began showing footage of the Eiffel Tower, Notre-Dame, and tourist boats on the Seine.

"Imagine! April in Paris! All four ladies, and their husbands, will be going to Paris for two weeks, where they will stay in a luxury apartment in the very trendy Marais district, and . . . there's more!"

The pictures on the screen changed, and it now showed a professional-style kitchen and a chef wearing a tall white toque. "While enjoying all the attractions of the world's most beautiful city, they will also get a week's worth of lessons at Le Cooking School from renowned pastry chef Larry Bruneau!"

Lucy glanced at Sue, thinking that her friend looked as if she'd died and gone to heaven. "I can't believe it," mouthed Sue, nudging the others.

Sidra must have been behind this, thought Lucy. Only Sidra would have known how much Sue, a gourmet cook, would enjoy lessons from a genuine chef. And Paris, that was another of Sue's enthusiasms. Sidra had come up with the idea for her mother, and the rest of them were tagalongs. But that was okay with her. She didn't care about cooking classes; she was more interested in gardens and museums. But she was finally going to get her dream of seeing Paris, and more importantly, she'd be able to spend time with her unhappy daughter. She was smiling, she realized, and she couldn't seem to stop. Now she was actually jumping up and down, right along with her three friends. They were all holding hands and jumping up and down like sorority sisters who all had dates for Spring Fling. They were going to Paris!

Chapter Two

It was the light. There was something special about the light in Paris, thought Lucy as the minivan rocketed along the Seine River. Maybe it was the time of year, April, or maybe all the gray buildings and the stone embankments that bounded the Seine, but the sunlight wasn't at all like the hearty, dazzling blast you got in Maine. It was thinner somehow, gentler and more liquid, as if it were coming through a filter.

"That's Notre-Dame," said Sue, poking her in the ribs and pointing out the window.

So it was. Lucy had seen the cathedral only in pictures, but there it sat, solid and massive, complete with those amazing flying buttresses, right on an island in the middle of the river. "I can't believe I'm really here," she said.

"Well, you are," said Bill, who was seated behind her in the crowded van.

The van driver had been waiting for them when they got through immigration, holding a sign that read TINKER'S COVE EIGHT. *A touch of humor from Norah,* Lucy had thought, *or, more likely, Sidra.* The driver, Henri, had led them through the chaotic terminal at Charles de Gaulle Airport and through the automatic doors to the even more disorganized scene outside, where roadway repairs were forcing buses, cars, taxis, and vans to jostle for space at the curb.

"This would never happen in the U.S.," Sue's husband, Sid, had declared when a tiny Renault simply stopped in the middle of the single open lane to discharge a passenger, who took his own sweet time saying good-bye to the driver, heedless of the tie-up he was causing. Sid's voice was full of disapproval. At home he designed and installed closet systems and liked everything to be in its proper place.

The four American couples had followed Henri, pulling their wheeled suitcases to a quiet parking area, where he'd helped them load their luggage into the van, arranging it like a puzzle. Then they had all squeezed inside, fitting their American-size bodies into the European-size van.

"I give you tour of Paree, no?" Henri had said, flooring the accelerator and zooming into traffic to be greeted with a chorus of beeps from the other drivers.

The first part of the drive had hardly been scenic. It was the sort of grimy autoroute that you'd find in the United States, leading into Boston or New York. But then they were in the city proper, and it looked exactly like Paris ought to look, with parks and shops and six-story buildings with tiled mansard roofs, French windows, and tiny balconies. Lucy could hardly take it all in.

"La Tour Eiffel," announced Henri, pointing at the iconic structure. Then they crossed the river and were whizzing around the l'Arc de Triomphe, where a huge blue, white, and red French flag hanging from the center of the arch fluttered in the breeze, surrounded by a whirling ring of traffic. Horns blared as Henri took a right, cutting off several miniscule Smart cars, and headed right down the Champs-Élysées.

Then Lucy caught a glimpse of the famous glass pyramid in the courtyard of the Louvre, so quick she would have missed it if she'd blinked, and then they were battling traffic once again on the rue de Rivoli.

"Fantastic shopping here," said Sue, adding in a reverential tone, "Bay Asch Vay. It's the very French version of a hardware store."

"Looks like BHV to me," said Pam. "Whatever could that mean?"

"It means expensive," said Sid with a sigh, resigned to Sue's passion for shopping.

Then they were caught in another whirling roundabout, this time around the tall verdigris column that now stood in place of the Bastille prison, which was destroyed by an angry mob in 1789, sparking the French Revolution.

"They make such a big deal about it, but there was only a handful of prisoners inside," said Ted Stillings, Pam's husband. As editor and publisher of the *Pennysaver*, he had a journalist's commitment to the facts.

"It was symbolic," said Bill, yawning. Lucy knew her husband needed his eight hours every night, and he hadn't been able to sleep on the overnight flight. Neither had she, for that matter.

"I always feel so badly for poor Marie Antoinette," said Rachel, who could probably find something nice to say about Idi Amin. "She seems so sweet."

"I think you're thinking of Kirsten Dunst in the movie," said Sue.

"She was married to a fool. Louis XVI was a terrible king," said Ted.

"The whole system was rotten," said Rachel's husband, Bob Goodman, who was a lawyer. "The king could get rid of anybody he didn't like. He would simply issue a lettre de cachet with some poor devil's name on it, and off he went to prison until the king decided to let him out."

"It's still rotten," said Henri, surprising them all with his command of English. He took an abrupt turn down a quiet, very narrow street and braked in front of a pair of double doors, like old-fashioned garage doors, that were covered with unsightly graffiti. "Voilà. Neuf rue Roger Verlomme."

They all scrambled out onto the sidewalk and stood awkwardly, looking down the empty street, which was lined with blank walls punctuated here and there with similar doors, all tightly closed. A few windows boasted window boxes planted with ivy and spring flowers, but even they were heavily curtained and offered no clues to the rooms within. Charming streetlights, styled like lanterns, hung here and there from the buildings.

"What do we owe you? How much?" Ted asked Henri as he reached for his wallet.

"No problem. All paid," said Henri, but seeing Ted replacing his wallet in his pocket, he added pointedly, "Did you enjoy the tour of Paris?"

Sid was on it. He had a couple of euro coins he was intending to give to Henri, but Sue stopped him. "Give him a twenty," she hissed.

Sid gave her a look as if she were completely mad, and Bill stepped up, slipping Henri a twenty-euro bill. "All set?"

"Merci," replied Henri. "Have a nice time in Paris." He paused, indicating a small treed plaza at the end of the street, filled with chairs and tables. "That's a nice café," he added before jumping into the driver's seat.

Then the van was gone, and the eight Americans, tired from the overnight flight, as well as the struggle at the baggage carousel and the long lines at immigration, were standing on the street, next to a pile of suitcases, apparently locked out of their promised luxury apartment.

"What now?" asked Rachel.

"Try the buzzer," advised Sue, pointing out a keypad fixed to the wall beside the doors.

Rachel pushed the one button that didn't have a letter or number, and moments later one of the big doors popped open and a slender woman of a certain age, her gray hair beautifully coiffed, and wearing a flattering blue scarf around her neck, welcomed them. "*Bienvenue,*" she said. "I am your concierge, Madame Defarge. This way, please."

Lucy, somewhat giddy from a lack of sleep, stifled a giggle. She remembered reading Dickens's *A Tale of Two Cities* in high school, with its unforgettable portrait of a fictional Madame Defarge, who knitted as the guillotine did its gruesome work eliminating the nobility, as well as anyone who opposed the revolutionaries during the Terror.

This Madame Defarge held the door for them, waiting as they gathered up their bags and stepped into a spacious cobbled courtyard, where a tree was leafing out, pots of spring flowers were lined up along the walls, and a few bicycles stood in a metal rack. The courtyard was bounded by several separate buildings, each with a doorway marked by a letter. Their doorway was labeled A, and once inside they found themselves faced with a rather treacherous-looking spiral staircase.

"One flight up," said Madame, pointing. "First floor."

"Isn't this the first floor?" asked Pam.

"No, no. This is the *rez-de-chaussée,*" said Madame. "First floor is one flight up."

"Better not all go at once," cautioned Bill, drawing

on his experience as a carpenter. "I don't think it will hold us."

"Nonsense," said Madame, leading the way. "This *escalier* has been here since the last century, maybe longer."

"Probably longer," sighed Sid, taking in the crooked tilt of the landing.

"The key is special, very dear," said Madame, holding up an enormous piece of brass hardware.

"I'll say," agreed Sid admiringly.

"There's only one?" demanded Sue. "For eight people?"

"There's another inside." Madame adopted the attitude of a teacher. "Now, you must pay attention. In Paris we are very careful to lock the door because of thieves. So you must not, not ever, carry the key and the address together, because then a pickpocket or thief could steal your things."

Lucy and Rachel found their eyes meeting, somewhat in disbelief. In Tinker's Cove nobody locked their doors, and residents often had to search for their forgotten keys when they wanted to leave for a long vacation. Some people even left their keys in their car when they ran into the Quik-Stop for a gallon of milk.

"And now I want to tell you about the entrance keypad," continued Madame. "The code is one-five-two-three-A, and you must never divulge it to anyone, or you will put all your courtyard neighbors at risk."

"One-five-two-three-A," repeated Lucy.

"Not out loud," hissed Madame, implying Lucy was revealing a state secret.

"Sorry," said Lucy, repeating the code to herself like a mantra.

"Now we go in."

As Madame busied herself with the key, which had to

be turned several times, Lucy imagined what the apartment would be like. Over the years she'd collected a number of *Country French* magazines and catalogs, and she pictured a cozy interior filled with comfy chairs and sofas upholstered in toile de Jouy fabric or perhaps Provençal prints, copper pots hanging from beamed ceilings and plenty of those mustard-colored crocks.

"*Entrez,*" announced Madame, opening the door and revealing featureless gray walls, a huge expanse of parquet flooring, a pair of enormous white leather sofas, a Lucite block serving as a coffee table, and French windows covered with severe blinds. "Very luxurious, no?" she asked.

Lucy bit her lip, trying to hide her disappointment.

"Very modern," enthused Sue. "Roche Bobois, n'est-ce pas?" she asked, naming a high-priced French furniture company with a store in Boston.

"*Peut-être,*" replied Madame with a shrug. "*La cuisine, c'est ici,*" she said, leading them around the corner of the L-shaped space to point out a sleek modern kitchen.

At least that was what Lucy thought it was. There was a huge white marble island streaked with gray, which held a tiny sink and a cooktop, but not even a spoon was in sight. One wall was lined with pale wood cabinets, but the joinery was so subtle that Lucy never would have guessed their function had Sid not picked a spot and pressed against it, popping open a door. "Very nice," was his verdict.

"The bedrooms are this way, down the hall," trilled Madame. They followed her through the dining area, which featured a Parsons table and white leather chairs, and down a long hall, where she opened a door, revealing a huge bed covered with a shaggy white fur spread and a sleek mirrored armoire. "The bath is beyond," she said, pointing to a door that was hidden in the wall. "Who will take this room?"

"We will," said Sue, shouldering her way past her friends.

"*Bien.*" Madame led them to the opposite room, similarly outfitted, which Rachel and Bob agreed would do fine for them.

Pam and Ted got the next room, which left only one door remaining in the hallway. It had a stained-glass window, and when Lucy opened it, she found a rather dated, old-fashioned bathroom with a rolltop tub. "Where's the bed?" she asked.

"The sofa," replied Madame. "The sofa is also a bed."

"This apartment is supposed to sleep eight," said Bill. "That's what we were told."

"*Bien sûr.* Three *chambres* and one sofa bed in the salon."

"We don't have a bedroom?" asked Lucy.

"No, madame. You have the sofa and this bath."

Bill peered into the bathroom. "The tile is cracked," he said. "It needs renovating."

"It is a charming period *salle de bain,*" insisted Madame.

"It's fine," said Lucy, who knew when she was beat. "I've seen worse."

"In a gas station," muttered Bill.

"*Quoi?*" asked Madame, eyebrows raised.

"Nothing," said Lucy, turning to Bill. "I guess we'll stash the suitcases here. What do you think?"

"I think I'd like a nap," said Bill, yawning and heading back down the hall to the living room.

"I hope you'll be very *confortable,*" said Madame. "The second key is in the kitchen drawer. And now I will leave you."

Lucy took advantage of the bathroom, which had a certain boho charm and was actually more to her taste than the rest of the ultramodern apartment, and freshened up. Then she returned to the living room, where Bill had stretched out on one of the sofas. "You shouldn't nap," she said. "It's better to tough it out and keep going."

"Who says?" asked Bill, yawning.

"The travel experts."

"She's right," said Sue, joining them. "How's your room?"

"This is our room," said Lucy.

"You're kidding!" exclaimed Rachel, rubbing lotion into her hands as she joined them.

"What a bum deal," added Pam, seating herself on the other sofa.

"What's a bum deal?" inquired Bob.

"Lucy and Bill have to sleep on the couch," said Pam.

"That stinks," said Sid.

"What stinks?" asked Ted.

"There's no room for Lucy and Bill, just a sofa bed. At least I think it's a sofa bed," explained Sue.

"It's a sofa bed," sighed Lucy, who was leafing through a loose-leaf notebook she'd found in the kitchen, one containing instructions for the apartment, and came upon a lengthy explanation of the operation of the sleep sofa. "But it's not the kind we're used to. It's going to be tricky."

"France is tricky," said Bill before dozing off with a snore.

"No, no, no," said Lucy, shaking him. "It's noon and . . ."

"It's actually six in the morning U.S. time," said Bob.

"Our bodies think it's six," agreed Ted, "and they're wondering why we've been up all night."

"Well, whether it's six or noon, it's mealtime, and my body is wondering when it's going to be fed," said Pam.

Sue, who had been exploring the kitchen, found the refrigerator concealed behind a wooden panel. "There's at least a case of champagne in here," she announced. "And a huge tub of pâté de foie gras."

"Terrific cabinetry," said Sid, who was busy opening doors and drawers. "And lookee here. All kinds of gourmet stuff." He was sorting through a number of cans and jars. "Olives and mustard and looks like jam."

"My goodness," said Pam, looking over his shoulder. "It's like an entire grocery store. There's coffee and tea."

"And caviar," said Sue, examining a tiny can.

"There's a case of red wine, too," said Ted, who had found it stored in a utility closet containing controls for the electricity, heat, and hot water.

"Is this all for us?" asked Rachel.

"I think Norah must have arranged it," Sue said, speculating. "We're going to be living high on the hog, but we can't live on champagne and caviar alone. We'll need to shop for meat and vegetables and bread."

"There's supposed to be a Monoprix grocery store on the rue Saint-Antoine," said Lucy, who was still studying the notebook.

"I can't wait. I'm starving," complained Pam.

"The café on the corner?" suggested Lucy. "It says here it's the closest restaurant."

"The driver recommended it," said Sid.

"D'accord," said Sue. *"Allons-y!"*

"Whatever," grumbled Bill, hauling himself off the sofa.

The café, Chez Loulou, was hopping when they opened the door and stepped into a crowded bar. "Huit pour le déjeuner?" inquired a tall black man, speaking over the heads of the people standing at the bar.

Lucy glanced around at the crowded room, doubtful they could be accommodated.

"Is there a table?" asked Sue, also doubtful.

"No problem," he replied, snapping his fingers. In minutes a couple of young waiters dressed in black had appeared and rearranged the tables, lining several together for the group.

"Wow. That was fast," said Pam, slipping into a bentwood chair.

"I am Loulou," said the host, distributing menus. "I am afraid today we are out of wine," he said with a shrug.

"No wine?" wailed Sue. "How is that possible?"

"It is not possible. It is just a joke," Loulou said and laughed as a waiter arrived with a couple of carafes of house red. "Today the special is *bœuf bourguignon*, Provençal-style."

"Sounds terrific," said Pam, and they all nodded their heads in agreement. All, that is, except Sue.

"I'll have salad," she announced.

After lunch the members of the group went their separate ways. Sue wanted to go straight to BHV, and Sid agreed somewhat halfheartedly to accompany her. "It's a hardware store," she told him. "Really. French hardware. You'll love it. And it's not far. We can walk, stretch our legs after the flight. We can also look for that Monoprix grocery store."

Rachel and Bob wanted to visit the Mémorial de la Shoah, commemorating the French Jews killed in the Holocaust, but couldn't interest the others.

"Pam and I have a college buddy here in Paris," said Ted. "Richard Mason. He's at the *International New York Times*. He told us to call him first thing, as soon as we got here."

"And I want to see Elizabeth," said Lucy. "She got the afternoon off to spend time with us."

"Not us," said Bill, covering an enormous yawn with his hand. "I'm going to take a nap."

"You'll be sorry," advised Sue.

"Your metabolism will never adjust if you do that," agreed Ted.

"I don't care," said Bill. "I've got to get some sleep."

"Elizabeth will be so disappointed . . . ," protested Lucy.

"You know you're dying to have a mother-daughter chat," said Bill, and Lucy had to admit he was right.

After a quick phone call to make arrangements, Lucy agreed to meet Elizabeth at the Cavendish Hotel on the boulevard Haussmann. The Métro posed no threats to Lucy, who had grown up in New York City. In fact, she was quite impressed by the clean station and the trains, which arrived every five minutes. She had no trouble at all finding the hotel, but there was no sign of Elizabeth at the concierge's station in the beautifully decorated lobby. Instead, there was a large framed photo of a bespectacled middle-aged man propped on the chair behind the ornate Louis XIV desk.

There was also a stack of printed brochures with the same photo, which identified the portly man in the photo as Ahmed Fouad II, king of Egypt. Intrigued, Lucy picked one up and read the text, which claimed that Fouad, his preferred name, ascended the throne in 1952, when his father, King Farouk I, abdicated in his favor, hoping to appease antiroyalist forces. It apparently didn't work, as Colonel Gamal Abdel Nasser rose to power and the royal family remained in exile in Europe.

Lucy read on, straining to recall her high school French, not to mention her world history class. She knew there had been some sort of Suez crisis a long time ago, and that tourists had been massacred in Egypt at some point, but now the country was in turmoil as popular demonstrations brought down succeeding governments. Perhaps, she thought as she replaced the brochure, this faction hoped to restore stability by reestablishing the monarchy.

"Mom!"

Lucy turned to greet her daughter, exchanging the requisite two *bisous,* or kisses, one for each cheek, which made her feel terribly sophisticated.

"I'm sorry I wasn't here," apologized Elizabeth. "I have to help prepare for this conference. Les Amis du Roi de l'Égypte." She picked up the framed photo and the stack of brochures. "I just have to take these to Monsieur Fontneau. He's my boss. I'll be right back."

Lucy watched as Elizabeth hurried off down a long hallway leading to various function rooms, then strolled around the luxuriously appointed lobby, pausing to examine an enormous arrangement of fresh flowers set on a marble table. Crystal chandeliers glittered above, a plush patterned carpet was underfoot, and conversational groups of furniture were scattered about.

One such grouping, she noticed, was occupied by a group of men deeply engaged in a discussion. Lucy couldn't understand whatever language they were speaking—it certainly wasn't French—but it was clear that there was a difference of opinion. She observed a lot of head shaking and waving of hands, until two of the participants stood up, facing off angrily. One, a distinguished-looking man in his midsixties with gray hair, dressed in a beautifully tailored but somewhat out-of-date suit, was attempting to lay down the law to a younger man, who suddenly turned on his heel and marched off in a huff. She watched as he crossed the lobby, guessing that he'd picked up his ill-fitting sport coat in a flea market, and thinking that he looked as if he was going to cry. "Malik!" called the older man, but he didn't stop.

A slice of life, thought Lucy, who was about to sit down when Elizabeth returned, beaming. Her smile reminded Lucy of the times she had taken her out of school early for one reason or another. Back then, even a dentist appointment was preferable to spending another hour in school. She found Elizabeth's cheerful attitude reassuring and was relieved to see she hadn't spent all her time in Paris crying on the phone. She had had her hair styled in a chic new cut and had clearly done some shopping. She was wearing a new chunky scarf slung around her neck, topping an adorable black coat and a pair of high-heeled ankle boots.

"Love your coat," said Lucy, studying the flattering coat as they went down the stairs to the Grands Boulevards station. It was tightly fitted across the shoulders and bust but fell into loose gathers around the hips.

"Wish I could say the same about yours," replied Elizabeth, commenting on Lucy's orange and brown plaid jacket. "You're not in Tinker's Cove now, you know."

"I see you've lost none of your, um, spark," said Lucy as they boarded the train. "I can't wait to see your apartment."

"It's a dump," grumbled Elizabeth, grabbing the pole as the train started with a jerk.

Lucy glanced around the train, which was filled with people, mostly reading newspapers or consulting their smartphones. They looked quite a lot like New Yorkers, she thought, mostly dressed in black, with well-worn walking shoes. "I have a theory that the people in big cities are all alike," she said. "They're citizens of the world. It's only the country folk who are true to what we think of as French or American."

"I don't think that's necessarily true," said Elizabeth. "Believe me, Parisians are not at all like Bostonians or New Yorkers. You'll see what I mean when you meet Sylvie."

Lucy shrugged and continued studying the ads plastered on the walls of the Métro car, which were mostly for English lessons. *Same as in New York,* she thought, following Elizabeth out of the train at the next stop and up the stairs. Then she was hurrying along, panting to keep up with Elizabeth's city strides. How did she manage in those heels? Lucy wondered when they finally stopped in front of another set of graffiti-covered doors and Elizabeth punched in her security code. This time the courtyard wasn't very pretty at all. It was filled with motorcycles and trash cans and kids' toys, and laundry was hanging from lines strung from window to window. The paint on Elizabeth's door was peeling, and the spiral stairs inside were even ricketier than the ones in Lucy's place.

"We're on the top floor," said Elizabeth, charging up the first flight. Lucy followed, pacing herself on the climb, pausing now and then to catch her breath.

"I bet you've got a nice view," said Lucy, panting as she finally reached the top-floor landing.

"You'd bet wrong," snapped Elizabeth, unlocking the door.

Stepping inside, Lucy saw that Elizabeth hadn't exaggerated. The apartment was every bit as grim as she'd claimed: the walls were covered with hideous dark green wallpaper, and the windows opened onto the courtyard, with its array of laundry.

"I'll give you a tour," said Elizabeth, taking Lucy's coat and tossing it on the futon. "My bedroom." She added her own coat, then pointed to the round table with four chairs, which filled most of the room. "The dining room. Also the living room. It's multipurpose."

"Open space," said Lucy.

"And not much of it," said Elizabeth, opening a door. "The kitchen." Lucy peered into a tiny, dark room that was mostly filled with an ancient prefab unit combining sink and cooktop. Elizabeth opened another door inside the kitchen, announcing, "*La toilette.*"

Indeed, inside the small space, which would be a closet back home, she found a toilet, sink, and rusty metal shower. "It's got everything you need," said Lucy, determined to look on the bright side.

"Except space to towel off," said Elizabeth. "I have to do that in the kitchen."

"How European," said Lucy, grinning.

"It's not funny," grumbled Elizabeth. "I'd show you Sylvie's room—she's got the only bedroom—but she keeps it locked."

"Locks are a big deal here," ventured Lucy. "Our concierge, Madame Defarge, gave us a very stern lecture about how important it is to lock the doors. I mean, really, what's the big deal? What do we have that anyone would want?"

"You'd be surprised," muttered Elizabeth, cocking her head to the sound of keys rattling outside the apartment door. A moment later the door opened, and her roommate stepped in.

"Elizabeth," she cooed in a deeply accented voice. "Is this your *maman?*"

"I'm Lucy Stone," said Lucy, noticing that Sylvie was a very attractive, petite blonde with flawless skin, delicately arched brows, and a self-satisfied smile. Like Elizabeth, she was wearing a black coat, black tights, little boots with heels, and a chunky scarf.

"And I'm Sylvie, Sylvie Seydoux." She extended her chin, and Lucy realized it was the *bisous* thing, requiring two kisses, and cooperated in the exchange.

"Shall we go for *café?*" suggested Sylvie. "It's not so nice here."

Lucy would have been perfectly happy to remain sitting on the saggy, musty futon, but it seemed there was to be no rest for her. She put on her coat and followed the girls down the four flights of stairs and through the courtyard and down the street to the corner café. Cafés, it seemed, were everywhere.

"Inside or out?" asked Sylvie, and they decided to sit outside, in the weak Parisian sunshine.

Coffee wasn't served in the big cardboard container Lucy was used to getting at the Quik-Stop. It was a tiny china cup of black sludge, which Sylvie and Elizabeth tossed back in one gulp. Lucy sipped hers, grateful for the caffeine jolt, even though she suspected it would keep her up half the night.

"So what are your plans while you are in Paris?" asked Sylvie, lighting a cigarette.

"I'm here with friends, so I guess I'll go along with whatever they want to do. And we're all signed up for cooking classes."

"That should be interesting," said Sylvie, blowing smoke. "But what do you like to do? *Les musées? Les jardins?* Shopping at Printemps and Galeries Lafayette?"

"I'm on a bit of a budget," admitted Lucy, finishing her coffee. "No, you know what I'd like to do? I'd like to go to the flea market. I've always heard about how wonderful it is."

"Les Puces!" exclaimed Sylvie. "Of course! We must all go next weekend. I will show you, okay?"

"That would be great. Thanks," said Lucy.

"Great," grumbled Elizabeth.

"Well, I have to go," said Sylvie, glancing at the smartphone that was permanently fixed to her hand and stubbing out her cigarette in the ashtray. She rose and distributed *bisous* to Lucy and Elizabeth, then trotted off down the street, attracting admiring glances from every man she passed.

"She attracts them. I don't know how she does it," said Elizabeth, watching her make her way down the street. "She's got a man in her room every night, a different man. It's disgusting."

"She seems nice enough," said Lucy.

"You try living with her," advised Elizabeth. "Sometimes I'd just like to kill her."

"Don't say things like that," said Lucy, spying a florist shop across the way. "Come on," she said, standing up. "I'll buy you some flowers to brighten up that apartment."

"It'll take more than flowers," said Elizabeth.

"Well, it's a start," said Lucy, determined not to let her daughter spoil her vacation. "Look! Lilies!" She pointed to the price, which was displayed on a card. "And so cheap!"

"It's euros, Mom, not dollars," said Elizabeth, adding, "Believe me, nothing here is what it seems."

Chapter Three

I never should have had that coffee with Elizabeth and Sylvie, thought Lucy, and she was doubtful that the waiter's promise that her after-dinner *café Américain* was decaf was actually true, because here she was, wide awake on the sofa bed in the great gray room, lying beside Bill, who was snoring steadily despite his afternoon nap. It was an odd feeling, she decided, being absolutely bone-tired and still not able to sleep.

She reached out to the Lucite coffee table and checked the time on her cell phone: 2:30 a.m. That would be something like 9:30 or 10:30 p.m. at home, which was her usual bedtime. So why wasn't she asleep?

Pounding the pillow, she flipped over and closed her eyes tight, determined to will herself to sleep. Finding that impossible, she rolled over onto her back and decided to work out what was bothering her. She was physically tired, the bed was comfortable, and she was tucked in beside the man she loved. Check. So the problem was emotional; some unresolved issue was preventing her mind from shutting down. Everything was fine back home in Tinker's Cove. She'd spoken to her son, Toby, earlier that evening, and he had assured her that her daughters Sara and Zoe were settling in fine with him and his wife, Molly, apparently enjoying the chance to spend time with their little nephew, Patrick.

No, she knew perfectly well it wasn't anxiety about the situation in Tinker's Cove that was keeping her awake. It was her worries about Elizabeth. She had hoped that when she actually saw her daughter in Paris, she would discover that her complaints were largely unfounded, that she'd been exaggerating about her unhappiness. But now that she'd seen the apartment, and the roommate, she had to admit that Elizabeth's situation was less than ideal.

Another girl would shrug her shoulders and get on with her life, making the best of things, but that girl was not Elizabeth. Elizabeth was a perfectionist, she tended to see things as black or white, and she had a priggish streak. She rarely ate meat, she didn't smoke or drink, she certainly didn't indulge in drugs, and Lucy suspected she was rather prudish when it came to sex. She'd had a serious boyfriend in Florida, Chris Kennedy, but hadn't mentioned him much lately, except to say he had achieved his lifelong dream of becoming a government agent and was involved in some sort of lengthy training program. But Lucy had no idea whether it was the FBI, CIA, or some other agency.

Lucy could see that Sylvie—who had what she assumed was a very French attitude about life—was not the roommate Elizabeth would have chosen. The smoking and the male guests were bad enough, but Lucy thought it was the secretiveness that probably bothered Elizabeth the most. She'd had roommates in college, and Lucy remembered the open doors in their dorm suites, and the constant discussions dissecting their most personal problems. For Elizabeth, that locked bedroom door was an insult, a constant reminder that Sylvie didn't trust her.

Sighing, Lucy rolled over and reached for her phone, checking the time once again. Almost three thirty. She yawned. *A promising development,* she decided, snuggling up to Bill. Maybe now she'd sleep.

Several hours later she woke to find Bill bringing her a cup of steaming coffee. "Sue and Sid went out and bought croissants for breakfast," he told her. "We're supposed to be at the cooking class at eight o'clock."

"What time is it now?" she asked, reaching for the coffee.

"Almost seven."

"I didn't get to sleep until after three," she said, grumbling.

"I slept great," said Bill, who was dressed and freshly shaved.

"I know," grumbled Lucy.

"Up and at 'em," said Bill in an encouraging tone. "The bathroom is all yours."

When the Americans arrived at Le Cooking School, which was located only a few blocks away from their apartment, they found their teacher waiting for them outside, standing on the sidewalk in front of his pastry shop. Chef Larry Bruneau was easily identifiable. With his curly red hair and flamboyant mustache, he looked exactly like the cartoon-style portrait on the Le Cooking School sign that hung above the door. Lucy guessed he was about thirty, and noticed he was wearing expensive-looking sports clothes rather than chef's whites.

Le Cooking School was upstairs, he explained, above the patisserie that bore his name in swirling gold letters. The window was filled with a luscious display of baked goods: glossy fruit *tartes,* tempting éclairs, and pastel-colored *macarons,* as well as simpler offerings, like madeleines, *palmiers,* and the delicious butter cookies called cat's tongues, or *langues de chat.*

"They're absolutely gorgeous!" exclaimed Sue. "Look at those gorgeous Napoleons. I've always wanted to learn how to make puff pastry. When do we start?"

Chef Larry gave her an indulgent smile. "We're going to begin at the beginning," he told them, speaking unaccented American English. "We're going straight to the Marché des Enfants Rouges."

"Did you say red children?" asked Lucy, puzzled.

"Commies?" joked Ted.

"There used to be an orphanage in the area," explained Chef Larry, "and the children wore red uniforms."

"Oh," said Rachel. "And what are we looking for at the market?"

"*Les pommes,* apples, in particular, and the general experience, to get a flavor of the French approach to food and cooking," replied Chef Larry, leading the way through the narrow, twisting streets, past trendy boutiques and tired-looking cafés.

"This reminds me of SoHo," said Sue, who paid frequent visits to her daughter Sidra in New York City. "And not in a good way. It's very touristy."

"Not the *marché.* It's the real thing," announced Chef Larry, leading them past some tacky sidewalk stalls featuring watches and jewelry and into a covered area where fruit and vegetable vendors had set up lavish displays of fresh produce.

"My goodness," sighed Lucy, taking in the huge, colorful arrangements boasting varieties she'd never seen except in garden catalogs. "White eggplant. And look at all that gorgeous asparagus, green and white, too. And the pears and apples . . ."

"Today," announced Chef Larry, holding up his hand, "we're going to make a traditional French apple tart. . . ."

"Tarte tatin," said Sue, letting the teacher know she was no novice when it came to French cooking.

"Just so," agreed Chef Larry, looking bemused. "And what varieties of apple would you suggest?"

"At home I always use Northern Spies," said Sue.

"Here we look for a sweet apple, an Auslese or a Tokay. And, of course, this time of year, they are imported."

"I thought those were grapes," muttered Ted as Chef Larry led them down the concrete-floored aisle to a stand featuring nothing but apples. All sorts of apples: red and green, yellow and striped.

"Ah, madame," cooed Chef Larry, approaching the proprietor, a plump woman wearing a flowery, ruffled apron over her gray sweater. "Qu'est-ce que vous avez pour moi aujourd'hui?"

She replied in rapid-fire French, and the two engaged in a lively discussion, punctuated with much gesturing and pointing to the various kinds of apples. In the end, she filled a large bag for him, he handed over an astonishing number of euros, and they all headed out of the market.

Lucy paused, her eye caught by a particularly beautiful display of lettuces, and found she had to hurry to catch up to the others, who were now gathering on the sidewalk outside the market. She was intent on the group and didn't notice a man who was also approaching the narrow opening between the stalls that served as an exit, and bumped into his shoulders. She glanced at him, expecting him to yield, perhaps with a charming French version of "Ladies first." Instead, he glared angrily at her, giving her a fleeting impression of dark eyes beneath a flourishing unibrow and a three-day beard, then rudely brushed past without an apology. She watched, stunned, as he charged ahead and went straight for Chef Larry, yelling something at him and giving him a shove. Chef Larry staggered but managed not to fall, the apples spilled, and she heard Bill shouting, "Hey, there!" Then the guy was gone, running down the sidewalk, and they all scrambled to gather up the apples, which were rolling every which way.

"What was that about?" she asked, handing Chef Larry an apple that had rolled in front of her feet.

"Nothing, nothing at all," he said with a dismissive shrug. "I guess he was in a hurry."

Lucy wasn't convinced the assailant was merely in a hurry. She thought he'd attacked Chef Larry on purpose. "Do you know him?" she asked.

"Why would I know him?" he countered. "He probably saw his girlfriend with another man or something. He's just some thug, a *sale mec*. This sort of thing happens all the time." He was taking his time, concentrating on inspecting the apples as he replaced them in the bag. Finally, when the last one had been retrieved and stowed in the bag, he declared, "No damage done. *Allons-y.*"

The group trailed along, exchanging glances but avoiding discussing the incident, following Chef Larry back to the cooking school. They clustered together outside a door squeezed between the patisserie and the neighboring beauty salon while Chef Larry dealt with the security keypad, then continued on up three long flights of dusty stairs to the school. Lucy shrugged out of her jacket and tied on a starched white apron, which boasted an embroidered version of the same Le Cooking School logo that was on the sign. As she tied the tapes around her waist, Lucy decided that the classroom resembled the home ec classrooms of her youth, with a modern upgrade: the instructor's demonstration area boasted a huge video screen. The rest of the room was divided into six separate mini-kitchens for the students, each equipped with a generous counter, a sink, a stove, and a tiny refrigerator. The couples distributed themselves around the classroom and waited while Chef Larry got the video system running.

Lucy was tired and found her mind wandering, reviewing the incident at the market, while Chef Larry demonstrated the correct way to cut the apples. He began by peeling and coring them, then divided them into perfectly smooth hemispheres. When the demonstration was complete, he distributed the apples and set the students to work. Lucy yielded the knife to Bill and let him handle the slicing. Chef Larry circled the room, checking on the students' progress. He corrected Bill's technique and then went on to observe Sue and Sid.

"*Très bien, madame,*" he told Sue, giving her neat paring job an approving nod.

"Thanks." Sue put down her knife. "I make a similar tart at home, you know. I hope we'll be trying some more advanced recipes."

"Absolutely. Tomorrow we will advance to *pâte à choux,* and on Wednesday I will teach my foolproof method for classic pastry dough, *pâte brisée.*"

"But don't we need *pâte brisée* for the tarte tatin?" asked Sue as Chef Larry pulled his cell phone from his pocket and gave it a glance. "And I'm really eager to learn your method for puff pastry."

Chef Larry furrowed his brow and replaced his phone in his pocket. "Not today, madame. I have adapted the classic tarte tatin for my students. We will see how far we get, but *pâte feuilletée* may be a bit ambitious for this group."

"But you will teach us *pâte brisée?*" persisted Sue.

Chef Larry reached for his phone once again, giving it only a quick glance before slipping it once again in his pocket. "As I already mentioned, madame, *pâte brisée* will be taught on Wednesday."

"Terrific," said Sue. "And maybe you could demonstrate *pâte feuilletée?*"

"You are perhaps ahead of the other students," said Chef Larry, with a nod at Pam, whose attempt to core an apple had resulted in shattering it. "I will be with you in a minute, madame."

"How come you're teaching?" asked Sue as he started toward Pam. "I'd expect a young chef like yourself to be working at a top restaurant, apprenticing with a master chef."

"I like to be my own boss," replied Chef Larry, reaching into his pocket for the phone, which he glanced at and then turned off. "I don't want to chop carrots and onions for fourteen hours a day, getting yelled at by some petty tyrant and getting paid only peanuts for doing it." He stowed the phone in a drawer. "Besides, pastry is my true love."

"I don't blame you," said Sid. "I wouldn't work for anyone but myself." He paused. "I've heard the taxes are real high here. Is that true?"

"True enough," said Chef Larry, taking the knife from Pam and demonstrating the correct way to core an apple. "You want to caress the apple," he said in a velvety tone, "coax it to give up its core, like so. And then we will cook it ever so gently, bathing it in butter and sugar and a touch of vanilla, allowing the true essence of the apple to be revealed in the most delicious way."

Pam's chin dropped, and she seemed to loose her footing, almost swooning until Ted grabbed her by the waist. "That sounds wonderful," she said with a sigh.

"It's just an apple tart," snapped Ted.

"Not *just* an apple tart," said Chef Larry. "Believe me, your palate will be amazed!"

It was well after one o'clock when the tarts finished baking and were turned out to cool. The aroma was heavenly, and the tarts themselves were beautiful, topped with glistening caramelized globes of apple.

"Tomorrow we will eat!" declared Chef Larry, dismissing the rather disappointed students.

"What now?" asked Lucy as they all made their way down the stairs.

"I vote for lunch at a café," suggested Rachel. "There's one across the street."

Lucy followed her pointing finger and noticed a man lurking in a doorway opposite the patisserie. He was wearing a leather jacket, and she thought he looked a lot like the guy with the unibrow who had attacked Chef Larry in the market, but she couldn't be sure, because of the distance.

"There's always a café across the street," cracked Sue, pulling a Zagat guide out of her purse. "The question is whether it's any good."

"We're in Paris. They're all good," said Ted.

"That's not necessarily true," said Sue. "There's quite a lot of second-rate tourist food around. We shouldn't go anywhere that has menus printed in English, German, and Chinese."

"We don't need to be too picky," said Bob. "I'm so hungry, I could eat a horse."

"That could probably be arranged," said Sid with a wry grin.

"Let's try Les Deux Magots. I read about it in a travel magazine," suggested Pam. "It's famous."

"Nobody goes there anymore," said Sue, brushing off Pam's suggestion.

Pam's face reddened at the put-down. "It was just an idea. . . ."

"The Flore will be crowded," said Sid, who was reading over Sue's shoulder.

Lucy didn't like the way things were trending. As a mother of four, she'd refereed plenty of squabbles, and that wasn't the way she wanted to spend her vacation. She tapped Bill on the shoulder and whispered in his ear, "I'm too tired for this. Let's go."

He nodded in agreement. "I think Lucy and I will head over to the Left Bank," he said. "I read that Hemingway used to shoot pigeons for his dinner in the Luxembourg Park."

Sue raised her eyebrows and inquired in the voice that had made her such an effective preschool teacher, "Do you mean the Jardin du Luxembourg? That's not far from the cafés in Saint-Germain."

But Bill didn't answer. He and Lucy were already halfway down the block. Lucy felt her spirits lifting, almost as if school was canceled due to snow. "They're great friends," she began. "I love them all."

"But it's good to be on our own," said Bill, taking her hand. "Now, the question is, how do we get to this jahr-dan?"

"Let's not worry about it," said Lucy. "Let's just wander a bit and see where we end up."

"But first, let's eat," suggested Bill, leading her into a tiny, crowded café. They squeezed themselves around a free table, lined up with other tables, all occupied. A waiter appeared, gave them menus printed only in French, a bottle of water, and a basket of bread. Lucy consulted the list of specials and quickly decided on the *croque-monsieur,* which, the menu stated, was made with famed Poilâne bread. Bill skipped the menu and pointed to the dish the neighbor at his left elbow was eating with great enjoyment, and announced he would have the same. Lucy noticed the waiter's reaction; he seemed both surprised and impressed at this American's choice.

The food came, and Lucy chewed her way through a lovely toasted cheese sandwich, while Bill dove into his huge plate of winter stew.

"Parsnips," he said with approval.

"Do you know what else?" asked Lucy.

"Some sort of meat," he said, spearing a chunky piece. "Pork?"

"No," said Lucy, nibbling on a *frite.* "Veal. It's actually calf's head."

Bill dropped his fork. "What?"

"*Tête de veau.* That's what the menu said. It means 'head of calf.' "

Bill studied his dish, slowly turning over a few vegetables and choosing a piece of carrot. "Well, I'll be darned." His eyes sparkled, and he grinned. "It's awfully good. Want to try some?"

Lucy's first inclination was to decline; then she rose to the challenge. "Okay. When in France . . ."

"Open wide," said Bill, choosing a piece of meat for her.

Lucy obeyed, expecting something horrible, but was pleasantly surprised. "I don't think I'd choose it," she said, "but it's not bad." She chewed. "It's actually delicious."

After lunch they found themselves walking along the quais lining the Seine River, broad banks paved with stone and dotted here and there with trees, which were now covered with tender green leaves. They weren't alone. The quais were popular with strollers and dog walkers; from time to time they watched a barge or tourist boat chug past. Eventually, coming to a bridge, they noticed the metal fences looked very odd, and climbed up the stone steps from the quai to investigate. Reaching the bridge, which was near Notre-Dame, they discovered the metal webbing on both sides was filled with locks, many with names and initials, sometimes even a crudely scratched heart.

"I think lovers put them here as a token of everlasting love," said Lucy. "I bet they throw the keys into the river."

Bill peered over the side, down into the murky water. "Down there with the rusty bikes and rotting bones . . ."

"It's a romantic gesture," said Lucy. "We should do it."

"I'm surprised the city puts up with it," said Bill, studying the thickly packed locks with a builder's eye. "That's quite a bit of weight. I wouldn't be surprised if all this metal is putting stress on the bridge."

"It seems fine," said Lucy. "I wonder if there's any-place nearby that sells locks."

"I don't see a hardware store, but I do see Shake-speare and Company."

Lucy followed his gaze and saw the famous English-language bookstore that had served as a temporary home to so many authors, including Hemingway and Fitzgerald. "Let's go," she said, forgetting about the locks.

They spent a happy hour browsing among the books, both new and used, and Bill bought himself a used copy of *A Moveable Feast,* the book Hemingway wrote de-scribing his life in Paris as a young writer.

Lucy disapproved. "Hemingway was kind of a jerk, always punching people out," she said as they wandered through the twisting, narrow streets. "And he kept leaving his wives for other women."

"You don't think he would have put a lock on the bridge?"

Lucy considered the matter. "Nah, he'd spend the money on a drink."

"Good idea," said Bill, spotting another corner café.

Clouds were filling the sky and the afternoon light was fading when Bill finished his beer and Lucy drank the last of her Bordeaux. They were tired of walking, so they joined the commuters descending into the Métro station. There was quite a crowd surging through the turnstiles, and the platform beyond was packed with people, as was the train when it arrived. Lucy doubted there was room on the train for them, but found they were carried along by the pressure of the crowd. The doors closed and she let out a sigh; she'd never been in a rush hour crowd like this, not even in New York. But, she decided, looking on the bright side, she didn't have to worry about pickpockets, because they were all so tightly crammed together that there was no room for a pickpocket to operate. The train sped along the track, and Lucy checked the map on the wall above the windows and discovered they could get off at the next stop, the Gare d'Austerlitz, and switch to the line that ran near their apartment.

When the doors slid open, Lucy was able to worm her way through the packed bodies, but Bill, she realized with horror, wasn't able to make it out of the train before the doors closed. She stood, horrified, on the platform, watching helplessly as her husband was carried away.

What to do? She knew that Bill depended on her to navigate the complicated system and wasn't at all confident that he could manage on his own. It was like that silly song about Charlie who got lost on the MTA and had to ride forever beneath the streets of Boston. But no. Bill was smart. Bill was sensible. He'd surely manage to get off at the next stop. Hopefully, he'd remember to cross over to the other side of the tracks, and he'd show up on the next train. Hearing the announcement that the train for Saint-Ouen was approaching the station, she ran up the stairs and over to the other side, making it just as the doors closed and the train swooshed away. She glanced up and down the platform, but there was no sign of Bill in the crowd of debarking passengers.

Her chest was tightening, and her anxiety was growing. What if he got confused? Who could he ask? He didn't speak French. She doubted he even knew the address of the apartment, so he couldn't even take a taxi. She sat down on one of the benches and tried calling him, but her cellphone didn't work in the underground station. Lucy tried to calm herself, watching as a train arrived on the opposite side. She checked the electronic sign on her side, learning the next train was in three minutes.

It seemed a very long three minutes, and she could feel her heart pounding in her chest when the light appeared in the tunnel and the train finally pulled into the station. She crossed her fingers and closed her eyes, and when she opened them, the train was leaving and Bill was making his way through the crowded platform to her. "Maybe we should have done that lock thing," he said as she threw her arms around his neck.

Lucy was beginning to think that Elizabeth was right and Paris wasn't the fairy-tale city she'd imagined. It seemed a hostile place, teeming with people who were not the least bit friendly, who'd knock you over for a spot on the subway. There was so much she didn't understand—her high school French wasn't much help—and even the food was weird!

When they arrived back at the apartment, Lucy was exhausted and wanted a bit of peace and quiet. That was impossible, however, because Ted had invited his friend from the *International New York Times,* Richard Mason, to join them for dinner. Richard was a good-looking man in early middle age. His temples were graying, but he took care of himself and was fit and trim in dark pants and a leather jacket, with a scarf looped around his neck in the French manner.

Sue and Sid had gone shopping at the nearby Monoprix supermarket and had whipped up a mushroom risotto, so they all gathered at the sleek white Parsons table to eat.

"To Paris and good friends," said Ted.

"And old friends," added Richard.

"Old friends are the best friends," said Pam.

They all joined in the toast and then settled down to fill their plates. The risotto was delicious, the salad crisp and fresh, and the bread was light on the inside and crusty on the outside. There was also plenty of wine, drawn from the stockpile in the apartment.

"We have dessert," announced Sue as Sid began collecting the dinner plates. "I stopped at the school and snagged a couple of *tartes.*"

"How'd you manage that?" asked Pam.

"You know Sue. She usually manages to get her way," said Sid with a nod.

Sue was quick to defend herself. "I happened to bump into Chef Larry on the street outside his patisserie and asked. There was no arm-twisting involved. He also said not to worry about drinking all the wine or eating up the gourmet groceries, because he can get us more at very good prices."

"So he supplied all the stuff that's here?" asked Ted.

"Yeah. He said he always makes sure Norah's cupboard is well stocked," replied Sue, lifting a slice of tarte tatin onto a plate and passing it to Richard.

"It must be nice, living the good life at cut-rate prices," said Richard, accepting the plate.

The tarte tatin was a revelation. They all agreed they'd never tasted anything so delicious.

"Who knew apples could taste like this," mused Bill.

"The trouble is, you get used to it," said Richard with a wry grin. "Now when I go back to the States, I really miss French cooking."

"No McDonald's for you?" asked Pam.

"No trips to the American grocery for peanut butter and brownie mix?" asked Sue, referring to a Paris institution.

"Nope. I shop like the rest of Paris, at the market on Saturday morning."

"We went to the market today as part of our cooking class," said Ted. "As a matter of fact, some guy roughed up our teacher."

"Really?" Richard's tone was sharp, but he quickly added, "That's not at all typical. They must have a history."

"Apparently not," said Sue.

"I think he was an Arab," said Bob. "He was dark, swarthy. He had that look."

"Could be," offered Richard. "There is a lot of tension in the Arab community. It's spilling over from the Arab Spring. The old dictators, like Gaddafi and Mubarak, are gone, leaving a power vacuum. There's a lot of rivalry between different factions, even here in France."

"I don't think you should jump to conclusions," said Pam, sipping her decaf. "We don't know if he's Arab or Italian or Romany, or anything at all about him, except that he seemed to have some sort of issue with Chef Larry."

"Larry said not. He insisted he didn't know him," said Lucy.

"Maybe he was a pickpocket," suggested Rachel.

"Well, I have an issue with Chef Larry," said Sue, narrowing her eyes. "He's a nice guy, but I can't say I'm terribly impressed so far."

Lucy started to mention her suspicions about the guy she'd seen lurking in the doorway, but was cut off by Bob.

"Why are you defending that thug?" he demanded, challenging Pam. "He attacked Larry. It's a good thing we were all there. If Larry had been alone, I don't like to think what might have happened. These Arabs are out of control. They hate America, and they want to destroy Israel."

"We don't know what was behind the attack," said Ted. "It could be a woman, a debt, a grudge."

"And it was just a shoving match," said Bill. "High school stuff."

"Bob has a different perspective, that's all," said Rachel, eager to smooth things over. "When you visit the Mémorial de la Shoah, well, you see how intolerance and prejudice can have catastrophic results."

"That's right," said Pam. "But it's a two-way street. Isn't Bob being intolerant in this case?"

"Is that what you think?" demanded Bob. "Six million Jews died in the Holocaust, and these Islamic radicals want to finish off the rest of us! Remember nine-eleven? They call it jihad and think they'll go to heaven if they kill infidels."

There was a long silence until Sid spoke up. "This infidel found a rather nice bottle of brandy at the Monoprix. Who'd like a taste?"

"I'll bite," said Bill. "You wouldn't believe what I had for lunch. . . ."

Chapter Four

After a second bad night spent beside Bill, who slumbered peacefully, Lucy had to admit she wasn't really all that interested in the cooking classes. If she had her way, she'd skip the class and sleep in, but that was impossible since her bed was in the middle of the apartment's living room. The others tried to be quiet and tiptoed through on their way to the kitchen area, but Lucy found it difficult to ignore them. She'd hear a rustle or a footfall, and she'd have to lift her eyeshade and see who was there. After doing this several times, she gave up and got out of bed, reaching the kitchen just in time to get the last cup of coffee.

She was still a bit groggy and out of sorts, however, as the group of friends made their way to Le Cooking School. The others were walking ahead of Lucy and Bill. Lucy was eating her croissant breakfast as she walked, and it slowed her down. Rain was forecast, so she'd brought her travel umbrella, which was also a hindrance as it dangled on a cord from her wrist. The others had disappeared inside when they reached the school, and Bill couldn't remember the entry code.

"Is it one-oh-four-oh-A or four-oh-one-oh-A?" he asked.

"I'm not sure," said Lucy, who was watching the early morning parade of pedestrians making their way to the Chemin Vert Métro station. "Try them both."

Bill punched in one number, and nothing happened. "I guess it's the other one," he said. "Which one did I use?"

"I didn't see," said Lucy, who was staring across the street at a man standing in the doorway of the Harley-Davidson motorcycle shop, dragging on a cigarette. "Don't look now, but isn't that the guy from the market?" she asked, whispering. "Unibrow?"

Bill immediately turned his head in the guy's direction. "I'm not sure," he said.

"He's dark and has a three-day beard, just like that guy. And he's smoking."

"There are lots of dark guys with three-day beards in Paris," said Bill, poking at the keypad. "And they all smoke. I can't tell one from another."

"You have a point," admitted Lucy as the keypad buzzed and Bill pushed the door open. "But I'm pretty sure I saw him yesterday in the same spot, when we were leaving class."

Upstairs, in the classroom, Chef Larry was togged out in chef's whites, with a high toque on his head. The class was already under way. He was breaking eggs into a pot and whisking them furiously. "We're making profiteroles," he told Lucy and Bill, "beginning with *pâte à choux*."

"Sounds fabulous," said Lucy, tying on her apron.

"It's just a fancy name for cream puffs," said Sue scornfully. "I bet you've made them a million times."

"*Pâte à choux* is not complicated," admitted Chef Larry. "That is its beauty. But I am going to teach you my fabulous chocolate sauce—with a secret ingredient."

"Can't wait," muttered Sue, who was justifiably proud

of her own chocolate sauce recipe, which had just a hint of coffee.

"And today we will have a coffee break—very American, right?—and eat our profiteroles and tarte tatin," said Chef Larry, spooning the *pâte à choux* into a pastry bag. "The bag is not necessary," he said. "You can just spoon the *pâte à choux* into little balls for baking, but I like to make swans," he said, demonstrating with a flourish.

"Swans!" muttered Sue, rolling her eyes. "What a cliché!"

"I think they're cute," said Pam.

"And I can't wait to have another piece of that tart," added Bill.

"All that pastry will spoil your lunch," advised Lucy, who was a firm believer in three square meals a day and no snacks.

"I'll have salad," promised Bill.

But after eating generous helpings of tarte tatin, plus the profiteroles, which were absolutely delicious, containing a luscious brandy-flavored cream filling and topped with the amazing chocolate sauce Chef Larry had sprinkled with his secret ingredient, a special sea salt called *fleur de sel,* nobody was eager to face a large lunch.

The friends were debating the issue, standing in the tiny vestibule and watching the heavy rain that was pouring down outside, when two young men approached, engaged in a lively conversation. They were both wearing baseball caps pulled low on their heads, and like most men in France, they had scarves wrapped around their necks and had turned up their coat collars against the rain. They were carrying briefcases and packages, as well as umbrellas, so there wasn't a free hand between them with which to operate the security keypad. Realizing they were locked out and were getting pelted with rain while they fumbled with their stuff, Pam opened the door for them. The two ducked inside and passed the group without making eye contact and went straight for the stairs.

"You shouldn't have done that," hissed Bob, watching the two bound up the stairs. "What's the sense of a security system if you just let people in?"

"It was the polite thing to do," said Pam defensively.

"Well, in case you haven't noticed, the French aren't really big on politeness," huffed Bob. "They didn't even say thank you."

"What's your problem?" demanded Pam. "They were getting soaked."

"I'm sure Bob only wants to keep us safe," said Rachel, attempting to smooth things over.

"That's right. They could be up to no good," said Bob. "They had scarves covering their faces."

"I don't know how you've missed it, Bob, but all the men in Paris wear scarves," said Sue, who had pulled a small folding umbrella from her purse. "I think I'd like to do some shopping and work up an appetite," she said. "What do you think, Sid?"

"Sooner or later you'll hit your credit limit and this madness will stop," teased Sid.

"What do you say, Lucy? Want to come with us?" asked Sue.

"Sure," said Lucy, checking with Bill and getting a nod. "We can buy some presents for the kids at home."

Sid opened the door, and Lucy reached for her umbrella, discovering she didn't have it. "Oh, darn. I left my umbrella upstairs," she said.

"We'll wait," said Rachel in a philosophical tone. "Maybe the rain will let up a bit."

"That's Rachel," observed Pam. "Always the optimist."

"I'll get it for you," offered Bill.

"Don't bother. I could use the exercise," said Lucy, guiltily aware of the profiteroles and tarte tatin she'd eaten.

She heard their voices as she hurried up the three long flights of stairs, growing fainter as she climbed. When she reached the second floor—really, the third, because the French counted floors differently—she paused to rest and catch her breath, reading the sign on the landing that listed the various businesses on that floor: a lawyer, a dentist, a masseuse, and a podiatrist. One more floor to go. As she climbed, she wondered how many calories she was burning. *Probably not all that many,* she decided, recalling an article in a women's magazine that claimed you would have to run a marathon to burn off one Big Mac.

She hoped Chef Larry was still in the classroom. She'd be out of luck if he'd already locked up and left, though she didn't think he had, because they were all standing in the doorway and would have seen him. Of course, she speculated, there were probably other doors to the building, surely a back door for deliveries and garbage removal, and probably even a second flight of stairs. If only they'd thought to put in an elevator, she thought, hurrying down the hall.

She had passed the doors for Compu-Tech and Marie-Ange, Modiste, whatever that was, when she noticed the door to the cooking school was ajar. *Good,* she thought. *Chef Larry must still be here.* She called out his name and pushed the door open, but when she stepped inside, she found the classroom empty. It was a bit odd, she thought, but maybe Chef Larry was somewhere else in the building. Perhaps he was chatting up Marie-Ange, or shooting the breeze with the geeks at Compu-Tech, and hadn't bothered to lock up. Lucky for her. She grabbed her umbrella, which was hanging on the coatrack, where she'd left it, and turned to go, catching a glimpse of a tray of spilled profiteroles on the floor in front of the counter Chef Larry used for his cooking demonstrations.

Taking a closer look, she noticed a trail of red splotches leading behind the counter. A trail, she realized, horrified, that must be blood. *Okay, blood.* The morning class was a pastry course, but maybe the afternoon class involved some sort of meat recipe, something like *bœuf bourguignon.* But even a very juicy package of beef wouldn't produce this much blood, would it? She was already crossing the classroom, thinking she'd better investigate, just in case Chef Larry had accidentally cut himself while chopping up some meat or something. If he'd severed an artery, for instance, he would need immediate medical care.

But when she rounded the corner of the counter, she found Chef Larry was indeed bleeding, lying flat on his back in a growing pool of blood and smashed profiteroles, but he hadn't accidentally cut himself. Not unless he'd plunged a knife into his own chest.

Lucy immediately began yelling for help, unsure what to do, but nobody seemed to be coming. She started one way and then another, shocked and panicked. At home she would call 9-1-1, but this wasn't Maine. It was France. This was an emergency, she was yelling her head off, but where were all the other people in the building? She feared he was already dead, but then he groaned, and she realized she had to get help, fast. Looking frantically around the classroom, she noticed a phone on the wall. Beside it was a neat list of numbers: *sapeurs-pompiers, médecin.* . . . What to dial? The number twenty-five was large and printed in red, so she punched it in the keypad.

A bored voice answered, saying something she didn't quite catch. "Un homme b-blessé," she stammered, her voice quavering as she struggled to remember her high school French. "Vite! Vite! Beaucoup de sang!"

"Calmez-vous, madame," replied the voice. "L'adresse?"

Lucy couldn't remember the French words for numbers, so she gave the address in English, which didn't seem to faze the dispatcher at all. "Please hurry! *Dépêchez-vous!*" she pleaded. "I'm afraid he'll die. He was stabbed with a knife."

"Help is on the way, madame," said the voice. "Stabbed, you say? Is this a matter *criminelle?*"

"I don't think he stabbed himself in the chest," said Lucy.

"Do not leave," advised the voice. "That would be a matter *sérieuse.*"

"I'm staying," replied Lucy, hearing the varying *woo-wah* tones, which indicated an ambulance was on the way.

Hands shaking, she replaced the phone handset on its hook, noticing that Bill was in the doorway, wondering what was keeping her. "Don't come in," she warned as he was pushed aside by the arriving medics. Then the rest of the group of friends arrived, curious to see what all the fuss was about, and they were herded in a tight little bunch into one of the student cooking areas.

The medics seemed to take a long time doing whatever they were doing, and there seemed to be a good deal of discussion. Lucy felt her heart fluttering in her chest. It was time to get moving and get poor Chef Larry to the hospital.

"What's taking so long?" she asked, but got no reply from the medics.

It was Sue who replied. "It's the French way. They try to stabilize the patient before they transport him. Remember Princess Diana? They say she might have lived if they'd gotten her to the hospital sooner."

"Socialized medicine," snorted Sid, who was a member of the volunteer fire department in Tinker's Cove and had answered many an emergency call. "Back home, we'd have him at the hospital by now."

"And he'd get a huge bill," snapped Rachel. "Probably end up bankrupt."

"But he'd be alive," said Sid.

"There's really nothing for us to do here," said Bill. "You've done your duty, Lucy. Let's go. We're just in the way."

"The dispatcher said to stay," said Lucy.

"Well, I need a drink," said Sue, turning to leave and bumping into a short, dark man with the usual fashionable stubble of beard, wearing a scarf over his Burberry trench coat. "I think we should regroup at the café."

"*Un peu de patience,*" advised the man, shepherding the group away from the door as the medics wheeled the wounded man away on a gurney. "I am Commissaire Lapointe, with the police, and I have a few questions."

"We're happy to cooperate," said Bob, stepping forward. "I'm Bob Goodman. I'm a lawyer in the U.S., and I can assure you that none of us had anything to do with this unfortunate incident."

"I see," said the *commissaire*, blinking slowly. His eyes protruded a bit, and he reminded Lucy of a lizard, testing the atmosphere and waiting to pounce on whatever unwitting prey might come by. He almost seemed bored as he pulled a notebook from his pocket. "Can you give me your names and your addresses in Paris?"

When that bit of business was completed, he asked about Chef Larry. "What is your relationship to the victim?"

"His name is Larry Bruneau, and he is the owner of this cooking school," said Bob, representing the group. "We are all students. We had a class this morning."

The *commissaire* was no longer bored. "What was the subject of the class?" he asked.

"Profiteroles," said Sue.

"Ahhh," replied the policeman. "*Délicieuses, sans doute*. But hardly the sort of thing that leads to a stabbing."

"That's what I don't understand," said Rachel. "Why would anyone want to hurt Chef Larry?"

"There are many reasons for crime, madame," said Lapointe. "It is unfortunate, but people do many terrible things to each other for many different reasons. Perhaps he owed money. And then there are drugs, the black market. There is much that goes on in Paris that a visitor does not see." He paused, then shrugged. "Most likely, it is to do with a woman."

"I opened the door," said Pam, eager to confess and relieve her guilty conscience. "I know you're not supposed to, but it was raining and there were two young men getting soaked, so I opened the door for them."

"They did not know the code?" asked the *commissaire,* narrowing his eyes.

"They were carrying lots of packages, and their hands weren't free," said Pam. "They certainly didn't look like criminals."

"There's no reason to believe they were the assailants," said Ted, eager to defend his wife. "There are plenty of other people who work in this building. There are many businesses besides the cooking school."

"And there was that man who attacked Larry in the market," said Lucy, immediately wishing she hadn't spoken up.

"Madame Stone, you are Madame Stone?" asked the *commissaire*. "What attack are you speaking of?"

"We were at the *marché,*" began Lucy.

"The Enfants Rouges," added Sue.

"This guy came up and shouted at Chef Larry and shoved him."

"Have you seen this man again?" asked Lapointe.

"I think I did. I think I saw him yesterday and again today, standing across the street," said Lucy. "But I'm not sure. He was just average. He looked like a lot of other men. Dark, very short hair, unshaven." As she spoke, she realized she could be describing the *commissaire* himself.

"The guy in the market had a unibrow," said Sue.

"What is that?" demanded the *commissaire*. "Unibrow?"

"Very dark eyebrows that connected over his nose, with no space in between," said Sue.

"Mrs. Stone, did the man you observed also have this unibrow?"

"I didn't see. But he was wearing a leather jacket."

"Like these guys today," said Pam.

"It is the style," admitted Lapointe.

"I feel so guilty," said Rachel. "If I hadn't let them in . . ."

"Do not disturb yourself, madame. If they are in fact the assailants, they would have found another way. They could have simply waited for their victim to leave the building."

"I wonder," began Bob. "Is there a surveillance camera on the premises?"

"We will look into that," said Lapointe. "It is what

you say, early days. I can assure you there will be a thorough investigation, and in time we will, without doubt, discover the truth."

Bob was thoughtful, obviously considering the ramifications of Lapointe's statement. "How long do you think this investigation will take?" he asked.

Lapointe shrugged. "Impossible to tell. It will take as long as it takes."

"But we're going to be in Paris for only eleven more days. Our flight is one week from Saturday. Will this be a problem?"

"Not a problem," said Lapointe. "But I will need your passports."

"We won't be able to leave without our passports," said Bob.

"Exactly," said Lapointe, holding out his hand.

"So we will be able to leave on schedule?" asked Bob.

"Perhaps, perhaps not. It depends on the investigation."

"So we might not be able to leave?"

"As I said, it is impossible to know." Lapointe's voice became firmer. "Now I will take your passports. And you will receive notice in a day or two to come to the station to make formal statements."

"How much notice will we have?" asked Bob.

Lapointe considered the question. "Twenty-four hours, maybe less."

"We must have at least twenty-four hours' advance notice," insisted Bob.

"Ah, monsieur, you are not in America now. This is how we do things in France. When you are summoned, you must come."

Bob bristled. "I am familiar with the French justice system."

"Then you will most certainly want to cooperate.

And now the passports, please. And then you will leave so the investigators can proceed to examine the scene of the crime."

Seeing no alternative, they drew the required passports from pockets and purses and handed them over.

"À bientôt," said Lapointe. "And meanwhile, I hope you will enjoy your visit. There is much to see in Paris."

"Is that supposed to be a joke?" asked Bill as they began making their way down the stairs.

"If it is," said Sue, "the joke's on us."

Chapter Five

The café on the corner was still busy with lunchtime customers, but a large booth in the back was empty and they all squeezed in, borrowing a few chairs from nearby tables. No one was in the mood for a meal, but Sue ordered a few plates of *frites* to accompany their drinks.

"I plan to drink quite a bit," announced Sue, "so I'll need to eat something."

"Good idea," chimed in Lucy, who also felt the need for something alcoholic. Her hands were still shaking, and she couldn't erase the image of poor Chef Larry from her mind. He remained firmly in place, flat on his back, with the hilt of the knife sticking out of his chest.

"What did that cop mean?" asked Sid. "Can they really keep our passports and detain us here in Paris?"

"Oh, yes," answered Bob. "The French legal system is different from ours. There's no presumption of innocence, for example, and there are severe penalties for failing to cooperate. Our system is prosecutorial. The prosecution and the defense argue the case, and the jury decides. The French system is inquisitorial. A magistrate takes charge of each case and is responsible for determining the truth of the matter."

"It seems rigged, if you ask me," said Bill. "What if the magistrate is wrong?"

"Juries make mistakes, too," said Bob. "It's just a different system, but the ultimate goal is the same—to find the truth." He paused. "No system is one hundred percent perfect."

A waiter arrived with their orders, beer for the men and wine for the women, except for Rachel, who had a cup of tea. Sue was making fast work of the fries, a sure sign she was upset. She didn't even take umbrage when the waiter asked if she wanted ketchup. She merely shook her head and didn't criticize Bill when he said he sure would like some.

"Chef Larry wasn't teaching me anything I didn't know already," she said, "but I had hopes, you know? I was hoping to learn the secret of *pâte feuilletée*. Mine never comes out quite right."

"Why make it from scratch?" inquired Lucy. "You can buy ready-made puff pastry. It's in the freezer section. That's what I do."

Sue gave her a pained look. "Not the same thing at all."

"Well, maybe there'll be a substitute teacher," said Pam, who actually was an occasional substitute teacher back home in Tinker's Cove.

"I don't think so," said Bill. "Le Cooking School looks like a one-man show to me."

"What about the bakery?" wondered Pam. "Do you think it will close?"

"I bet Chef Larry has hirelings who do the baking," said Sue, signaling the waiter for another glass of wine. "And he has that wholesale grocery business, too. Remember? He said he could get us all the wine and caviar we wanted."

"At a very good price," added Sid. "That's what he said."

Lucy was thoughtful, but it was Ted who said what she was thinking. "I wouldn't be surprised to learn he dabbles in black market goods," he said. "Lapointe mentioned that as a possible motive."

"You think that wine and stuff we found in the apartment fell off a truck?" asked Sid.

"Something like that," said Ted.

"And I was going to ask him to get us another case of wine," said Sue. "I never thought it was stolen. I just figured he had connections in the industry and was getting it wholesale."

"I don't think so," said Lucy. "People don't get themselves stabbed for no reason."

"And there was that attack in the market," said Bob.

"I wonder if that guy was operating on his own," said Lucy, "or if he was part of some criminal organization."

"Like the Mafia?" Rachel's huge eyes were bigger than ever. "You think he was delivering a warning?"

"It could have been something like that, or even some terrorist group," said Ted. "Richard told me that's how a lot of them make money for their operations."

"He doesn't strike me as a man with a cause," said Sue. "I think Chef Larry is just out for Chef Larry."

"Well, I like him," said Pam. "And I hope he pulls through."

"We all do," said Rachel.

"You bet," agreed Bob. "The sooner he recovers and tells the police who attacked him, the sooner we get our passports back."

"Well, in the meantime, it looks like we've got plenty of time to fill," said Bill. "Any ideas?"

"We're in France," said Sue. "Like Lapointe said, there's plenty to see and do."

"I've always wanted to see Versailles," said Pam.

"Me too," added Rachel. "That's where they filmed

that movie about Marie Antoinette. There were just glimpses, but it was gorgeous."

"It's only a short train ride away," offered Sue. "Let's go. Tomorrow. It will take our minds off the current unpleasantness."

Everybody seemed to think a trip to Versailles was a good idea, except Bob. "Hold your horses," he advised. "Chances are we'll all be called in for questioning tomorrow."

"That soon?" asked Sid.

"I'd bet money on it," answered Bob, looking glum as he drained his glass and set it on the table.

Pam was having none of it. "This is crazy. We're Americans. We're the can-do people. We're not helpless here. We've got an embassy."

"You're right," said Bob, perking up. "I'll go this afternoon and see if they can't help us get our passports back, or issue temporary passports."

"Shall we all go?" asked Lucy.

"I don't think that's necessary," said Bob.

"Good," said Sue. "I have no desire to sit around in some waiting room all afternoon, not when I could be shopping."

"And I'm going to want to keep an eye on you," said Sid with a resigned sigh.

In the end it was decided that Lucy should go to the embassy with Bob, because she discovered the body, and Bill would also go, to support Lucy, but the rest of the group would spend the afternoon pursuing their various interests. They agreed to meet for dinner, at which time, it was hoped, Bob would have good news for them.

Lucy was much happier when she could take action, rather than sit and fret, so she was feeling quite chipper as she and Bill set out with Bob for the embassy. A quick check on Bob's smartphone revealed that the embassy was located on the avenue Gabriel, off the place de la Concorde, which was only a short ride away on the Métro.

The place de la Concorde was buzzing with traffic, which whizzed around the Egyptian obelisk in the center, making a sharp contrast to the fountains and classical buildings. When they walked past the Hôtel de Crillon, Bill remarked that Hemingway liked to drink there.

"I thought the Ritz was his favorite," said Bob. "They even named the bar after him."

"No, I'm pretty sure it was the Crillon," maintained Bill.

"I don't think there was a bar he didn't like," said Lucy, and they all laughed.

They were still enjoying the quip when they approached the embassy, which was next to the Crillon and surrounded by a sturdy iron and stone fence. At the gate they were confronted by a very serious U.S. Marine, dressed in camouflage and holding a scary-looking gun.

"What is your business?" he asked.

"We need emergency passports," said Bob.

"You know you can apply online," said the marine.

"It's a rather special case," said Bob. "We need to see a consular officer."

The marine looked them over, then advised them to proceed to the security checkpoint. There Lucy opened her purse for examination and they passed through a metal detector before they were allowed to enter the building. Once inside they were sent to a crowded waiting room and were given numbers.

"Maybe this is a mistake," said Lucy. "Our number is forty-seven, and they're only up to twenty-two."

"It will probably go quickly," said Bob.

"I doubt it," said Bill, opening a copy of the *International New York Times* that somebody had discarded. "Hey, look!" he exclaimed. "Your buddy Richard has a front-page story."

Lucy and Ted looked over his shoulders as he read the story, which was an account of the activities of Les Amis du Roi de l'Égypte to restore the monarchy. " 'Egypt is in crisis,' stated the group's leader, Khalid Sadek. 'Only the rightful king, Fouad II, can unite the various factions and prevent civil war.' "

The story went on to point out that Fouad II lived a quiet life in Switzerland and seemed to have little interest in reassuming the throne, which he had held briefly when he was less than a year old.

"That group was holding a conference at the Cavendish Hotel," said Lucy. "Elizabeth was helping to set it up." She pointed to the head shot of Khalid Sadek, whom she recognized as the gray-haired man in the old-fashioned suit. "I actually saw him. He was there."

"I wonder where they're getting their money," said Bob. "That place isn't cheap."

"Maybe they're selling their jewels, like the Russian émigrés," Lucy said, speculating. "Maybe this Fouad is like Anastasia, a fake, and that's why he doesn't want to claim the throne."

"More likely, he doesn't want to face an angry mob in Tahrir Square," said Bill, turning to the sports. After learning the Bruins had lost to the Canadiens, they went on to finish the crossword. They were playing a half-hearted game of hangman when number forty-seven was called. Their hopes were high, however, when they were finally allowed to see a foreign service officer.

"I'm Fox Carrington," he said, rising from his desk and leaning across it to shake hands. "How can I help you?"

"I'm Bob Goodman. I'm an attorney representing a

group of eight Americans. We all need emergency passports."

"All your passports were stolen?" asked Carrington, who looked as if he'd stepped out of a J.Crew catalog. He was clean-cut and smooth shaven and had a slight Southern accent. Lucy thought he was perhaps old enough to be in high school.

"Not exactly," explained Bob. "We were enrolled in a cooking school, and the teacher—the chef, actually—was assaulted. The investigating police officer confiscated our passports."

Carrington put down his pen. "Did I hear you right? You're involved in a crime?"

"Definitely not involved," said Bob. "We had nothing to do with it."

"But this French cop took our passports, which I don't think he is allowed to do," added Lucy.

"Did this assault take place while class was in session?" asked Carrington. "Were you all witnesses?"

"No, nothing like that," said Bill. "Class was over. We were leaving, waiting for the rain to stop."

"But I forgot my umbrella, and when I went back to the classroom to get it, I found Chef Larry on the floor, bleeding, with a knife in his chest."

Carrington tented his hands and nodded. It was as if he heard stories like this every day. Perhaps he did, thought Lucy.

"He would have died, except for my wife, here. She called for help," said Bill.

"And what thanks do I get?" asked Lucy. "None at all. Instead this cop took our passports and said we have to stay indefinitely, which is a real problem, because our flight is in ten days. And I have children at home, who need me."

"And you know what it's like to change flights," said

Bob, rolling his eyes. "We'll have to pay exorbitant fees."

"I didn't even think about that," said Bill.

"Did this cop give you a card or anything? Do you know his name?"

"Lapointe," said Lucy, proud of herself for remembering. "Commissaire Lapointe."

"No card? No phone or email?" asked Carrington.

"An unfortunate omission," admitted Bob. "I should have thought of that."

"You were taken by surprise," said Bill.

"We were all in shock," said Lucy.

"Without more information, there isn't much I can do," said Carrington.

"Well, they're going to be calling us for statements. We can get more information then," said Bob.

"Good," said Carrington. "You must cooperate, of course. You must cooperate with the French authorities."

"Does that mean we can't leave on schedule?" asked Lucy.

"Out of the question," said Carrington. "The French authorities are within their rights to detain you until they are satisfied with the case."

"That's outrageous," said Bob. "We had nothing to do with this attack. We didn't even know Chef Larry until yesterday."

"It's unfortunate, but that's how it is. When you travel outside of the States, you leave your rights as an American citizen behind and you're subject to the laws of the land you're visiting, which happens to be France. Believe me, it could be much worse. Take Italy, for example. Or Saudi Arabia." He shuddered at the thought. "Of course, the less you appear to know, the sooner you will get your passports back. Once they are satisfied you are not involved, they will return them and you will be free to go."

"How long do you think that will take?" asked Bob. "I mean, as a general rule."

Carrington considered the question. "I don't like to say. It could be wrapped up in a day or two, or it could go on for some time. We had a case, an American woman who married a French citizen and then killed him. She claimed self-defense, said he was abusive. It was a very sad thing. I think they finally did release her, but she was in prison for more than a year."

Lucy felt her chest tighten, picturing herself in a dark, dank prison cell. "That couldn't happen to us, could it?"

"I doubt it, but I'm not really in a position to say." He clapped his hands together and rose, signaling the interview was over. "Do feel free to contact me if you need assistance."

"But that's what we're doing. We're asking for assistance," said Lucy.

"Perhaps you should consult a lawyer. There are a number of American firms with offices in Paris. I have a list." Carrington opened a drawer and produced a sheet of paper, which he gave to Bob. "And take my card, one for each of you."

"Well, thanks for seeing us," said Bill.

"No problem, anytime," said Carrington, eyeing the clock. "And remember what I said. The more you cooperate, the better."

"Right," said Bob, extending his hand.

Carrington shook hands all around, his grasp firm and energetic. "And have a nice day," he said.

"I really hate that fake 'Have a nice day' thing," muttered Lucy as they left the embassy. "It's so phony. At least the French don't pretend to care whether you have a nice day or not."

"That Carrington was next to useless," said Bill as they gathered in a small knot on the sidewalk.

"I didn't really expect them to give us emergency passports, but I figured it wouldn't hurt to ask," admitted Bob. "At least now they'll start a file. They'll know about us, in case, well, things go south."

"What do you mean?" asked Bill. "Go south?"

"Well, in case Chef Larry dies and they decide to charge one of us."

"He means me," said Lucy, swallowing hard. "I'm the one who found Chef Larry. I'm the obvious suspect."

"Let's hope he recovers and identifies his assailant," said Bill.

"That would be the best-case scenario," agreed Bob. "So what do you want to do now? Reconnoiter with the others?"

"It's not even four," said Bill, checking his watch and opening his map. "This is a pretty central location. I bet there's something nearby."

"You could say that," offered Lucy, pointing at the horizon. "The Eiffel Tower is just over there."

"How about Les Invalides?" suggested Bill, pointing to a spot on the map. "Napoleon's tomb."

"And the Army Museum," said Bob. "I think they have Napoleon's hat there and a lot of other cool stuff."

Bill was definitely interested. "Sounds great."

"Ick," said Lucy. "I don't like Napoleon."

"We could do the Eiffel Tower," offered Bob.

But Lucy was already developing plans of her own. "No, you guys go and see the guns and stuff. I think I'll pay a visit to Elizabeth."

Bill furrowed his brow. "Are you still worried about her?" he asked.

"A bit," admitted Lucy. "I just want to touch bases

with her, make sure she's okay. And it's not far from here." She was already on her way, giving them a little wave and heading off in the direction of the Palais Garnier, but she wasn't really thinking about Elizabeth's problems. She was thinking about the hotel, the Cavendish chain, which was an economic powerhouse with branches all over the world. Perhaps someone in management, if Elizabeth asked politely, might be able to give her a lead to someone who could intervene on their behalf. Or even drop a word to someone influential. That was how things worked in Maine. Lucy had seen it plenty of times as a reporter for the Tinker's Cove weekly newspaper, the *Pennysaver*. And if networking was the key to getting things done in Maine, she suspected it was even more important in France.

The walk to the boulevard Haussmann was longer than she had thought, but Lucy didn't mind. She was enjoying walking along the streets of Paris, pausing here and there to examine a shop window or to witness a charming incident, like the bride in an enormous full-skirted wedding dress she saw stuffing herself into a tiny Renault.

Elizabeth was on duty at the concierge's desk when Lucy finally reached the hotel, but she was due for a break. She took her mother into the staff room, where there were coffee and snack machines, and bought two bottles of water.

"Are you having a good time in Paris?" asked Elizabeth, seating herself in an armchair with a cracked leatherette seat and unscrewing the cap on her bottle of Vichy water.

"We were until today," said Lucy, taking the adjacent seat, a similar chair covered in ugly tweed. "Our teacher at Le Cooking School, Chef Larry, was attacked. Stabbed. And now the police have taken our passports."

Elizabeth's mouth was full of water, and she swallowed hard. "What?"

"I found him and called for help. They took him to the hospital. I don't know if he's alive."

"So you might actually be involved in a murder?" asked Elizabeth. "That's bad."

"I know. That's why I came. There was a cop. He took our passports."

"Are you suspects? That's really bad, Mom. The French have this thing, *garde à vue*. It means they can lock you up for pretty much as long as they want, if they suspect you of committing a crime."

This was news to Lucy, but it confirmed her worst fears about the French system, so she forged ahead with her plan. "I thought . . . I'm actually hoping that maybe you could ask one of your supervisors for some advice. Maybe your boss, Monsieur Fontneau, could help us? Concierges have all sorts of connections, right?"

Elizabeth was quiet. Her index finger was running in circles, stroking the lip of the bottle. "He's my immediate supervisor, Mom, and I'm trying to impress him. I don't want him to know my family is involved in a crime."

"Well, what about the hotel manager?"

"Are you crazy? That would be worse. Monsieur Bertrand is terribly proper. Besides, I'm pretty low on the totem pole. I don't really get to talk to top management."

"Don't they have some sort of service for resolving employees' problems?" asked Lucy, who was growing rather cranky. She wasn't at all pleased with her daughter's attitude.

"I'll think about it," said Elizabeth in a rather doubtful tone, which convinced Lucy that no help was to be found in this quarter. She was about to say something she would probably have regretted when two young men in Cavendish blazers entered the break room.

"Mom, these are my colleagues, Adil Sadek and Malik Mehanna. They work on the front desk."

"*Enchanté,*" said Adil, giving her a little bow. He was extremely good-looking, tall, and slim, with caramel skin, jet-black hair, and amazingly long eyelashes.

"Your mother? I thought you were sisters," said Malik, who was shorter and heavier, but whose cheeks dimpled when he smiled. Lucy had the feeling she'd seen him before, his name sounded familiar, but she couldn't place him.

"Don't mind him," advised Elizabeth. "Malik can't help being charming. He does it to get tips."

"No, no," insisted Malik. "I was telling the truth. You could be sisters."

Lucy was blushing and shaking her head. "Does this sort of flattery really work?"

"You'd be surprised," said Adil, extracting a tiny paper cup filled with tarry liquid from the coffee machine. He sat at one of the tables and ripped open a packet of sugar, adding it to his coffee.

Malik joined him at the table, unwrapping a chocolate bar and breaking off a piece. "Would you like some?" he asked, offering it to Lucy and Elizabeth.

Elizabeth shook her head, indicating she didn't want any chocolate.

"No, thanks," said Lucy, sipping at her water. "I'm in a bit of trouble, and I wonder if you could help me," she began, getting a sharp look from Elizabeth.

"*Bien sûr,*" said Malik. "What do you need?"

"Just a bit of information," said Lucy, glaring at Elizabeth. "As it happened, I witnessed an, um, accident and I called for help. They took the victim away in an ambulance, and I want to know how he's doing. Do you know where they take people who've had accidents?"

"L'Hôtel-Dieu," said Malik.

"Where's that?" asked Lucy.

"Near Notre-Dame."

"The cathedral?"

"That's right," replied Malik, rising to his feet. "Back to work."

"Gee, I've got to go," said Elizabeth, realizing she'd overstayed her break and hopping up.

"I shouldn't have kept you," said Lucy, automatically accepting some of the blame.

"Let me know what happens," said Elizabeth, surprising Lucy with a quick peck on the cheek.

"I will," promised Lucy, replacing the cap on her water bottle as she followed Elizabeth and the two boys down the hall to the lobby. There she tucked her bottle into her purse and made her way to the exit, where a liveried doorman asked if she'd like a taxi. "I would," she said. "*Merci.*"

Moments later, rather expensive moments but worth every euro to Lucy, she was debarking in front of the hospital, which, she was puzzled to learn, was also a hotel. Handy, she decided, in case you wanted to be near a sick loved one, but rather weird if you were vacationing. Who would want to spend their vacation near a bunch of sick people? There was so much about France that she didn't understand. For instance, why did they have an enormous tomb for Napoleon, who had really brought an awful lot of grief to the French people?

Once inside, she followed the arrows on the *accueil* signs that indicated the reception desk and found herself in a hospital lobby that looked a lot like hospital lobbies in the United States, busy, with people coming and going. Some were obviously visitors, carrying flowers and gifts, others were uniformed health-care workers, and there were even a few departing patients being pushed to waiting taxis in wheelchairs. The reception desk was front and center, so Lucy approached, trying to dredge up the appropriate French words, which had long been buried in her mind.

"Bonjour, madame," she began, aware that failing to offer a greeting was considered rude in France. "Je cherche l'information d'un patient, nom de Laurence Bruneau," she said, feeling rather proud of her linguistic accomplishment.

The woman behind the counter replied with a string of rapid-fire sounds, which Lucy could not begin to comprehend.

"Parlez lentement, s'il vous plaît," Lucy said, getting a repetition of the same speech.

"She said that information is not available, because of patient confidentiality," offered a woman in line behind her. She was obviously wealthy, dressed in a suit that even Lucy recognized as a genuine Chanel, and carrying a large alligator handbag, which contained a ridiculously small dog sporting a pink bow in her topknot.

"*Merci,*" said Lucy, wishing she had enough facility in French to convince the receptionist to change her tune. But as it was, she didn't want to monopolize the receptionist's attention when others also wanted information. She stepped aside, yielding her place to the helpful woman, who gave her a smile and a nod at the same time that the little dog leaped out of the bag and onto the reception counter, going straight for a vase of flowers and knocking it over.

The receptionist jumped up to snatch the vase, the dog jumped to the floor and ran for the door, and the helpful woman dashed after her little pet. Everyone was reaching to help, picking up flowers and snatching papers from the expanding pool of water on the reception desk. Lucy also decided to help, picking up a clipboard that, she happened to notice, held a list of patients' names with their room numbers. *Bruneau, L.* was at the top, assigned to room number 710. She carefully placed the clipboard on the counter, which was high and dry, unlike the desk behind it, and headed for the elevators.

Room 710 was easy to find. When the elevator doors slid open on the seventh floor, Lucy had an unobstructed view of the closed door, with the number clearly visible on a plastic square. She also had a clear view of the uniformed police officer seated on a chair beside the door, guarding it. Unwilling to draw attention to herself, she remained in place, and the doors slid closed and the elevator descended.

It was while she was on the elevator that something clicked and she suddenly remembered where she'd seen Malik. He was the young man she'd seen arguing in the Cavendish lobby with the older, gray-haired man and then angrily stalking off. And his companion Adil's last name was Sadek, the same as the leader of Les Amis du Roi de l'Égypte, whom Richard had quoted in his news story. Could they be related?

Chapter Six

Leaving the hospital, Lucy found herself walking by Notre-Dame and, acting on an impulse, decided to go in. Her first impression was of the darkness inside and the scent of old dust and burning candles. The medieval cathedral was a sharp contrast to the Community Church in Tinker's Cove, with its white walls and large clear-glass windows, which allowed worshippers to see the green leaves and blue sky outside. Notre-Dame was dingy and crowded with sightseers, who followed a U-shaped circuit through the huge stone edifice. There were devout worshippers, too, kneeling in the various side chapels.

It seemed very strange to Lucy, who wondered at the immense effort involved in building the cathedral. How did the builders manage it, working in the thirteenth century, before cranes and power tools? she wondered. She thought of the incredibly strong hold faith must have had on medieval minds, faith that required people to create this tribute to Mary when they had so little and their lives were so miserable.

Of course, she thought, pausing before the crowned statue of Mary floating above a sea of flickering candles, they didn't know how awful their lives were, having nothing to compare them to. They didn't know about hot showers and Social Security and antibiotics; they knew filth and poverty and early death. The church, with its promise of eternal life, was their only hope.

Watching as a beautiful young woman lit a candle and knelt before it, crossing herself and murmuring a prayer, she thought of the millions of people who, even today, were believers. Maybe there was something in it, she decided, pulling a five-euro note from her purse and shoving it through the slot in the cash box. Feeling rather ridiculous, she pulled a thin taper from its holder and lit it from one of the burning candles. Then, making a wish, not anything she would dare call a prayer, but merely a simple plea that everything would be all right for herself and those she loved, she lit a candle. She had never done such a thing before and didn't know what to expect, but she was a bit disappointed when she didn't feel any sort of spiritual connection or transformation. It was just like taking her first communion at the Presbyterian church she attended as a child, which served cubic centimeters of white bread and tiny shot glasses of grape juice. But it couldn't hurt, she told herself as she left the church. It was a sort of insurance.

The gang was gathered in the living room when she returned to the apartment, where they were drinking wine and eating baguette slices spread with olive tapenade.

"I ate way too much, waiting for you," said Sue in an accusing tone. "It's all your fault."

"Don't believe her," said Rachel, filling a wineglass for Lucy. "She had two pieces, while the rest of us . . ."

"Who's counting?" said Pam, passing Lucy a slice of bread loaded with the savory mixture. "This stuff is delicious."

"Did you make it?" asked Lucy, savoring a bite.

"Bought it at the Monoprix," said Sue. "I wish we had one in Tinker's Cove. Even the bags of salad are better somehow."

"Drink up," urged Bill. "We have a reservation at Chez Loulou."

"What were you doing that made you so late?" Rachel asked Lucy as they all trooped down the stairs.

"First, I stopped at the hotel to see Elizabeth, and then I went to the hospital to see how Chef Larry is doing," she said as they crossed the courtyard and exited onto the street. It was only a short walk to the corner and Chez Loulou, but the sidewalk was narrow, which made conversation difficult. It wasn't until they were all seated at a long table in the restaurant that they were able to talk.

"And how is Chef Larry?" asked Pam.

"I don't know," said Lucy. "He's apparently alive, but there was a cop sitting outside his door."

"Did you talk to the cop?" asked Sid.

"Are you kidding?" Lucy's eyebrows shot up. "I got out of there as fast as I could."

They laughed, then got down to the business of consulting the menu, trying to decipher the French. "What is *magret de canard?*" asked Pam.

"Duck breast," said Sue. "But I don't have a clue about *cervelles en matelote.*"

"It sounds delicious," said Rachel.

"If you don't know what it is," advised Bill, wiser after his encounter with *tête de veau,* "I wouldn't order it."

"Point taken," agreed Sue. "I think I'll have a *salade niçoise.*"

"Better safe than sorry," agreed Lucy. "I think I'll have that, too. I'm not really very hungry."

"I've rather lost my appetite, too," said Ted. "I guess witnessing the bloody aftermath of a violent stabbing does that to you."

"It looks like we're going to have plenty of time to get acquainted with French cuisine," observed Bob. "From what the guy at the embassy said, the French cops can keep our passports for as long as they like and we have no recourse except to cooperate."

"I called Richard this afternoon, and that's pretty much what he said," offered Ted, reaching for the carafe to top off his glass just as the waiter arrived to take their order. When that business was done, he continued his report. "Richard said we should tell the truth, the whole truth, and nothing but the truth. He mentioned this politician quite high up in the government who was tried for corruption and actually cleared, but, get this, the guy's wife went to jail because she told some lies, attempting to cover up for him."

"I thought there's some rule about spouses not having to testify against each other," said Pam, taking a bite of bread.

"Not unless they want to," quipped Sue.

"That's back home," said Bob with a sigh. "But it seems it's not the case in France."

"Our only option is to cooperate," said Lucy. "Not that we wouldn't, of course. I asked Elizabeth if anybody at the hotel could help us."

"Good idea," said Pam, forever the cheerleader she was in high school.

"Don't get too excited," advised Lucy. "She was reluctant to get involved, and I guess I can't blame her. She was afraid of damaging her professional reputation."

"Well, I called Sidra," said Sue. "I figured that if anyone could help us, it would be Norah—and I was right. As soon as Sidra told her about our problems, she called me and promised to make arrangements with some big international lawyer she knows who can assist us. . . ."

"That's going to be expensive," cautioned Bob.

"Even better, Norah said she'd cover any additional expenses while we're detained here in Paris, including the lawyer."

"That's terrific," said Pam.

"I had a nice little chat with our concierge," offered Rachel. "She speaks quite good English, and I asked if it would be a problem if we wanted to keep the apartment a bit longer."

"I hope you didn't tell her we're involved in a police investigation," said Lucy.

"I didn't, but why not?" asked Rachel.

"Because I don't think she'd be very happy about renting to people who are under suspicion," said Lucy.

"Oh, don't be silly," said Rachel. "We're not under suspicion, for one thing. And she's really quite nice. She's a terrific knitter. She was working on an adorable little sweater for her dog. His name is Gounod, and he's very cute."

"And what did she say about the apartment?" asked Bob, intent on getting his wife back on track.

"Oh, she said she'd ask the owner," said Rachel, smiling at the waiter who was setting a steaming plate of *cervelles en matelote* in front of her.

"Ohmigosh," said Sue, laughing. "Do you know what that is?"

"Whatever it is, it's quite good," said Rachel after she'd swallowed a crusty mouthful.

Sue took a moment to spear a green bean. "They're brains, sweetie. *Brainsss.*"

"How offal," said Pam, unable to resist the joke and giggling at her own cleverness.

"No, really, they're very good. Anyone want a taste?"

Bill was the only one who was game, agreeing with Rachel that the dish was delicious. "Maybe I'll have them tomorrow," he said, "if we eat here again."

"Norah also said we shouldn't let this get us down," said Sue. "She said we should enjoy ourselves while we're here. So I say, if we don't get a summons tomorrow, let's head out to Versailles."

"I'm beginning to think Marie Antoinette was misunderstood," said Lucy.

"She was a victim of circumstance, caught up in events she couldn't control," said Bob, sighing. "Just like us."

But the next morning, as they got off the Métro at the Gare d'Austerlitz stop, Lucy felt quite cheerful. Perhaps it was just the fact that they were doing something and going somewhere. It was hard to get too depressed, she thought, standing in line at the ticket counter, when you were in France and on your way to see Versailles, with its Hall of Mirrors and fabulous gardens.

"Château de Versailles," she told the man at the ticket window, feeling a bit more comfortable with her mastery of French. "Deux billets pour aller et retour," she added, specifying two round-trip tickets. When he responded with the rapid-fire speech that she still found incomprehensible, she simply handed over her credit card.

Then, carefully tucking the tickets in her purse, she zipped it tight, checking the area for possible pickpockets. Not that she knew what a pickpocket looked like, she thought, noticing the usual mix of tourists and natives going their various ways in the station. One man, who was leaning against a pillar, turned his head quickly away, and she wondered if he'd been watching her. Was he a pickpocket? He was good-looking in the usual way, with very short hair and that stubbly, unshaven look they all had, and was wearing the required scarf over his black leather jacket, which was trimmed with metal studs. Or maybe he'd found her attractive? She'd heard that Frenchmen were more appreciative of older women, unlike the youth-obsessed Americans. It wasn't impossible that she might attract an admiring male glance, she thought, feeling her cheeks warm as she joined the others and headed for the platform.

The ten-mile ride to Versailles wasn't nearly long enough for Lucy, who could have sat on the train all day, gazing out the windows at the little towns and quaint houses, their stuccoed walls and clay-tiled roofs so different looking from the houses in Maine. When they arrived in Versailles, they discovered it was actually a small city, with buses and a busy open market.

"Oh, let's have a picnic," said Sue, and they were soon darting from stall to stall, stocking up on provisions for lunch. Then, carrying their bags of bread and wine and cheese and fruit, they followed the brown signs to the château, the gate of which was right on the tree-lined street.

"Somehow I thought it would be more isolated," said Ted. "This doesn't seem very secure at all."

"It wasn't," said Sue, who was consulting a guidebook. "There were guards, but anybody could go in if they had a sword and a jacket, and if they didn't happen to own them, they could rent them."

"If they'd had TSA screening procedures, France might still be a monarchy," said Pam. They were climbing the cobbled drive, gazing at the enormous château, which was golden in the morning sunlight.

"It's big, but it doesn't seem big enough," said Sue, referring once again to her guidebook. "This says that twenty thousand people lived here, from the royal family and their courtiers on down to the scullery maids."

"That's bigger than Tinker's Cove," said Ted, who

had a journalist's fondness for statistics and was always comparing population and circulation figures.

"It must have been grand," said Pam in a dreamy voice. "Imagine having your hair powdered and wearing a long silk dress and meeting your handsome lover, in his stockings and silk breeches. . . ."

"Great, until they chopped your head off," said Bob.

But even Bob had to admit it was quite a place when they'd finished the tour, which took them through the various royal apartments, the impressive chapel, and the enormous Hall of Mirrors. After seeing so much brocade and gilt and marble, Lucy found it was a relief to step outside into the well-ordered formal gardens. There didn't seem to be any place for a picnic among the neat gravel paths and geometric flower beds, but they followed a young couple toting a basket and found a grassy area beside the Grand Canal. There were lots of people picnicking on the grass. Others were rowing themselves around the Grand Canal in rented boats.

It was warm in the sun, and their lunch of bread and cheese and fruit and wine made them all sleepy. Lucy was lying down, and Bill was resting his head on her thigh. She was thinking that there was much more to see and that they really ought to get up.

"I'd like to see the Hameau," she said, lifting her head and shading her eyes from the sun. Squinting for just a moment, she thought she saw the guy from the Gare d'Austerlitz, the one she thought might have been admiring her. Or was it? Whoever he was, he didn't seem to be interested in her anymore; he was watching a couple of blond German girls in tight jeans toss a Frisbee back and forth.

"Come on," said Lucy, urging her companions on. "There's a little train we can take to the Trianons and

Marie Antoinette's little farm. Maybe there are lambs and chicks!"

"And a gift shop," said Sue. "We can't miss the gift shop."

Lucy loved the waterwheel and the thatched roofs of the houses in the Hameau, but she had to admit there was something ridiculous about a queen who dressed in a milkmaid's costume and herded perfumed sheep with a crook made of Sevres porcelain. And outside the Petit Trianon, the queen's private retreat, they stood in the stone grotto where she was informed that an angry mob of Parisian market women was marching on the château. The mob forced the royal family to go to Paris, where they were imprisoned, never to see Versailles again. The king and queen were eventually tried and beheaded, and their young son, the dauphin, died in prison of tuberculosis. Only their daughter Marie Thérèse Charlotte survived; after six long years of imprisonment she was finally released as part of an exchange of prisoners with Austria, then France's enemy.

Perhaps the group members were tired after their exhausting day in Versailles, or perhaps they were thinking about the violence that overtook France during the revolution, but they were quiet and subdued on the trip home. Lucy thought of the little dauphin, imprisoned in filth and neglected, only to die at the age of ten, and wished she could believe the human race had progressed from that sort of cruelty.

"The more things change, the more they stay the same," said Lucy as they made their way into the courtyard. "That's a French proverb, isn't it?"

"Ah, there you are," said Madame Defarge, popping out of her lodge by the courtyard entrance. She was waving a handful of papers and seemed decidedly uncomfortable. "These came for you," she said, narrowing her eyes suspiciously. "You are all required to report to the commissariat tomorrow." She paused, then hissed, "For questioning."

Turning on her heel, she disappeared as quickly as she had come, apparently unwilling to linger for the briefest of chats. There was no singsong "*Bonne nuit,*" no "À bientôt" with a little wave, no "Au revoir" with a smile, no farewell at all, only a firmly closed door.

"That was some cold shoulder," said Sue, turning to Rachel. "And you were saying how nice she is."

"She was," insisted Rachel. "But I guess Lucy was right. She doesn't want to get involved with suspected criminals."

They were somber as they climbed the twisting, uneven stairs to the apartment, each one dealing with this setback in their own way. Lucy amused herself by imagining what her friends were thinking: Sue was thinking of pouring herself a glass of wine or three, and Sid was hoping that this interview at the commissariat wouldn't take very long, because he wanted to visit the Eiffel Tower tomorrow. Bob was searching his mind, looking for legal loopholes, while Rachel was wondering what information she might possibly have that would help in the investigation. Pam was planning to do a calming yoga workout, and Ted was wondering if the *International New York Times* would be interested in a story about an average American's encounters with the French justice system. Bill was thinking of ways to level the stairs, while she herself was trying to think of some way she could crack the case and discover who attacked Chef Larry so they could get their passports back and go home on time.

When her cell phone rang, she grabbed it eagerly, noting the caller was Elizabeth and hoping her daughter had some good news for them. "What's up?' she asked, by way of greeting.

"Well, it's Sylvie's birthday and she's giving a party tonight for herself and you're all invited."

Lucy didn't understand. At home, a young person wouldn't dream of inviting members of the older generation to what would surely be a raucous, boozy celebration, one that would probably include a visit to a tattoo parlor. "Really?" she asked.

"Yeah. I know it seems weird, but she's quite insistent. She's been making little treats all day. She calls them petits fours, but I don't think they're cake. And she's got a case of champagne."

"Well, I like champagne," said Lucy in a doubtful tone.

"I'm afraid she'll take it out on me if you don't come," said Elizabeth. "She can be really bitchy if she doesn't get her way."

"Okay," said Lucy, thinking there were worse ways of spending an evening than drinking champagne and eating petits fours, whatever they turned out to be. And it would keep her mind off the present situation. "Who else is coming?"

"Tout le monde. That means everybody she knows," said Elizabeth.

"I know what it means," said Lucy, thinking that maybe she'd pick up some information about Chef Larry. If everybody in Paris was going to be there, surely somebody would know him, right?

Despite Lucy's urging, only Pam and Ted were willing to venture out to the party. Sue was cooking up French bread pizzas in the kitchen, Sid was absorbed in a soccer match on TV, Rachel was relaxing with a novel, and Bob was busy with his iPad. So the Stillingses and the Stones made their way to the Métro station, stopping first at the Monoprix to buy a box of fancy chocolates for Sylvie.

The party was in full swing when they arrived. They could hear music and voices as they climbed the stairs. Sylvie greeted them enthusiastically with double *bisous* and graciously posed for the birthday photos Ted insisted on taking with his smartphone. Elizabeth shooed some young people off the futon so they could sit down, and before they knew it, they had been given flutes of champagne and plates of assorted canapés.

Lucy was savoring a stuffed mushroom when she noticed Adil and Malik standing together in a corner, and went over to talk with them. "Lovely party, isn't it?" she said.

"Terrific," said Adil, looking past her and scanning the crowded room.

"How is your friend?" asked Malik. "The one in hospital?"

"I don't know. I wasn't allowed to see him," admitted Lucy as Elizabeth came by with a bottle of champagne and refilled her glass. Adil and Malik refused. They were drinking orange juice.

"Sylvie loves to entertain," said Elizabeth with a touch of sarcasm.

"I like the Western way," said Malik. "I like it that a woman can invite her friends for a good time."

"But you wouldn't want to marry such a woman as Sylvie, would you?" said Adil with a smirk.

"Not even a girl like my Elizabeth," said Lucy. "She would be too independent for you, right?"

Malik was gazing wistfully at Elizabeth, who was busy greeting people and filling glasses. "I might like a Western wife, but my family would not approve."

"Nor would I," said Adil in a pompous tone. "A wife should be submissive to her husband in all things."

"Would you let her drive a car?" asked Lucy, thinking of the women in Saudi Arabia who had been testing that country's prohibition on women drivers.

"Of course," said Malik, grinning easily.

"Only with my permission," said Adil. "She would have to ask me before she could take the car."

"Every time?" asked Lucy.

"Yes." Adil nodded, his expression serious. "I would want to know why she needed the car, where she was going, and what she was doing."

"I think you might have a hard time finding a wife who would agree to that," said Lucy. "At least in France, anyway."

"That's true. Even the Muslim girls are adopting Western attitudes," said Adil, who clearly disapproved. "But it is better for us to be in Paris. Things are not so good in Egypt now. There's no stability, and the mob is in charge, overturning one government after another. They need a strong leader."

"Is that why you're in France?" asked Lucy, who was curious. "Because of the Arab Spring?"

"Not exactly," said Adil. "Our families left Egypt with King Farouk in nineteen fifty-two,"

"Are you related to the king?" asked Lucy.

"No," said Adil. "But my family has always been close to the royal family."

"Adil's great-grandfather was Farouk's head of security, and my grandmother was the infant prince's nanny," said Malik, a note of pride in his voice. "When the royal family boarded the yacht to leave Egypt, she was ordered to walk in front of Farouk, carrying Fouad, because the baby was now the king."

"I know about this," said Lucy. "I read about Les Amis du Roi de l'Égypte in the paper, and I saw the preparations for the conference at the Cavendish."

"Adil's grandfather is the leader of Les Amis," said Malik. "He is a true believer."

"My grandfather is right. Only a strong leader can unite the Egyptian people and restore order."

"And you think Fouad is that strong leader?" demanded Malik, with a laugh. "He isn't interested in Egypt. He likes living in Switzerland with his Nelly. I heard he eats in the kitchen with the help."

"My grandfather says Fouad may be reluctant now, but he will come to realize his duty and will reclaim his birthright." Adil turned to Malik. "And now, excuse us, but we must go home. We have to be at work very early tomorrow. Isn't that so, Malik?"

Malik didn't seem as if he wanted to leave the party. He was about to take a bit of toast topped with pâté from the plate Sylvie was offering him, but he immediately dropped his hand. "*Désolé*," he said, apologizing to Sylvie. "You know how it is. We've got the early shift."

"D'accord," Sylvie replied with a shrug. "*À demain.*" She offered the plate to Lucy, who took a toast and, nibbling it, made her way through the crowded, tiny room to the futon, where Bill and the Stillingses were still sitting. Her place had been taken, however, by a young man, and they were deep in conversation.

"I am not surprised about what happened to Larry," he was saying. Lucy noticed his hands were rough and red, and he hunched his shoulders, as if expecting a blow. "He was asking for trouble."

"In what way?" asked Lucy, intrigued.

"Ah, Lucy, this is Émile," said Pam. "He worked with Chef Larry at the Cavendish Hotel."

"Really? I didn't know Chef Larry worked at the Cavendish."

"Only for a short time," said Émile with a smirk. "He didn't play by the rules."

"He seems very ambitious," offered Ted. "He told us he didn't want to spend hours and hours chopping carrots and onions. That's why he started his bakery shop and the school."

Émile raised one very dark eyebrow. "That's not why he left. He was fired."

"Why?" asked Pam.

"I don't know for sure," replied Émile. "But after he was gone, people were saying that a lot of stuff was missing. Expensive things, like caviar and truffles."

"They thought he was stealing?" asked Lucy.

"I don't know for sure," said Émile. "But that's what I heard."

Just then the lights were flicked off, and Elizabeth appeared in the kitchen doorway carrying a birthday cake, complete with candles in the American style, and everybody was singing the birthday song. *Definitely the birthday song*, thought Lucy, recognizing the tune but not quite making out the words.

Chapter Seven

Bob greeted them eagerly when they got back to the apartment. "I heard from Norah," he said, looking more cheerful than he had in days. "She referred me to a top-notch firm of international lawyers. I'm going to put a call in first thing tomorrow, before the interviews. If these guys are as good as I think they are, they'll want to represent us at the police interviews."

"That's great, Bob," said Lucy, her spirits lifting. She hadn't realized how depressed this whole thing was making her, but now she suddenly felt a lot more optimistic.

"If we hadn't drunk so much at the party, I'd suggest a champagne toast," said Pam.

"That's okay," said Rachel. "Bob's already celebrated...."

"It was only a beer," said Bob.

"Well, you deserve a big thank-you," said Bill, clapping him on the back.

"Hear! Hear!" added Ted.

But when she woke the next morning, Lucy found the atmosphere had changed.

"I don't understand it. They're not answering my

calls," said Bob when she went into the kitchen in search of coffee.

"It's early yet," she said, checking her watch and trying not to notice the fluttery feeling in her stomach. "It's barely seven o'clock. Their office probably isn't open yet."

"They start later here," said Rachel in a reassuring tone.

"If they're international, they have to deal with different time zones," said Bob.

"In France there's only one time zone," said Sue. "Theirs."

"They do seem to think they're the center of the universe," admitted Ted. "At least that's what Richard says."

"I've got the first interview, at nine," said Lucy, wrapping her hands around her coffee mug and realizing it was extremely unlikely that Bob could arrange for her to be accompanied by a lawyer so early in the day. "They're just looking for information, right? They don't consider me a suspect, do they?"

"Of course not," said Sue, patting her hand.

"No one could suspect you," said Rachel with an affirmative nod.

"Only if they're nuts," said Bill.

"I think you should be prepared for anything," said Bob, looking grim. "I wish they'd answer their g-d phone."

Lucy went pale, and Rachel hurried to give her a hug. "Don't mind him. Bob's always anticipating the worst."

"I hope he's wrong," said Lucy in a nervous whisper. Just the name of the place is scary somehow. Thirty-six, quai des Orfèvres."

"There's a movie with that title," said Sid. "It's one of those subliminal things. You've heard it, and it has negative overtones, but it's really just an address."

"It's in the Maigret books," offered Pam. "And he's such a nice man."

"I wonder what *orfèvres* means," mused Sue, reaching for her dictionary.

"Probably something like the Traitors' Gate at the Tower of London," suggested Pam.

"No! Not at all," crowed Sue. "It means goldsmiths! The quai of goldsmiths!"

"That makes me feel the teeniest bit better," admitted Lucy. "What do you think I should wear?"

"Avoid stripes," said Sue, attempting a joke but getting only dirty looks.

"Not funny," said Lucy, leaving the kitchen to sort through her suitcase. In the end, she chose a black sweater and pants, and Sue lent her a colorful Hermès scarf picturing hot-air balloons by way of apology for her bad joke.

When Lucy and Bill got out of the taxi at 36 quai des Orfèvres, they discovered it was just another gray Paris building, perhaps a bit plainer than most, with its orderly rows of windows. She thought fleetingly of the architecture back in Maine, which had a lot more variation: some buildings were brick and square, and others were rambling, had cedar shingles or clapboard siding, and often had a window stuck in an odd place or a roof that sagged. In Paris there was a strange uniformity. The buildings were all similar, they were even the same height, and you couldn't tell what was behind those neat facades. Apartments? Offices? Schools? They all looked alike, but sometimes you got a glimpse through one of those court-yard doors and were surprised to see a garden or a pile of junk or kids playing in a school yard.

Once inside the big square building, they had to pass through a thorough security check and then were directed upstairs, to the offices of the *brigade criminelle*. Bill was given a seat in a poorly lit hallway, and Lucy was taken inside a rather cluttered office crowded with desks, where Lapointe was waiting for her.

"Madame Stone, take a seat," he said, indicating a chair next to his desk. Unlike the other desks in the shared office, which were covered with stacks of papers, Lapointe's was bare, except for a phone and a computer. He didn't raise his eyes from the screen as she sat down, and his hands were busy on the keyboard. Noticing a card holder on one corner, Lucy took a card and tucked it in her pocket.

"I see from my notes that you were a student at the cooking school of Laurence Bruneau. Is that correct?"

"Yes," said Lucy, thinking this was an odd line of questioning.

"You came to France to study *la cuisine?*"

"Not exactly," said Lucy. "The trip was a sort of prize, an award. There is this TV show in America, *Norah!*, and the star, Norah Hemmings, rewards people who do good in their communities. My friends and I created the Hat and Mitten Fund in our town, which gives warm winter clothing and school supplies to kids who don't have them."

"In America children don't have hats and school supplies?" asked Lapointe, seeming puzzled.

"It's the sad truth," said Lucy. "Winter clothing is expensive, and kids grow fast. It's a problem for some families with limited incomes. It's the same with school supplies. Paper and pencils get used up."

Lapointe was clicking away on his computer, and his eyes never met hers. "And this Norah Hemmings, she gives you and your friends a trip to France? Wouldn't it have been better to donate that money to your Hat and Mitten Fund?"

Lucy had actually had the same thought but felt duty bound to defend Norah. "She made substantial donations to the fund in the past."

"This trip cost a lot of money. The cooking school alone is very expensive, thousands of euros," said Lapointe. "This seems very odd to me, all this money for you and your friends to come to Paris. Is there something you are supposed to do while you are here?"

"Only to take the cooking class," said Lucy. "The rest of our time is free, for us to do what we want. Yesterday we went to Versailles."

"Perhaps this trip was a way to hide a money transfer. Do you think this is possible?"

"Money laundering? You tell me," said Lucy, who found the idea ridiculous. "I don't know how these things work, but I don't think Norah would be involved in anything like that." She bit her lip. "Look, all I know is I was on the TV show, they gave us this prize, and I packed my bags and got on a plane. That's it."

"You'd be surprised what you might know," said Lapointe, peering around the side of the computer screen and resting his bulging reptilian eyes on her. "I will find the truth bit by bit," he said, quickly licking his lips. "It will emerge, and the guilty will be punished."

Lucy thought of Elizabeth's warning about *garde à vue* and had a brief image of a dark, dank cell. "I am only too happy to tell you what I know. You haven't asked me anything about the crime or the man at the market who attacked Chef Larry. And I think someone has been following us—a sinister-looking man in a leather jacket."

"If you are as innocent as you claim, why would anyone be following you?" he asked. "I think you must be mistaken."

"I'm sure you're right," said Lucy, who didn't think any such thing. Her thoughts turned to the rumors she'd heard the night before, at Sylvie's birthday party. "Do you think Chef Larry was involved in the black market? Perhaps he angered someone? In fact—" she began, about to mention Chef Larry's offer to get cut-rate delicacies for them when Lapointe cut her off.

"Madame, I am the one who is supposed to be asking the questions." Lapointe blinked slowly. "But for the time being, I am satisfied. You may go, but I may need to talk to you again."

"How long do you think this investigation will take?" asked Lucy. "We have a flight home on the seventeenth."

"That is not my concern," said Lapointe. "You may send in Monsieur Stone, *s'il vous plaît.*"

Lucy went out to the hall, where Bill was leafing through his guidebook. "He wants to see you."

"How'd it go?" he asked her.

"I don't know," she said. "I have no idea where this is heading."

"Damn," he said, giving her the book. "Something to read while you wait."

But when Lucy sat down, she didn't open the book. Her mind was busy going over the interview. Money laundering? Could it be possible? All indications were that Chef Larry was involved in the black market. Could he also be operating a money-laundering scheme? And had they, and perhaps even Norah, been drawn in? The more she thought about it, the more anxious she got, and when Bill emerged, much sooner than she had expected, she jumped on him.

"What did he ask you?" she demanded.

"Nothing much. Just name and address, occupation, that sort of thing."

"Really?" she asked, surprised, as they stepped out of the notorious building and into the weak Paris sunshine.

"Yeah," said Bill, exhaling a big sigh. "But even so, it was pretty stressful. Let's find a café. I'm wicked thirsty."

"I feel like we're being set up," muttered Lucy as they headed for the café on the corner. "Lapointe was asking me about money laundering. I think he's on the wrong track. Norah would never be involved in something like that."

"Beer, see voo play," he said to the waiter, who was hovering inside the door.

"Deux bières, s'il vous plaît," said Lucy, holding up two fingers as they settled themselves at a window table. At home she'd never think of drinking beer in the middle of the morning, but in Paris . . . Well, she noticed, there was plenty of company in the café, and they certainly weren't all drinking coffee.

Lucy was still working on her beer when Sid and Sue joined them, having seen them through the window.

"Has Lapointe questioned you?" asked Bill. "Are you done already?"

"Yeah. He only asked a couple of questions," said Sue. "He asked about the trip and the cooking school. I told him Chef Larry wasn't much of a teacher."

"Didn't you tell Lapointe about the wine and gourmet goods?" asked Lucy.

"No, I didn't," said Sue. "As far as I know, that was all on the up-and-up."

Lucy shook her head. "You should have told him."

"Why didn't *you* tell him?" asked Sue, challenging Lucy.

"I should have," admitted Lucy. "The truth is, he didn't give me a chance."

"Lapointe gave Lucy a hard time," said Bill. "She was in there for quite a while."

"He just asked me about our address, confirmed the information on my passport," said Sid. "That was it."

"You do have an honest face," said Sue, reaching across the table and stroking his cheek.

Sue had just finished her coffee when Ted and Pam arrived and joined the group.

"How did it go?" asked Lucy.

"Much better than I expected," said Ted. "Richard warned me that the French police can be pretty hard-nosed, but all Lapointe wanted was basic stuff, name and address, stuff like that."

"He didn't ask about the cooking school?" asked Lucy.

"Oh, sure," said Pam. "But just basic stuff, again. How did we learn about it? That sort of thing."

"So do you think we're off the hook?" asked Sid.

"I asked if we'd be able to leave on the seventeenth," said Lucy. "He said that was not his concern, whatever that means."

A glum silence fell on the group, but it was broken when Rachel arrived. Her jacket was unbuttoned, with the ends of the unfastened belt flapping loosely, and her long, dark hair was coming loose from its clip.

"What's the matter?" asked Sue, who was always quick to pick up on clues from a person's appearance.

"Lapointe's been talking to Bob for a long time," she said, slipping into a chair and squeezing her big purse against her chest. "I'm afraid Bob started mouthing off or something. He was spoiling for a fight when he went in. He doesn't like the French justice system, he hates feeling powerless, and he can't believe that all his law school training and experience don't count here."

"Well, that's not illegal," said Pam. "They can't charge him with disliking the system."

"I'm not sure that's true," said Ted. "They put a big premium on cooperation, and if he seems to be obstructing their investigation, they could hold him."

"Oh, no!" wailed Rachel. "Can they put him in jail?"

"I don't know," said Ted. "I guess it depends on whether or not they think he's got important information. I could call Richard and ask."

"What about those international lawyers Norah recommended?" asked Lucy, picturing Bob confined in that dark, dank cell, kept in *garde à vue*.

"I have their number," said Rachel, rummaging in her big brown leather bag. "Somewhere."

"And the embassy guy," offered Bill, reaching for his wallet. "I've got his card."

Lucy dialed the embassy at the same time Rachel called the lawyers, but neither got much help. Fox Carrington at the embassy said he was sorry, but Americans didn't have the same rights in France as they did in America, and were expected to abide by French law. If they broke a French law, they could certainly be prosecuted and punished.

"We're not trying to break the law," said Lucy. "We just need some help dealing with the system. Don't you offer some sort of legal aid to distressed American travelers?"

"It depends on the case," said Carrington. "Give me a call if anything develops."

"Something *has* developed. Our friend is being detained by the police," said Lucy, but Carrington had already ended the call.

Rachel was quick to mention Norah's name when she called the law firm of Mayall & Poulin, and she did get to speak to a junior partner. The junior partner explained that the firm really didn't get involved in criminal matters but specialized in visas, real estate transactions, that sort of thing. When asked if they could provide a reference to a criminal law practice, the junior partner seemed shocked. "I suppose I can look into it," he said in a doubtful tone.

"I would appreciate that," said Rachel, giving him her cell phone number before ending the call. "When pigs fly," she said, expressing her disappointment.

"Why don't we have an early lunch, while we wait?" suggested Pam.

Bill was the only one with any appetite; the rest just picked at their sandwiches and salads. Rachel tried to keep up a brave front, but she revealed her anxiety when she ordered a second cup of tea. Finally, when the dishes had been cleared away and the bill paid, Lucy offered to accompany Rachel back to the police headquarters to inquire about Bob.

This time, the officer at the reception desk did not send them upstairs, and he simply shook his head when they asked about Bob. Lucy produced the card she had taken from Lapointe's desk, and tried calling him on her cell phone, but her call went straight to voice mail.

"What do you want to do?" she asked Rachel.

"I'm going to sit here and wait for him," said Rachel, indicating a wooden bench that was situated against the lobby wall.

"You're sure you don't want to go back to the apartment? You'd be a lot more comfortable there."

"No. I'm going to wait right here."

Lucy sighed. "Then I'll wait with you."

Rachel looked at her with her big doe eyes. "You don't have to. I'll be fine."

"Don't be silly," said Lucy. "I'm not leaving you all alone. I'm staying right here."

Rachel squeezed Lucy's hand. "Thanks."

Lucy found that sitting in the lobby at 36 quai des Orfèvres was quite interesting, and watched as suspects in handcuffs were brought in and hustled upstairs by the flics. The cops were easily identifiable, even the ones in plain clothes. There was something about their confident attitude and their aggressive physicality. Lucy found most of them quite good-looking and wondered if being handsome was a requirement, like minimum height. There was also a steady stream of citizens, either presenting themselves for questioning on some matter or reporting a crime. From time to time she and Rachel used their cell phones, attempting to call Bob or Lapointe, but never succeeded in making contact.

But even though she found these mini-dramas quite absorbing, time dragged in the intervals when nothing was happening and the wooden bench was hard and uncomfortable. It was almost six o'clock when Bob finally appeared, looking drained and tired.

Rachel jumped up and hugged him, demanding, "What happened?"

Before Bob could reply, Lucy took him firmly by the arm and dragged him to the door. "Let's get out of here. You can tell us all about it outside."

Rachel wouldn't let go of Bob's hand. She held it as they walked along the sidewalk to the Métro station. "I was so afraid they were going to lock you up," she said.

"Me too," admitted Bob. "I think Lapointe was just yanking my chain, showing who was in charge. Most of the time he wasn't even questioning me. He just kept me sitting there."

"Mucho macho," muttered Rachel. "I hate that stuff."

"What was his line of questioning?" asked Lucy. "Did he try to place you at the crime scene? Was he trying to implicate you in the stabbing?"

"No, nothing about that. It was all about money. How much money did I bring to France? How much did I have access to? Was I carrying money for somebody else?" He paused, shaking his head. "It was so crazy. I mean, I do okay financially. I'm a professional, after all, but it's not like I'm rolling in dough. And the little bit I've managed to save is tied up in my IRA. And here he is, asking me about suitcases stuffed with cash." He exhaled sharply. "Weird."

Lucy didn't like the direction the investigation was taking. Once again she had the sinking feeling they were involved in something they didn't understand.

"Well, it's over. At least I hope it is," said Rachel. "Let's get home and see what Sue has cooked up for supper."

"She said something about lemon roasted chicken," said Lucy, smacking her lips.

The Métro was crowded with workers heading home for the night, and there was no opportunity for conversation. Lucy was left to her own thoughts, and they weren't comforting. From what Bob had told her, and judging by her own interview with Lapointe, it seemed certain that the authorities believed Chef Larry was involved in money laundering. She didn't have the foggiest idea how something like that worked, but at Sylvie's birthday party she had heard rumors that Chef Larry had been stealing goods from the Cavendish Hotel, rumors that were substantiated by the array of gourmet goodies they had found in the apartment and by Larry's offer to get more. Lucy doubted that stolen caviar and truffles generated the amount of money that Lapointe was talking about.

In the States, she'd heard that stolen goods were often sold at flea markets, but the sums involved were so small that the police generally ignored them. She had certainly never heard of any police raids at the weekend flea market out on Route 1. Of course, she thought, there was that VAT, or value-added tax, in France, and maybe that made black market dealing more profitable. And in France, there was more interest in luxury foods. Truffles, for example, could cost thousands of euros for a kilo, which she thought was less than a pound, but she wasn't actually sure.

She wondered if Lapointe had actually accused Bob of bringing "suitcases stuffed with cash" into France, or whether Bob had come up with the phrase. That was an awful lot of money, the sort of money that came only from dealing in drugs. Was Chef Larry involved in illegal drugs? It hardly seemed likely, but then, you never really knew people. You always thought other people were like you: you projected your own values and ideas onto others. If you were a good person, you tended to expect other people to be good, too. There was a term for it, "mirroring." It was mirroring that made people give their money to con artists or dismiss the funny smell coming from their neighbor's backyard. "He seemed so nice," they would tell reporters after the serial killer had been arrested, "but he always kept to himself."

"C'mon, Lucy," said Rachel, breaking into her thoughts. "It's our stop."

The long, anxious day had taken a toll on Lucy, and

she was tired as she climbed the stairs from the Métro station and followed Bob and Rachel along the narrow sidewalk to the apartment. The curb was quite high and the pavement uneven, so she had to concentrate on putting one foot in front of the other. She was hoping there would be a chilled glass of white wine waiting for her, and maybe Sue had cooked up some cheesy things or stuffed mushrooms. Her mouth was watering when they reached the double doors that led to the courtyard, and she could hardly wait for Bob to punch the code into the keypad. The buzzer finally sounded, and she pushed the door open, only to be met by Madame Defarge on the other side.

"Finally, you are back!" she cried, wringing her hands. "It has happened. *Je suis désolée*. I am sorry, but there was nothing I could do. The police came, and you were all out. I could not stop them."

"The police came here?" asked Bob.

Madame Defarge nodded.

"They searched the apartment?" asked Bob, sounding as if he were cross-examining a witness.

"*Oui*. They insisted. They had official papers. I had to let them in."

"What time was this?" asked Lucy.

"In the morning. They came just as I was on my way out to do my shopping."

"Did you observe them?" asked Bob. "You accompanied them, right? To make sure they didn't steal anything?"

Madame Defarge looked down at the cobblestones, then raised her eyes to meet Bob's. "I was running late," she said in an apologetic voice. "If I don't get to the market by ten, the quality is poor. The best food has all been sold. It's gone. What is left is not so good." She shrugged. "And," she added, cocking her head toward the window where her fluffy little white dog was sitting, watching with a toothy smile, "I wanted to get some fillet for my petit Gounod."

"Of course, quite understandable," said Bob, heading upstairs to assess the damage.

Chapter Eight

When Bob unlocked the door, it was all too clear that the apartment had been searched. Ransacked was more like it, thought Lucy. The suitcases that she and Bill had zipped and stacked neatly in a corner of the living room had been opened, and the contents tossed every which way. In the kitchen, bags of flour and sugar had been dumped into the sink, and Carte Noire coffee was all over the floor. Bob and Rachel's bedroom had been treated in the same way, the doors of the armoire hanging open and the clothes thrown everywhere. The bed had also been tossed, the sheets and duvet yanked off and the mattress left askew. In the en suite bathroom Rachel's jars of face cream and bath salts had been emptied into the sink, making a gooey mess.

Bob stood in the doorway to the room he shared with Rachel, shaking his head. "I can't believe the cops did this," he said. "This would never happen in America."

Lucy wasn't so sure, but she wasn't about to argue. "What were they looking for?"

"Maybe it was a routine procedure," suggested Rachel in a doubtful tone.

"I don't think so, but what do I know?" said Bob in a defensive tone. "From what I can see, the flics can do whatever they want. Citizens don't seem to have any rights at all."

"I'm sure that's not true," murmured Rachel, who was busy picking up clothes and replacing them on hangers in the armoire. "I could use a hand, Bob. Can you get that mattress back on the bed?"

Lucy left them to it and made a quick tour of the apartment, discovering that the rest of the bedrooms and baths were in the same condition. She returned to the living room, where she began gathering up clothing and refolding it. She heard a key turning in the lock and looked up to see the rest of the group arriving home.

"What the hell!" exclaimed Bill, taking in the sofas, with cushions askew, and the clothes scattered about.

"The police searched the apartment while we were out," said Lucy. "Everything's a mess, the kitchen, the bathrooms. . . ."

They quickly hurried down the hall to check on their rooms, and Lucy heard their cries of dismay as they discovered the mess.

"My Crème de la Mer," said Sue, showing Lucy the empty jar. "Two hundred dollars, dumped in the bathtub."

"Well," said Lucy, "the tub's gonna look great."

Rachel was already starting in the kitchen, dustpan and broom in hand. "The coffee!" she exclaimed, mourning the loss. "That stuff was so delicious!"

After they all pitched in and cleaned up the kitchen, Sue spread out the dinner she'd bought on the way home: rotisserie chickens from a stand on the rue Saint-Antoine, green salad, and a couple of baguettes. "I was going to roast chickens myself, but I ran out of time," she said, wielding a carving knife.

"How did you all spend the afternoon?" asked Rachel.

"On the Batobus," said Sid. "It's a tourist boat on the Seine. You can get on and off."

"We checked out the Musée d'Orsay. We even got in line, but it was too long and didn't move, so we gave up and got back on the Batobus," said Bill. "How did you guys make out at the police headquarters?"

"Bob was there all afternoon," said Lucy.

"Are you kidding?" asked Sid.

"No, they just kept me sitting there at Lapointe's desk."

"Rachel and I waited in the lobby," said Lucy.

Sue's eyes widened. "All afternoon? That's terrible. You deserve a treat, which I happen to have," she said, unwrapping a beautiful chocolate cake and setting it on the table. "I thought we might need something sweet and chocolaty tonight."

"It's too pretty to eat," said Rachel, admiring the swirls of icing and the fresh raspberries that topped the cake.

"No, it's not," said Bob, holding out his plate.

"But you haven't eaten your dinner," protested Rachel.

"I'm learning that life is short and unpredictable," he countered. "I'm eating dessert first."

After dinner, the friends spent the rest of the evening tidying up their rooms and making lists of things they needed to replace. Lucy found the police had somehow overlooked the bathroom she and Bill used, which was hidden away in a back hall. She remembered her mother once saying that there was nothing a good bath couldn't make better, so she decided to have a good soak in the big rolltop tub and poured in half a bottle of bubble bath.

Lying there in the suds, gazing at her pink toes poking through the bubbles, she wished she could just wash away her worries, but they persisted. As an American, she took a lot for granted, she thought. It wasn't as if she was an innocent who'd never been touched by crime.

She was a newspaper reporter, and she'd been involved in numerous investigations back home in Tinker's Cove. But there the system was quite different. Chief Kirwan didn't detain random suspects for hours at a time, the Tinker's Cove Police Department didn't toss people's homes in pointless searches, and suspects were presumed innocent until proven guilty. And in America they didn't grab your passport, not unless you were actually indicted on a very serious charge. She wasn't actually positive about this—it hadn't really come up in Tinker's Cove—but she had read about high-profile cases in which the defendants were ordered to surrender their passports, and the news reports always made much of it.

Her thoughts turned to a favorite old movie that she and Bill had watched a few weeks ago, *Casablanca*. She remembered the European refugees who gathered in Rick's café during World War II, waiting desperately for letters of transit that would allow them to leave Morocco for someplace safer, like America. They were like those frantic refugees, she thought, scrubbing her face with a terry-cloth bath mitt. They were stuck in Paris until the French police decided to return their passports.

She was beginning to think Elizabeth was right: France was a horrible place. She thought of King Louis XVI and Marie Antoinette and their two children, chased out of their beautiful palace at Versailles and dragged to prison in Paris. She could understand why the common people detested the aristocrats, but it was possible to see the royal family and their circle as victims of circumstance, unaware of the poverty and suffering taking place outside the palace gates. Mob rule was terrifying. She'd read of the September Massacres, when the queen's friend, the beautiful princesse de Lamballe, was literally torn limb from limb. And when they'd finished, Lucy recalled, they stuck her head on a pole and paraded it back and forth beneath Marie Antoinette's prison window.

Poor Marie Antoinette. What a dreadful end. Stuck in jail for years, cruelly separated from her children, then carted through the streets of Paris to the guillotine. And the guillotine . . . How horrible was that? And to think it wasn't mothballed until 1981, which really wasn't very long ago. Suddenly cold, Lucy climbed out of the tub and wrapped herself in a towel. All she really wanted, she realized with a shiver, was to go home.

Next morning Lucy woke with a plan. If the police thought they were involved in some sort of illegal dealings with Chef Larry, the only way they were going to get back to Tinker's Cove was if she could discover what Larry had been up to. In other words, she decided, she had to talk to him and get him to tell her who had attacked him and why.

She realized this was easier thought than done. After all, Chef Larry had been under police guard at the hospital and probably still was. And she didn't know if he was recovering or if his condition had worsened. But she'd never know unless she tried, and she did have a few ideas as to how she could sneak into Larry's room.

She felt a certain sense of excitement when she went into the kitchen, looking for breakfast, but she wasn't about to share her plans with the group, and especially not with Bill. She'd make some excuse, she decided. Perhaps she'd express a desire to visit the Musée Edith Piaf, the tiny singer's two-room apartment, or to seek out the graffiti-covered home of pop star Serge Gainsbourg. Something that none of the others would have the slightest interest in doing.

The TV in the kitchen was on when she poured herself a cup of coffee, and Sue and Pam were watching intently.

"What's happening?" she asked.

"General strike," said Pam.

"The potato farmers are protesting a cut in their subsidy or something," said Sue. "And this being France, everybody's joining in. The Métro's shut down, truck drivers are on strike, and of course, so are the college students."

"I've never seen the point of student strikes," said Pam. "What difference does it make if they skip classes?"

"That's the point," said Sue. "It's an excuse to cut classes."

"That means we're stuck here," said Lucy as the coffee took effect, clearing her brain. The TV screen was showing crowds of protesters filling the streets, and the occasional shoving match with police. "We can't go out in that."

"Yup." Sue poured herself another cup of coffee. "Everything's closed, anyway."

"Is there anything to eat?" asked Lucy.

Sue nodded. "*Tartine.*"

"And what is that?"

"You toast up yesterday's baguette and put jam on it," said Sue.

"Sounds good," said Bill, joining them.

Fueled by *tartines* and coffee, the friends found ways to occupy themselves, while keeping an eye on the TV. The guys sat around the table, playing poker, placing small bets with pocket change. Rachel settled down with a book, Pam practiced yoga, and Sue studied the French edition of *Vogue*. Lucy found herself wandering around the apartment, going from window to window, checking that all was peaceful outside.

"The demonstrators will hardly come here. This is a

residential area," said Sue. "All the action seems to be on the Champs-Élysées."

"That's true," admitted Lucy, pulling the map of Paris out of her guidebook and studying it. Much to her surprise, she discovered that the apartment wasn't really all that far from the Île de la Cité, where the hospital was located.

"I've got cabin fever," she said, testing the water. "I think I'll see if the Monoprix is open, or maybe one of those little *tabacs.*" Nobody protested or warned her not to go, not even Bill.

"You could pick up something for lunch," suggested Sue. "We're kind of low on food—except for pâté de foie gras and Mariage Frères tea."

"Okay," promised Lucy, donning her plaid coat. "I'll be back soon."

Once outside, she noticed the streets were emptier than usual, but a few stores were open, including an ethnic grocery on the next block. She'd stop there on the way back, she decided, and get some couscous or stuffed grape leaves for lunch. But first, she was determined to get to the hospital and see Chef Larry.

It felt good to be out on her own, she decided, striding along the mostly deserted streets. Many businesses were shuttered, there were no taxis and no buses, and few people had bothered to go out. She thought it was a big improvement from a usual day, when the streets were packed with traffic and the sidewalks full of people, as she crossed the Pont de Sully to the Île Saint-Louis. This was a tony residential area, a small island east of the larger Île de la Cité, filled with *hôtels particuliers,* large private town houses, most of which, she guessed, had been converted into pricey apartments. It was peaceful here. The quaint streets were lined with trees, now producing tiny, fresh green leaves.

The Île de la Cité was busier, containing not only the Cathédrale Notre-Dame, the Sainte-Chapelle, and the Conciergerie, which attracted tourists from all over the world, but also the courts in the Palais de Justice, the police headquarters at quai des Orfèvres, and the hospital. Police cars were coming and going, no doubt due to the farmers' demonstration. There also seemed to be more ambulances than usual, with their braying horns.

The lobby of the hospital was quiet, with only a few visitors. Nobody was manning the reception desk, which Lucy took as a very good sign. She marched right on past, took the elevator to the seventh floor, and stepped right out, disregarding the cop who was sitting in front of the door to Chef Larry's room. He gave her a cursory glance, then returned his attention to his iPhone.

Lucy continued on down the hallway, past the nurses' station, trying to think of a way she could get into Chef Larry's room. Setting off a fire alarm came to mind, but that was terribly irresponsible, and if she got caught, she'd be in big trouble. Back home she'd try to chat up the cop and convince him she was Chef Larry's sister or something, but she knew her mastery of French wasn't up to the task. She was about to give up and go home when she saw a cleaner coming out of a closet, wearing a smock and pushing a mop.

The closet wasn't locked, so she popped in and discovered a row of hooks holding smocks just like the one the cleaner was wearing. She slipped one on right over her coat. It made her look rather chunky, but she thought that made her disguise even more realistic. Her shoulder bag was a bit of a problem, but she didn't dare leave it in the closet, in case she needed to make a quick exit. She tried shifting it around so it hung in front of her waist, and decided it made her look pregnant. *A meno-pause baby,* she thought with a grim smile.

There was also a wide array of cleaning tools and products to choose from. She grabbed a spray bottle of cleanser and a rag. Back in the hallway, she squirted some cleanser on a framed Impressionist print that was intended to brighten up the place, keeping an eye on the cop. They were the only two people in that stretch of hallway, at least for the moment. Then, unbelievably, the cop stood up and stretched, then ambled off in the direction of the lavatories.

In the blink of an eye she popped into Chef Larry's room, where she was disappointed to find he was deeply unconscious, hooked up to a lot of tubes and machinery with blinking lights. She hadn't expected this. She'd hoped he would be recovering nicely and would be able to talk. It was awful, absolutely tragic, to find a young man in this condition, but, she reminded herself, she didn't have time for sympathy. She opened the locker, hoping to find his clothing, but it was empty. Of course, his clothing was in a crime lab somewhere. What about the drawer of his nightstand? Also empty. Her hands were shaking, and her heart was pounding. She had to get out of there before she was discovered. She'd been foolish to take such a risk, she thought, giving him a good-bye glance as she turned to leave. Much to her surprise, his eyes were wide open.

"What are you doing?" he asked.

"I came to see you," she said, reaching for his hand and squeezing it. "There's a cop outside, so I borrowed this cleaning smock."

"They say I'm going to be okay," he said.

"That's great news," said Lucy, wondering if he knew who had attacked him, and whether it would upset him if she asked. "Do you remember the attack?" she asked in a gentle voice. "I was the one who found you. I called the medics."

"I don't remember it at all," he said. They tell me it's normal after a traumatic event. You repress the memory."

Lucy was disappointed. If only he were able to remember his attacker, he could clear her and her friends from suspicion. She also wondered if he was telling the truth, but didn't want to press him. "Is there anything I can do for you?" she finally asked.

"Yeah," he said. "Can you make a phone call for me?"

"Sure, but why can't you do it?" asked Lucy.

He shook his head. "Not allowed. The cops took the phone."

It was true. There was no phone on the nightstand, and she'd found no sign of a cell phone in her brief search.

"Okay," said Lucy, reaching under her smock for her bag and producing a scrap of paper and a pen.

He gave her a phone number and told her to ask for Serge. "Tell him I need to see him," he added quickly. They could both hear approaching footsteps and turned toward the door, which was beginning to open.

Lucy realized she was trapped and got busy with the rag, cleaning the sink in the corner of the room.

It wasn't the cop, thank goodness. It was a nurse, and she spoke sharply to her in French. Whoever said French was a beautiful language hadn't been chewed out by an officious nurse, that was for sure, thought Lucy, ducking her head and scurrying out of the room. The cop was coming back down the hall, and she smiled at him, hoping desperately the nurse would check on the welfare of her patient rather than chase her down the hall. The elevator doors were opening, and she hopped inside and was carried down to the lobby. There she went straight to the ladies' room, ditched the smock and cleaning supplies. Congratulating herself on her foresight in keeping her coat and bag with her, she left the hospital through the lobby.

Once outside, she started to retrace her steps, heading home. As she walked, she studied the phone number Larry had given her. Why was it so familiar? She didn't know any phone numbers in Paris, but for some reason this number was setting off chimes in her head. Maybe it was similar to a number back home?

Stunned, she stopped in her tracks. Of course! It was the phone number for the Cavendish Hotel. Chef Larry wanted to contact somebody named Serge at the Cavendish Hotel. Who was Serge? And why was he the one person Chef Larry wanted to contact? *Only one way to find out,* decided Lucy, reversing direction and heading toward the boulevard Haussmann.

Chapter Nine

It was a bit of a hike to the Cavendish, and Lucy stopped at the Vélib' station outside the hospital, which was stocked with gray bicycles available for rental. She wasn't sure how the system worked and was leery of inserting her credit card without understanding the charges, and she thought the bicycles themselves looked heavy and cumbersome.

"Go ahead," said a voice, and she turned to see Richard standing beside her and wearing a big grin.

"I don't think so," said Lucy, smiling back. "It's been a while since I rode a bike, and Paris traffic is really crazy."

"It's a great system. I use them all the time," said Richard. "I'll show you how it works."

Lucy shook her head. "I think I'll stick to shank's mare, my own two feet." She paused. "I suppose you're here covering the general strike."

"No." He shrugged. "Believe it or not, I'm doing an investigative piece on the French health system. I've got a meeting with some big-shot doctor who says it's on the verge of collapse." He shrugged again. "I suspect he believes he's not getting paid enough."

"Your suspicions are probably right." Lucy laughed.

"So, do you want to get a bike? All you need is a credit card."

"No, but thanks. I'm getting used to walking."

"Paris is a great city for walking," he agreed. "There's always something to see. You should stay clear of the Champs-Élysées, though. These strikes can get violent." He paused. "Where's the rest of the gang?"

"Back at the apartment," said Lucy. Noticing his questioning expression, she added, "I got restless. They're great friends, but sometimes I need to be by myself."

He nodded. "Well, take care."

"I will," said Lucy, giving him a little wave and starting off in the direction of the boulevard Haussmann. Richard was such a nice guy, and he'd certainly scored a great job, working for the *Times*. If only Elizabeth had a small portion of his enthusiasm for life in Paris.

Fortunately, her route was some distance from the demonstration on the Champs-Élysées, but she was aware that there were more flics about on the street and fewer pedestrians. Not even the general strike, however, seemed to discourage the motorists, who swarmed through the streets at breakneck speed, driving with little regard for the rules of the road.

At the Cavendish, Lucy found Elizabeth alone at the concierge desk, looking both terribly professional in the green Cavendish blazer and rather uneasy. "I'm always nervous when Jean-Claude goes on break," she confessed.

"So your boss is now Jean-Claude? You must be getting on pretty well," said Lucy.

"He's been great," said Elizabeth. "He keeps telling me that it's good to have someone who can communicate so well with the Americans and the English, but I'm terrified of the French guests. I'm sure they think I'm an idiot and wonder what I'm doing here."

"It's a learning curve," said Lucy. "I'm sure you'll catch on pretty soon. One day, voilà, you'll understand everything, as if you were born here."

"It can't come soon enough," said Elizabeth. "Meanwhile, let's pretend you're a guest and I'm busy helping you, just until Jean-Claude comes back."

"Fine with me," said Lucy, seating herself gratefully in one of the curvy chairs provided for guests. "I really do need your help. Is there anybody here named Serge?"

"Serge d'Amboise? The assistant manager? Why do you ask?"

"I think he may know Chef Larry, that's all," said Lucy.

"Well, that's him over there," said Elizabeth, indicating a very tall, dark, and handsome man standing in front of the reception desk. Unlike the other employees, who were all wearing the Cavendish blazers, Serge was dressed in a beautifully tailored suit that emphasized his broad shoulders and slim waist. "You can ask him yourself."

Lucy had to admit that Serge's splendid appearance was rather intimidating, and she suddenly felt terribly self-conscious in her plaid coat. "I can't just walk up to him and start asking questions," said Lucy. "Can't you introduce us?"

"Sure," said Elizabeth with a shrug.

Lucy followed her daughter across the expansive lobby, noticing how Elizabeth always turned heads. It was true, she thought, that beautiful people had an advantage over ordinary folks, and she wondered if they knew it. Elizabeth simply expected everyone to give her the attention she believed she was due, and they usually did. No wonder she didn't get along with Sylvie, who expected pretty much the same thing. There couldn't be two queen bees in the same hive, and Lucy didn't expect the two roommates to stay together much longer.

"Serge," Elizabeth was saying as the tall man bent his head toward her, "I'd like you to meet my mother, Lucy Stone. Mom, this is Serge d'Amboise."

"*Enchanté,*" said Serge, taking her hand. For a moment Lucy thought he might actually kiss it, but he contented himself with a gentle squeeze. "You must be very proud of your beautiful and accomplished daughter."

"Of course, I am," said Lucy. "This job is a wonderful opportunity for Elizabeth."

"We think very highly of her here. She is so American, so fresh."

"*Fresh* is the right word to describe her," said Lucy, smiling, "but in America it has a different connotation."

"Mom!" protested Elizabeth.

"What do you mean?" asked Serge, furrowing his brow. "I must know this. It is so hard to pick up slang and idioms."

"*Fresh* can mean naughty," said Lucy. "Sassy. My mother used to say, 'Don't be fresh with me, young lady,' and then I knew I was in trouble."

"Elizabeth is fresh like a spring morning. She's not in trouble," said Serge.

"That's good to know," said Lucy, tremendously pleased that Elizabeth seemed to be doing so well at her job. "I asked Elizabeth to introduce me because I think we may have a friend in common, Larry Bruneau."

"Chef Larry? How do you know him?" asked Serge. "He is in hospital. Someone attacked him."

"I was taking a cooking class from him. I was actually the one who found he'd been stabbed and called for help."

"You saved his life. I am sure he is very grateful for that."

"I was just at the hospital," said Lucy, suddenly unwilling to admit she'd actually been in his room and had spoken to him. "They say he's doing much better, but he's still under police guard."

"That's for the best, I suppose," said Serge.

"Maybe in a day or two he'll be allowed to have visitors. I'm sure he'd be eager to see his old colleagues," said Lucy, delivering Larry's message in a roundabout way.

"Of course," said Serge. "Perhaps I will organize a visit when he is well enough."

Lucy wondered whether he was simply mouthing platitudes or if he actually cared about Chef Larry. And if he did care, was it because he was genuinely concerned about Chef Larry's well-being, or because he himself was involved in the black market scheme at the hotel and was fearful that the hospitalized man might incriminate him?

"I'm sure he would appreciate it," said Lucy, watching Serge closely and probing for some clue to his true feelings. "I suppose he'll be in increased danger when he recovers enough to tell the police who attacked him."

"*Bien sûr,*" said Serge with a nod. "It is a problem for him, whether to tell or not. Maybe he doesn't know or remember."

"If he can't, or won't, name his attacker," continued Lucy, "my friends and I will remain under suspicion. I am here with seven others, and the police have taken our passports. We're in limbo until this case is solved."

"I am very sorry for you, but, bien entendu, you must cooperate with the police. You have no choice but to tell them everything you know. Believe me, crime is taken very seriously here, especially crimes against a person."

"I understand that, and we've all been trying to cooperate, but the police don't seem to believe us. They even searched our rooms and made a terrible mess."

"Mom, you didn't tell me that!" exclaimed Elizabeth.

"It's true. When we got back from police headquarters yesterday, we found the apartment had been ransacked, completely tossed."

A worried expression flickered across Serge's face but quickly disappeared. "There are worse places to be detained than Paris, no? You must make the most of this time and enjoy our beautiful city."

"It is beautiful, but I would enjoy my visit more if I knew for sure that I'd be able to return home on schedule. I have other children, other responsibilities," Lucy said. "Is there anything you could tell me about Larry that would help?"

Serge seemed to withdraw, physically distancing himself the slightest bit. "What do you mean?"

"Was he in trouble in the past? I know he used to work here. Were there problems? Was he fired, or did he quit?"

"I don't know. I think he left because he wanted to start his own business. He told me he didn't like being told what to do."

"Were you close friends?" asked Lucy. "Have you known him long?"

"No." Serge shook his head. "Colleagues, I think that is the word. We worked together for a brief period, that is all."

"You didn't hang around together after work? Go for a beer?"

"Nothing like that," said Serge, taking a step backward.

Lucy knew that time was running out. She couldn't think of any way around it, so she just had to come out and ask. "I've heard rumors that Chef Larry was involved in the black market. . . ."

"Mom!" protested Elizabeth, embarrassed by her mother's questioning.

Lucy ignored her. "And a lot of employees here seem to be from the Middle East, where there's so much terrorist activity. It's no secret that these groups traffic in the black market. Do you think there could be some connection and that's why Larry was attacked?"

"I don't know where you got these ideas, but you are mistaken," said Serge, a note of warning in his voice. "I think perhaps you Americans are a bit paranoid about Muslims, but not every Muslim is a terrorist. The Cavendish Hotels have a strict policy of nondiscrimination, for both guests and employees. We do have a lot of immigrant workers. It's the nature of the business. If they do their jobs well, they are not a problem. However, if their work is not satisfactory, we let them go." He paused. "And now, I'm afraid I must go and attend to my duties. It was lovely to make your acquaintance, Mrs. Stone. And, Elizabeth, I think a guest wants your attention."

Glancing at her daughter's empty desk, Lucy saw a well-preserved woman of a certain age wearing a gorgeous fur jacket, tapping one red-soled Louboutin shoe. Lucy wouldn't have recognized the brand, but Sue had bought herself a pair and had proudly showed them off after one of her shopping trips.

"Gotta go, Mom," said Elizabeth, already on the move.

"Just a minute," Lucy said, hustling to keep up with her. "Don't you think Serge was being a bit cagey?"

Elizabeth stopped and faced her. "What did you expect? You practically accused him of being complicit in a black market scheme. I'm sure he was offended. I just hope he figured you're only another rude American."

"I didn't mean to offend him," said Lucy, her cheeks reddening.

"Don't worry about it," said Elizabeth. "He's used to dealing with all sorts of people. I think the French take a smug sort of comfort in the idea that they are the most civilized people in the world."

"Well, I have news for them," said Lucy. "We Americans think the French are rude." To her horror, she realized that she'd been speaking, rather loudly, to nobody in particular. Elizabeth was already at her desk, slipping gracefully into her chair and greeting the woman with a big smile. The only thing she could do, she decided, was to make a hasty retreat.

She hurried to the door, which was opened for her by a liveried doorman. With no taxis, buses, or Métro, Lucy realized she had a long walk ahead of her, and her back was beginning to bother her. Thank goodness she had disregarded all that advice about looking like a Parisian and had worn her comfy running shoes, she thought, producing a small packet of ibuprofen from her purse and popping a few tablets into her mouth.

As she strode along the Grands Boulevards, looking in the store windows, she decided she wasn't convinced that Serge had been completely truthful with her. For one thing, he didn't seem genuinely upset that Chef Larry had been attacked. Sure, maybe they were only colleagues, as he'd insisted, but she knew that if her colleague at the *Pennysaver,* Phyllis, was nearly stabbed to death and was lying unconscious in a hospital, she'd be very worried. Frantic, even.

He was smooth, she decided, and charming and terribly handsome, and those were good things, right? Except maybe they could be used as camouflage to hide his true nature. Her mother used to say, 'Never trust a handsome man,' but then, her deceased mother seemed to have had something to say about everything, and the pity was that she remembered all her pronouncements, even when they were ridiculous, as this one clearly was. Of course you could trust a handsome man. Why ever not?

On the other hand, thought Lucy, it was the ones who knew they were handsome that you had to watch out for, and Lucy was pretty sure Serge had a very good idea of his effect on others and wasn't afraid to use his good looks to his advantage. No, she thought, turning onto the boulevard de Sébastopol, she had a feeling that Serge was hiding something, and she suspected it was something to do with Chef Larry. She remembered talking to that prep cook at Sylvie's birthday party, who had said Chef Larry was stealing luxury foods and selling them on the black market, and she wouldn't be at all surprised if Serge and probably other employees were in on the game. You didn't get yourself stabbed for nothing. Chef Larry must have gotten somebody very angry, and she wouldn't be at all surprised if that somebody turned out to be Serge.

It was quite a hike from the Cavendish to the apartment near the place des Vosges, and Lucy was dragging a bit when she turned onto the rue Rambuteau. It wouldn't be so bad, she thought, if she could stop and rest in a café, but they all seemed to be closed, expressing solidarity with the farmers. Only in France, she thought, could the problems of a few potato growers cause the entire country to shut down in a general strike.

The rue Rambuteau eventually turned into the rue du Pas-de-la-Mule, which, she guessed, meant that sometime long ago it was a path for mules, perhaps used to transport cargo from the Canal Saint-Martin. Only a few blocks more and she'd be back at the apartment, where she intended to give her feet a good, long soak in Epsom salts. Finally reaching the place des Vosges, she walked under the arcade, ducking through the passage by the Hôtel Pavillon de la Reine and down the rue Roger Verlomme to the apartment. It was a tiny street that opened at the other end into a small treed plaza, where Chez Loulou set out tables. It was rather chilly these days for eating outside, and the tables were usually occupied only by a few hardy souls. Today the bistro was closed because of the general strike. So why was that man sitting at one of the tables, leaning his chair backward against the wall? And why did he look so familiar?

Of course. It came to her in a flash. He was the guy who had followed them to Versailles. The closer she got, the surer she was. It was definitely him lolling in the chair, smoking, looking like someone who had nothing better to do. He must be keeping an eye on them, but why? And for whom?

She was tired and cranky. She was really beginning to hate Paris, which wasn't at all what she had thought it would be. She wanted it to be like the Lancôme ad that she'd seen playing on a giant screen at the airport, in which Natalie Portman skipped along the cobblestones in a filmy chiffon dress, only to be wrapped suddenly in a handsome man's arms. Only she wanted to be wrapped in Bill's arms, kissing him passionately beneath the Eiffel Tower. But instead, the entire city was shut down in a general strike, and she was involved in a sordid crime.

Making a quick decision, she marched right over to the guy, who watched her approach coolly through dark sunglasses, taking a long drag on his cigarette and slowly inhaling the smoke.

"Why are you watching us?" she demanded, arms on hips and bright white running shoes planted firmly on the paving.

He wasn't the least bit fazed, just flicked his cigarette. "Those shoes are terrible," he said.

"They're very comfortable, and I'm glad I brought them, because I've had to walk a long distance because of the general strike. Now, answer my question. Why are you following us?"

"I am not following anyone," he said. "I'm just getting some fresh air."

"I don't believe you care the least bit about fresh air," said Lucy, challenging him. "If you did, you wouldn't smoke, would you? And besides, I know you're following us, because I saw you in the train station the other day, and then I saw you in Versailles."

"Ah, you were in Versailles, too? *C'est magnifique.* Did you enjoy it?"

"Quite frankly, it seemed a bit over the top."

"Over the top?"

"Too much. *De trop.* I think that's the term."

"Ah, yes. But now the château belongs to the people of France."

"You still haven't answered my question," said Lucy, refusing to be charmed. He wasn't good-looking, like Serge at the hotel, what with the sunglasses and the stubble of beard and the shaved head, which she didn't like. Nonetheless, there was something appealing about him, and that disturbed her. What was it? His accent?

"But I have. I have told you I am not following you. It is a coincidence that we were both in Versailles, nothing more."

"You were sightseeing?" asked Lucy in a rather satirical tone.

"Ah, sadly, no. I was visiting Grand-mère."

"Oh, for Pete's sake!" Lucy rolled her eyes. "Can't you come up with something better than that?"

"The truth, madame. What is better than the truth?"

Lucy had definitely had enough. "Listen, buddy," she

said, glaring at him. "I don't want to see you again. You stop hanging around. Get that?"

"What? This is not a free country? I cannot go where I want?"

"You can go wherever you want, preferably far, far away. Just leave us alone!"

And with that, she turned on her heel and marched back down the empty street to the double doors, which were still covered with graffiti, and punched the security code into the keypad. The buzzer sounded, and she opened the door, looking over her shoulder before she went inside and noted with satisfaction that he was gone and the little plaza was empty.

When she entered the apartment, everybody rushed to greet her.

"Where were you?" demanded Bill in an accusing tone of voice. "You were gone for hours."

"You look exhausted," said Rachel.

"Did you find any food?" asked Sue.

"Oh, the food! I forgot all about it. I'm sorry. But that little ethnic store is open. At least it was when I went by."

"Maybe there's hope for dinner," said Sue, grabbing her jacket. "C'mon, Sid. Let's check it out."

"Where have you been?" persisted Bill. "Why didn't you call?"

"Didn't think of it," said Lucy. "I started walking, and I found myself near the hospital, so I thought I'd see how Chef Larry's doing, maybe pay him a visit, but he's still under police guard. Then I decided I might as well visit Elizabeth at the hotel and check on her. . . ."

"You walked all that way?" Rachel's eyes were round with disbelief.

"You must be exhausted," said Pam.

"I am," admitted Lucy, unsure whether she should

tell the others about her encounter with the guy outside the café.

"I can't believe you just went off like that," said Bill angrily. "I was really worried. You better not be up to your tricks, investigating the attack on Chef Larry. This is France, not Tinker's Cove, and you're just going to get yourself in a lot of trouble."

"And us, too," added Bob.

"Yeah, you've got to leave the investigation to the police," said Ted.

Lucy didn't much like this united front of male opposition. "You know, I am a grown-up," she said. "I don't need a bunch of men telling me what I should and shouldn't do."

"Right," Pam said, chiming in. "You guys are acting like male chauvinist you-know-whats."

"I think we should all have a glass of wine and let Lucy relax," suggested Rachel. "Let's all try to relax."

"That sounds like a good idea," said Lucy. Her feet were now aching, as well as her back, and she was dying to sit down. She had almost reached one of the sofas when there was a knock at the door.

"Who could that be?" Rachel wondered aloud. "Did Sue and Sid forget their keys?"

"I'll get it," said Pam, opening the door and revealing Madame Defarge, neat as ever in her usual twinset, skirt, and pumps.

"Bonjour," she began in a formal tone. "I am so sorry to disturb you."

"Not at all," said Pam. "Come in. We were just about to have an aperitif."

"Oh, no. I couldn't. I am just here to deliver some papers to you." Her voice became quite frosty. "From the police."

"Really?" Bob stepped forward. "I'll take them. It's probably our passports."

"Perhaps, monsieur," said Madame Defarge, giving him a thick envelope, "but I don't think so."

"Well, thank you for your trouble. Are you sure you won't join us for a glass of wine?" asked Bob.

"Thank you, but no," she said. "I must go."

Pam had just closed the door behind her when Bob ripped open the envelope, pulling out a sheaf of white papers.

"Not passports," said Ted.

"No," answered Bob, studying the printed documents. "My French isn't very good, but these seem to be orders to return to police headquarters for more questioning. . . ."

"We've done that," fretted Rachel. "What could they possibly want now?"

"I'm not sure, but I have an idea," said Bob. "Does *mort* mean what I think it does?"

"It means 'dead,' " said Lucy.

"Well, then, we're in big trouble, because Chef Larry *est mort.*"

Chapter Ten

Dead? How could that be? thought Lucy, struggling to comprehend the terrible news. She had just seen him a few hours ago, and he'd been very much alive. Not in great shape, but definitely alive and on the road to recovery.

"That's terrible! Poor Chef Larry!" exclaimed Sue when she heard the news, dropping full plastic shopping bags on the marble island. Tears sprang from her eyes, and she fumbled in her purse, producing a cute vintage handkerchief picturing poodles and the Eiffel Tower.

"I didn't think you thought very much of Chef Larry, rest his soul," said Rachel.

"I definitely had that impression, too," added Lucy.

"Oh, he wasn't much of a chef," said Sue, blowing her nose, "but the classes were fun, weren't they?"

"I guess," said Sid. "Personally, I was kind of relieved when we didn't have to go to the cooking classes. . . ." Sue gave him a look, and he quickly added, "But I'm really sorry he died. I mean, I didn't wish him any harm. He seemed like a really nice guy."

"I've got to call Sidra," said Sue, pulling her cell phone out of her pocket. "I'm sure Norah will want to know."

"Why do you think that?" asked Lucy.

"Well, it was obvious, wasn't it? Chef Larry was one of her protégés. That's why she included the cooking classes in the trip."

"I think I saw him on one of her shows," said Pam. "He made crepes."

"Well, be sure to let Sidra know that this puts us in a real pickle," said Bob. "Now it's a homicide, and we're really at the mercy of the system. They can arrest and detain us without cause. There are no limits to search and seizure, no plea bargaining, no jury, and no presumption of innocence."

"When you put it that way, it looks like we're in deep doo-doo," said Bill.

"Oh, make no mistake about it. We are in it up to our necks," said Bob.

Sue had done her best to come up with an appetizing supper, but the ethnic store's offerings were meager, and all she'd managed to find was couscous, stuffed grape leaves, and tzatziki, with sticky dates and pistachios for dessert. It didn't sit well with Lucy, who blamed her sleepless night on the unusual dinner, but she knew it wasn't really the food that was keeping her up. It was her nerves. She was definitely feeling shaky in the morning, when she presented herself once again at 36 quai des Orfèvres, a feeling that only got worse when she wasn't sent up to the fifth floor as before but was directed to the office of the *procureur de la République*.

She was literally shaking with fear when she presented herself to a receptionist, whose only greeting was a curt nod. "*Suivez-moi,*" she said, rising from her chair and leading Lucy down a short hallway to the office of the *procureur,* or *proc*.

The *proc* didn't share her office, as Lapointe did. She had a spacious carpeted room with a large window and was sitting on a generously padded leather chair behind a beautifully grained wood desk. "Please sit down, Madame Stone," she said, speaking perfect English in a lightly accented voice and indicating a Danish modern chair with a subtly manicured hand.

No bright red polish here, thought Lucy. *Just the slightest tint of pink.*

"My name is Giselle Hadamard," she said, "and I will be asking you a few questions about Laurence Bruneau. I have been involved since the beginning of this investigation. As *procureur,* it is my responsibility to supervise the police and to determine the truth of the matter. You could compare my role to that of a district attorney in the States, with an understanding that a *procureur* has considerably greater flexibility and more far-ranging powers than a district attorney. I would also add that this is now a homicide case and you must give me your complete cooperation."

"Of course," said Lucy, sitting down a bit more heavily than she would have wished, as her legs had suddenly given way beneath her.

The *proc* didn't seem to notice. Her head was bent as she studied the papers in a thick file. That gave Lucy plenty of time to take in her beautifully coiffed white hair, cut short. She was wearing what Lucy suspected was a genuine Chanel jacket, the same blue color as her eyes and trimmed with an intricate silver braid. When she looked up, it was obvious she treated her olive skin to frequent facials and was faithful about cleansing and moisturizing. She wore only a bit of makeup, concealer beneath her eyes, perhaps, with a touch of mascara and lip gloss. Lucy found her absolutely terrifying.

"Pardon me, Madame Stone, but I am interested in your shoes."

Lucy glanced down at her feet, clad in her favorite

white running shoes, and wondered if wearing them was actually against the law. "I wore them because they're very comfortable, and because of the general strike, I've had to walk a lot."

"They do look comfortable," said the *proc*. "I have some foot problems. Bunions, I think they are called, and I wonder . . ."

"Shoes like this would definitely help," said Lucy.

The *proc* bit her lip, then shrugged, shaking her head. "But no, I couldn't." She glanced at the papers, then leveled those steely blue eyes on Lucy. "Now to the business at hand, the murder of Monsieur Bruneau. I understand you found the wounded man and called the medical squad. Is that right?"

So Lucy went through the whole story again, beginning with the rain and the two young men and going back to the classroom to fetch her forgotten umbrella and finding Chef Larry bleeding on the floor.

"And I see here that you paid an unauthorized visit to Monsieur Bruneau in the hospital shortly before he was pronounced dead," said the *proc*. She didn't sound accusatory. She spoke in her normal voice, but Lucy felt as if the chair she was sitting on had been pulled out from under her.

"How do you know that?" she asked, gasping for air.

"It is in the file. You were observed, wearing, it says here, a cleaning smock. Why did you do this? You understand it puts you in a very bad position. You were the first to find Monsieur Bruneau after the attack and the last to be with him before he died."

Lucy did understand only too well and pictured herself spending long years in a dark cell with damp walls, barely surviving on bread and water. "I wanted to talk to him," she said, "but there was an officer outside his room, so I had to use a disguise."

"And why did you want to talk to Monsieur Bruneau?"

"I wanted to know who stabbed him. I thought that if I could figure that out, we'd get our passports back and be able to go home."

"What exactly did you do when you were in Monsieur Bruneau's hospital room?"

Lucy took a deep breath. This was embarrassing, for sure, but she knew there was no option but to tell the truth, the whole truth, and nothing but the truth. "I looked around a bit," she began, inwardly wincing as she recounted her foolish behavior. "His eyes opened. He asked me to call a friend for him, to ask Serge to pay him a visit. He gave me a phone number. Then a nurse came, and I left. That's all. I didn't do anything to Chef Larry. He was definitely alive when I left the room."

"Where did you go after leaving the hospital?"

"I went to visit my daughter, who works at the Cavendish Hotel."

"*Mon Dieu!* You walked all that way! Why, may I ask?"

"Well, because I recognized the number he gave me as the number for the hotel. I thought Elizabeth might know this Serge."

"And did she?"

"Yes. I met him. His name is Serge d'Amboise, and he's the assistant manager."

"Did you tell him Larry wanted to see him?"

"Sort of. I said there was still a police guard, but perhaps in a few days he would be able to have visitors."

"And his reaction to your suggestion?"

"Definitely noncommittal."

"This is good information. Do you think he is the one who killed Monsieur Bruneau?"

"I certainly hope not," said Lucy, finding it was one thing to harbor a vague suspicion and quite another to hear an official investigator voice it. She didn't want to entertain the possibility that Elizabeth had stumbled into a ring of criminals and was working beside thieves and murderers.

"Are you certain it was murder?" asked Lucy. "Perhaps Larry simply took a turn for the worse."

"I suppose that is possible, but unlikely," said the *proc.* "We must wait for the medical examiner's report."

"Serge has a position of some responsibility at the Cavendish," Lucy said, quickly adding, "But I can tell you that nobody in my group had anything at all to do with Chef Larry's death. Nothing. We are simply tourists, nothing more. I understand your investigation has to be thorough, and I don't mind that the police searched our apartment, but it would have been better if we had been notified and could have been present for the search. And I really don't think they should have left it in such a mess."

For the first time in the interview the *proc* showed a flicker of emotion. She furrowed her beautifully shaped brows, as if troubled. "But that is impossible," she said. "I was just going to inform you of the necessity of a search and arrange a time."

"Well, you can do it again, of course, but this time we'd really appreciate it if the searchers would leave things the way they found them. I mean, dumping bags of flour into the sink and spilling coffee all over the floor . . ."

"Madame, I am telling you that there is no record of a search in this file. Now that we are investigating a homicide, it is a necessary procedure, but we have not done it yet."

"The concierge said it was the police," said Lucy, standing her ground.

"She was clearly misinformed."

"Well, if it wasn't the police, who was it?" asked Lucy.

"We will endeavor to find out," said the *proc,* "but in the meantime I am warning you, Madame Stone, that it is a very serious matter to interfere in a police matter. I suggest you limit yourself to sightseeing while you are here in France."

"I certainly will," said Lucy, struggling with the idea that Chef Larry's murderer, or murderers, had been in the apartment and had rifled through their things. Why? Quite a few moments passed, her mind busy trying to figure out what this meant and whether they were in danger, before she realized the *proc* had fallen silent and was making notes in the file. "Um, pardon me, but may I go?" she asked.

"Will tomorrow afternoon—let's say three o'clock—be convenient for the search?"

Lucy didn't feel as if she really had much choice in the matter. "Okay," she said.

The *proc* didn't look up from the form she was filling in with a slim gold pen but dismissed her with a wave of the hand. "You may go."

"Before I go, I think I ought to mention that someone's been following us," said Lucy. "Kind of a rough-looking fellow."

"You are very observant," said the *proc* with an amused smile. "I believe the police have been keeping an eye on your group. It's for your own safety, of course."

Lucy's jaw dropped; she didn't know how to respond. Should she be grateful for the protection or appalled at the intrusion? And was it even true? The *proc* had said only that she *believed* the police were watching them.

"Did you order this surveillance?" asked Lucy. "And

on what grounds? Was there a warrant? In the U.S. police have to go to a judge—"

"Madame Stone," interrupted the *proc*, "might I remind you that you are not in the USA. You are in France, and we have our own way of doing things."

"Right," said Lucy, deciding that nothing was to be gained by irritating the *proc*. It was definitely time to go. "Good day to you," she said, heading for the door and not looking back.

The general strike had lasted only for a day, and the Métro was working again, although on a partial schedule. When she finally emerged from the station by the Bastille monument, she thought she was beginning to understand the anger that had driven the Paris mob to destroy the hated prison. She herself would happily join a mob bent on tearing down the police headquarters at the quai des Orfèvres. But that would have to wait. She would begin her counterattack by questioning Madame Defarge.

Madame was sweeping the courtyard, dressed rather oddly for the job in her skirt and kitten-heeled pumps, with a string of big pearls dangling around her neck instead of her usual scarf.

"Bonjour, Madame Stone," she said. "Your companions are all out except for Monsieur Stone."

"*Merci*," said Lucy. "I have just been interviewed at the police headquarters . . . ," she began.

Madame Defarge clucked her tongue, and Lucy wasn't sure if it was an expression of sympathy or disapproval. *Probably both*, she decided.

"The *proc* told me that the police did not search our apartment. In fact, she wanted to make arrangements for a search in the next few days."

"*Impossible*," said Madame Defarge, shaking her head.

"They were policemen. They showed me their credentials."

"Were they wearing uniforms?"

"No. They were detectives. They had black wallets, and they held them up for me to see."

"Did you examine their IDs?"

Madame bristled. "There was no need. They were police."

Lucy understood completely. The concierge hadn't wanted to get involved, which was only natural. She probably gave the IDs a cursory glance and went about her business, putting as much distance between herself and the flics as possible. And now, after all she'd been through, Lucy couldn't blame her. She'd like nothing more than to forget all about Chef Larry and get on a plane and fly home. "They weren't police," said Lucy, "but the police will be coming tomorrow."

"We must cooperate with the police, of course," said Madame, using a broom to gather up a few bits of debris that had strayed from the pile, "but I hope this investigation will not take much longer. I have consulted the owner, who told me your group has the apartment for only one more week. After that I must prepare it for a new group of tenants."

Ah, thought Lucy. *The new tenants, the nice tenants, the tenants who aren't involved in a murder.* "I understand," she said, tempted to walk right through the small pile of sweepings, scattering them, but instead walking carefully around them.

"How'd it go?" asked Bill when she entered the apartment. He was sprawled on one of the sofas, watching a soccer game.

"Well, I didn't get to talk to Lapointe this time. Instead, they sent me to see his boss, the *proc.* She was a really scary woman. She didn't throw me in jail, but I think she would have liked to," said Lucy, unwilling to confess that the police knew she'd gone to the hospital to see Chef Larry. She sat down on the other sofa, slipping out of her plaid coat. "But get this. It wasn't the police who searched the apartment."

Bill swung his legs off the sofa and sat up. "Who was it, then?"

"I don't know, but probably somebody involved in the murder, don't you think?"

"I don't know what to think," said Bill.

"It only came to light when the *proc* wanted to arrange a search and I said it had already been done."

"So the police are going to search again?"

"Well, not again. This will be the first time for the cops, but another search. We can be here and observe this time. It's set for three o'clock tomorrow."

"This sucks," said Bill, clicking off the TV with the remote. "And you know what? The game's over, and the score is nil. That means nobody scored. Nobody. What kind of sport is that? I ask you. Like they never heard of sudden death overtime?"

"No more talk of death," said Lucy. "What do you want to do this afternoon?"

"My interview isn't until five o'clock, so in the meantime, let's forget all this," said Bill, pulling her to her feet and wrapping his arms around her. "Let's wander where we will and see where we end up."

"We'll be flaneurs," she said, causing Bill to adopt his Groucho Marx impression.

"Speak for yourself," he said, waggling his eyebrows and pretending to tap ash from a cigar.

It was corny, but Lucy found herself laughing as they left the apartment, practically skipping down the stairs.

Water presented an irresistible attraction to these

homesick Mainers, and Lucy and Bill soon found themselves walking once again on the quais that bordered the
Seine. It was a gray day, but not dark, and the soft light
gave a monochromatic hue to the cityscape. The river
streamed by, lapping at the stone quais, offering changing patterns of light and dark. It was also a surprisingly
busy thoroughfare, and they watched with interest as
bateaux-mouches and tugboats and barges all chugged
by. They passed the Louvre and wandered on into the
Jardin des Tuileries, buying sandwiches and drinks from
a snack bar for lunch. They ate at an outside table,
watching the passing parade, mostly old people, young
children with caretakers, and the inevitable tourists.

"The Orangerie is just over there," said Lucy. "It has
Monet's water lily paintings. I've always wanted to see
them."

"Okay," said Bill, draining his glass of beer and getting to his feet. "I'm game."

"Water lilies are called *nymphéas* in French. Isn't that
a beautiful word?"

"Sounds sexy," said Bill, nuzzling her neck.

Lucy was surprised by this public show of affection.
"What's with you?" she asked as they walked along
hand in hand.

"Paris, I guess."

"I've read about these paintings," Lucy told Bill.
"Monet created a beautiful garden at his home in Giverny,
with the intention of using it as a subject for his paintings.
He dug a pond and built a Japanese bridge and planted
tons of flowers, and he painted them in all seasons, at
different times of day. It's about the colors and the
light."

"Yes, Professor," said Bill.

"I just want you to be able to appreciate them.
They're supposed to be amazing," said Lucy defensively.

"Besides," she added with a sigh, "it will be nice to look at something beautiful. It will be a welcome distraction."

The Orangerie itself was a rather plain stone building and had once been used to winter over the potted orange trees that were so popular with eighteenth-century aristocrats. There was the usual security system, and Lucy's bag had to be checked and they had to go through a screening device before they were allowed to enter the two galleries containing the water lily paintings. The first gallery wasn't crowded and there were benches to sit on, so Lucy sat down and gazed at the huge canvases, which she thought must be at least ten feet high and perhaps eighteen or twenty feet wide.

"Whoa," said Bill, sitting beside her. "They're big."

"Monet built a special studio for them," she said, consulting her guidebook. "They're in sequence. They're supposed to be different seasons."

"That really green one is probably spring," suggested Bill.

"I guess the dark one is winter, and the very green one must be summer."

"That one with the big orange and yellow area would be fall."

"And the one with pink is *Soleil Couchant*, which means 'sunset.' All those brushstrokes . . . There must be millions, and by themselves they don't look like anything. But when you get a bit of distance, it all comes together, sort of."

"Yeah, see, that must be the bridge." Bill pointed to a green arc in the middle of one of the paintings.

"And those drapey things are willows, I think. I like the paintings with willows best. It gives a sense of perspective."

"Are you disappointed?" asked Bill.

"Well, it's a lot of swirly colors. Maybe too chaotic for me right now," admitted Lucy. "Though you have to admit the man was a genius."

"Absolutely," said Bill, standing up and taking her by the hand. "But I think I know a better way of taking our minds off our troubles."

"What do you mean?" asked Lucy.

"Well, my interview isn't until five. I think we should spend the rest of the afternoon like Parisians. You know, the apartment might be empty." He leaned close, his beard tickling her neck, as he whispered, "I'm thinking of a romantic matinee."

"We can't," said Lucy, shaking her head. "What if they come home? That sleep sofa is the first thing they'd see."

"I was thinking of the *salle de bain*," said Bill. "The door has a lock. I checked."

"The bathtub? That would be kind of cramped. And cold."

"No. The floor."

"The floor!"

"It's been done before, you know. We could bring in some pillows and blankets and make a little love nest."

Lucy gave him a little sideways glance. "The bathroom floor . . ."

He was nibbling on her ear. "What do you say?"

She giggled. "I guess the Métro would be the quickest way home."

Chapter Eleven

Sue had good news to announce at breakfast on Saturday morning. "I got a call from Sidra last night," she began, "and you won't believe this, but Norah actually called the president and told him about our situation! She's a big supporter. Remember, she not only gave tons of money to his PAC, but she also interviewed him on her show, showered him with praise. Sidra said the president promised to instruct the ambassador himself to look into the matter and see what he can do." She paused to refill her coffee cup. "So I think we can expect this whole mess to go away. There's nothing like knowing somebody who can make things happen."

"That's super!" exclaimed Pam. "Now we can stop worrying and can actually enjoy our vacation."

"That's if the ambassador can actually fix things," grumbled Bob. "We're not out of the woods yet."

"Oh, Bob, give it up," snapped Sue. "He's the ambassador. He can fix it."

"I hope you're right, Sue," said Rachel. "It's definitely a positive sign that the ambassador is looking out for us."

"But his influence is limited," said Bob. "This is

France, and they do things differently, and they're not all that happy with the U.S. right now."

"Or ever," added Bill, who had minored in modern European history.

"We've got Norah and the president and the ambassador on our side," said Sue. "Between the three of them they ought to be able to come up with something."

"It's a very encouraging development—thanks to you and Sidra," said Lucy, who was only too aware that she wasn't out of the woods, not by a long shot. For one thing, she was the only one of the eight who had been subjected to an in-depth interview by the *proc*. All the others, including Bill, had merely been asked to confirm their identities and contact information. She was afraid that she was the prime suspect in Chef Larry's murder, and remembering Elizabeth's assertion that you weren't suffering from paranoia if they really were out to get you, she was pretty sure she wasn't being paranoid.

But while she still had her freedom, she was determined to enjoy it. "I, for one, am going to forget our troubles . . . for the day, anyway. I've always dreamed of going to the Paris flea market, and now I'm actually going," she said, thinking it would be a day to remember when she was confined to a dark and dank French prison cell.

"I know," said Sue, grinning broadly. "I can't wait for someone visiting my house to notice some adorable little treasure, maybe a watercolor or a Quimper plate, and being able to say, 'Oh, I picked that up in Paris, at Les Puces.' "

"You've got the tone right," said Pam approvingly. "It has to be offhand, like you spend every weekend combing the Paris flea markets."

"Absolutely," agreed Lucy. "Like, oh, it was nothing. It just caught my eye at Clignancourt."

"What do you suppose they'll have?" Rachel wondered aloud. "I hope I can find something small and packable."

"If I could find one of those gorgeous aged-wood wine-bottle racks, I'd gladly pay to have it shipped," said Sue, earning a groan from Sid.

"Shipping something like that would cost a small fortune," he protested. "I thought you were going to look for a 'little treasure.' Isn't that what you said?"

Sue ignored him, lost in an interior design fantasy. "And I bet I could carry a grape-picker's basket on the airplane. I could even hold it in my lap, if I had to. I can just picture it on the wall in my dining room, filled with sunflowers or dried hydrangeas."

"Okay, ladies," said Lucy, checking her watch, "we've got to get moving, or we'll be late for meeting Elizabeth and Sylvie. Sylvie said we should get there early if we want the best pickings."

The four women wasted no time, leaving the men to clear up the breakfast things, and headed out to the Métro. They had agreed to meet Elizabeth and Sylvie at the Strasbourg–Saint-Denis station, where they would change to the number 4 line, which ended at Porte de Clignancourt.

Their spirits were high when they met the girls on the platform, but Sylvie cautioned them. "It's a—what you say?—rough sort of neighborhood. You'll need to watch out for pickpockets and, even worse, bag snatchers."

When they exited the station, they saw she hadn't exaggerated the case. This neighborhood was far from the heart of Paris. It reminded Lucy of the Bronx and Brooklyn neighborhoods she'd been warned to avoid as a girl growing up on the East Side of Manhattan, the neighborhoods where her father made sure the car doors were locked when he had to drive through them to get to the zoo or the beach.

"Sylvie wasn't kidding," Sue murmured in Lucy's ear, with a nod at the tough guys, who seemed to be everywhere. "I've never seen so many shaved heads and leather jackets in my life."

"Keep your bag close," whispered Lucy, thinking that if they were still being followed by that guy she'd seen tracking them at Versailles, it would be very easy for him to blend into the crowd.

"It's this way," said Sylvie, leading them down a street lined with stores offering low-priced, low-quality goods and with street vendors, who urged them to buy illegal, fake designer scarves and "Rolex" watches for twenty euros.

"Keep moving," urged Elizabeth. "Don't make eye contact."

Reaching an intersection, they had to wait for the traffic light to change, and Lucy made sure to glance around, keeping a wary eye on her surroundings. It was then that she saw the three black men, their arms loaded with counterfeit purses, dashing through traffic, with a couple of flics in hot pursuit. "Watch out!" she warned as one of the vendors crashed through the crowd of pedestrians waiting to cross the street. While Lucy and her friends were shocked and alarmed, nobody else seemed at all disturbed by the scene, so she guessed it was a frequent occurrence.

Making a left turn, they followed Sylvie down a grimy side street that ran along a highway exit ramp and that was lined with stall after stall of junky knockoffs, fake Levis, and cheap T-shirts and shoes.

"This is not at all what I expected," declared Sue. "Where are the antiques? The *brocante?*"

"Just up here," said Sylvie, leading them into a covered arcade with a sign identifying it as the Marché Dauphine.

It was chilly in the market, which had a cement floor and metal stairs that reminded Lucy of the stairs leading to the elevated train lines in New York.

"The best antique shops are mostly down here, on the *rez-de-chaussée*," explained Sylvie. "Upstairs, on the mezzanine, that's where you find old posters, books, costume jewelry, the less expensive *brocante*."

They soon discovered the shops on the main floor were far beyond their budgets, featuring shabby Louis XV armchairs, fragile sets of Sevres china, gleaming gold vermeil flatware, and shimmering crystal chandeliers.

"I love those," said Sue, pointing out a pair of bird sconces, "but not for four thousand euros."

"And not a wine-bottle rack in sight," said Pam.

"Let's try upstairs," urged Rachel. "I have a thing for Bakelite bangles."

Even the Bakelite bangles were too expensive for Rachel, who declared she could get the same at home for less, but Lucy fell hard for a pair of 1950s educational posters picturing the city and the country in bright primary colors. "I could have the country in my kitchen and give you the city for your apartment," she told Elizabeth. "How much?" she asked the vendor. "Combien pour les deux?"

"Deux cent cinquante," replied the seller, a well-padded woman who was the exception proving the rule that Frenchwomen don't get fat, and who was dressed against the chill in several sweaters and a pair of fingerless gloves.

"Two fifty? Too much," said Lucy as Sylvie stepped up. "Cent cinquante, c'est juste," she said in an authoritative voice.

"Non, c'est trop peu," said the vendor with a dismissive shrug. "Deux cents."

Then Lucy lost track of the negotiation until Sylvie seemed satisfied. "One seventy-five. Is that okay?"

Lucy thought it was too much, well over two hundred dollars, but then again, she might never get back to Paris. "Okay," she agreed, emptying her wallet and producing a handful of bills.

The vendor carefully counted them, coming up ten euros short.

"Oh, gee, that's all I've got," said Lucy. "Will you take a credit card? *Carte de crédit?*"

The woman recoiled, looking as if Lucy was proposing to pay with a handful of wriggling pythons.

"Oh, let me," said Elizabeth, digging into her pocket and producing a fistful of change. "I'd like to get rid of these, anyway, since they're so heavy," she said, counting out five golden coins.

The woman examined them closely and returned one to her, shaking her head.

Elizabeth took it back and tucked it in her jeans pocket. "Oh, sorry. That's my good luck piece," she said, producing another two-euro coin, which the woman accepted.

Then she rolled up the posters, wrapped them carefully in brown paper, and handed them to Lucy with a flourish, as if they were da Vinci originals.

"That could have been a tragedy if she'd taken my good luck piece," said Elizabeth as Lucy presented her with the city poster. "Thanks, Mom."

"I didn't know you were superstitious," said Lucy.

"I know it's silly, but I found it in the apartment when a loose tile fell in the bathroom, and since then my luck really has changed. Now, how about some lunch?"

"Somebody has to pay for me," said Lucy hungrily. "I don't have a sou."

"Not to worry," said Rachel. "We've got you covered."

Following Sylvie's lead, they all trooped through a maze of narrow side streets to a corner café with a cute little car parked outside. "A Deux Chevaux," said Sylvie as they admired the antique auto. "It's in excellent condition, the sort of car you would see in a Jean-Paul Belmondo film."

"Remember Jean Seberg hawking newspapers?" asked Pam, reminiscing. "What was the name of that film?"

"I don't remember the name of the film, but I do remember Jean-Paul Belmondo with that cigarette and those bedroom eyes," said Sue.

"*Breathless*," said Lucy as they entered a tiny restaurant with only ten or twelve tables, all crowded together. Up a step, some very small booths were arranged along the mirrored walls, giving the restaurant the air of a theater. They were filled with singles, who nursed coffees or brandies and read the newspaper.

"Do you need to sit down?" Rachel asked Lucy, looking concerned.

"No, it's the name of the movie. *Breathless*. Belmondo plays a thief."

"That's right," said Sylvie, who had gotten the nod from the bartender and was pushing two tables together, pausing a moment to let a tall, gray-haired man squeeze by on his way to the door. Lucy saw him only from behind, taking in his silver hair and pin-striped suit, but she noticed the obvious way he gave Sylvie the once-over. These Frenchmen, she thought, didn't they ever get too old to cherchez les femmes?

Sylvie, she noticed, didn't seem to relish the attention. Her usual smug expression changed briefly, and she seemed troubled or perhaps anxious. But almost before Lucy could register the change, the clouds cleared and the sun was shining once again.

"We could use some menus," said Sue when they were seated, but Sylvie shook her head.

"This sort of place doesn't have menus. You get whatever they've prepared, the *plat du jour.* Today it's *lentilles avec saucisses et jambon.*" Sylvie seemed the slightest bit distracted, plucking at her napkin and glancing past Sue's head at the windows. Lucy followed her gaze but saw only a couple of heavyset guys, probably deliverymen who worked for the antique dealers in the area.

"How did you figure that out?" asked Pam, puzzled.

"My nose," said Sylvie, laughing. "I can smell it. Like my mother makes. *Délicieux.*"

"Okay," said Lucy, noting that the diners at the tables around them seemed to have no complaints and were happily tucking into lunch, all the while keeping up lively conversations.

The barman soon delivered baskets of bread and bottles of water and inquired if they wanted wine. They did, and a big carafe of red appeared, along with big plates of lentil stew with sausage and ham.

"I never much liked lentils, not until now," confessed Rachel.

"It's a classic dish, and they do it very well here," said Sylvie with an approving nod. She had a few mouthfuls and then rose. "Excuse me, please. I will be back in a moment." Then, moving quickly, she disappeared behind the bar, in the direction of the kitchen, following the arrow on the TOILETTE sign.

Lucy cast an inquiring glance at Elizabeth, who responded with a whisper, "The toilet. She must really need to go, as it's considered rude to absent yourself from the table while people are eating."

"Bulimia?" asked Rachel, also whispering. "She's very thin."

"No." Elizabeth shook her head. "It's the smoking that keeps her thin. Believe me, if they didn't smoke, a lot of skinny Frenchwomen would be a lot fatter."

"Maybe she's smoking in there, like we used to do in high school," said Pam.

Elizabeth laughed. "I don't think so." But as time passed and Sylvie failed to return, they began to grow concerned.

"Do you think she's sick?" asked Rachel.

"Maybe she's pregnant," said Pam, speculating.

"Or shooting up," offered Sue, getting disapproving looks from the group. "Just a thought," she added, defending herself.

"I'll go check on her," offered Elizabeth, taking the same circuitous route behind the bar, where the barman was busy slicing up a couple of baguettes and filling the bread baskets.

When she returned a few moments later, her expression was puzzled. "The toilet is empty. She's gone."

"Gone?" asked Lucy. "Are you sure?"

"Yeah. There's just one bathroom, and it's tiny. There's no place for anybody to hide. She must have left through the kitchen. There's a back door."

"Did you ask the cook?" demanded Lucy. "Did anyone see her go?"

"I did ask," said Elizabeth, "but he just shook his head."

"I'll ask the barman," said Lucy, popping up. "*La jeune fille qui . . . uh . . .*"

"No, Mom, I'll do it," offered Elizabeth. "I don't think your French is up to it."

But all Elizabeth was able to get from the barman was a shake of his head and a muttered "*Désolé.*"

"People don't just disappear," said Rachel, her eyes huge. "Do you think she was kidnapped?"

"No way," insisted Elizabeth. "She probably just encountered some guy. Could be the pot washer. I wouldn't be surprised. She'll go with anything in pants."

"Really?" asked Rachel. "She seems like such a nice girl."

"She seems to me like a girl who knows her way around," said Sue.

"You can say that again," agreed Elizabeth. "Honestly, I never know who's going to be tiptoeing through my room in the morning, shoes in hand, heading for the door."

Rachel's eyebrows shot up. "I can't believe it."

"That's very risky behavior," said Lucy, remembering how the old guy had looked Sylvie over. Was it that simple? Was a look enough to initiate an assignation? Did Sylvie really just go off with anyone? She found the idea disturbing. "She could be putting you in danger, you know, bringing strange men into your apartment."

"I know, Mom, and I've asked her not to do it, but she just tells me it is none of my beez-nees," said Elizabeth, mimicking Sylvie's accent.

"Well, what do we do now?" asked Sue.

"Back to the *marché?*" suggested Pam.

"I've spent all my money," Lucy reminded her.

"I can't afford anything I want," said Sue.

"My feet hurt," complained Rachel.

"Then I guess we're done here," said Elizabeth, signaling for the check. "I'm going to go home and hang up my poster, and then I'm going to spend the afternoon washing my clothes at the *laverie automatique*."

"You'll get no sympathy from us," said Lucy, earning a few chuckles. "Between the four of us, we must have washed thousands, maybe millions, of loads of wash."

When the footsore group straggled back to the apartment, they found Bill and Sid in the courtyard, cutting up wood, constructing a closet for Madame Defarge.

"A real American-style closet," she announced, beaming. "All my friends will be very jealous."

"It's not a big deal," said Bill. "We're repurposing this door she had."

"And we found some plywood in the shed. When it's painted, it will blend in with the walls," added Sid. "We're not going to have to mess with Sheetrock at all."

"Sounds good," said Lucy, who suspected that constructing the closet was a peace offering to Madame Defarge, who had made it quite clear that she wasn't thrilled about the group's involvement with the police. Or maybe the two contractors simply couldn't resist an opportunity to saw wood and bang nails and show off their abilities. "How long is it going to take?"

"The rest of the afternoon probably," said Bill, releasing his tape measure, which rewound with a snap.

"We didn't expect you back so soon," said Sid. "Where are the packages?"

"I had them sent," teased Sue. "I bought a dining table and a set of Louis XV chairs. Only fifty thousand . . ."

Sid clutched his heart. "You didn't!"

"No, I didn't," admitted Sue as the doorbell sounded, and Madame Defarge went to answer it. She returned with a couple of uniformed policemen, one of whom was carrying a very official-looking warrant.

"Is Monsieur Goodman here?" asked the first cop, a very good-looking young man with dark hair.

"No," answered Sid. "He went out with Ted. Didn't say where they were going."

"I'm his wife," said Rachel, determined to be helpful and cooperative.

"No matter. We are here to search your premises. It will take only a few minutes, and you may accompany us."

"I'll go," offered Rachel. "I don't think we all need to be there."

"D'accord," said the second cop, who was shorter and darker than his colleague.

"It's this way," said Rachel, leading them to the entryway.

"*Mon Dieu!*" exclaimed Madame Defarge when the door had closed behind them. "I am so embarrassed. Those other men, they weren't police at all, were they? But I was in a hurry to get to the market, and they looked like policemen. They were in uniform. I would not have let them in otherwise."

"It's understandable," said Pam. "They must have been in disguise."

"What did they look like?" asked Lucy.

"Young men. They looked like flics. Good-looking. Polite. I never thought . . ."

"Were they dark? Blond? Beards?" persisted Lucy.

"Je ne me souviens pas!" wailed Madame Defarge.

"She doesn't remember," said Lucy, translating.

"It doesn't matter," observed Sue. "We don't know many people in Paris. We probably wouldn't recognize them, anyway."

Lucy didn't agree. "A description would help the police. Whoever searched our place is probably connected to Chef Larry's murder, right? They could even be the murderers."

"I didn't think of that," admitted Sue.

"But wait! We have a camera," said Madame Defarge. "A TV camera." She pointed upward, to a corner of the courtyard, where a small surveillance camera was perched on a windowsill.

"You have CCTV?" asked Bill.

She nodded. "It's part of the security system. I don't bother with it, but a man comes every month and checks it."

"Can we look at the film?" asked Lucy.

"*Bien sûr,* that is, if you know how to . . ."

"Let me take a look," offered Sid. He followed Madame into the concierge lodge and a few minutes later appeared in the doorway, beckoning to the others.

They gathered inside the cozy living room, all eyes on Madame's tiny TV. Sid used the remote to fast-forward through the grainy black-and-white images, which were as jerky as old silent films. They laughed, recognizing themselves, looking very tired and jet-lagged on the day they arrived, and they saw themselves coming and going in the days since, as well as the other occupants of the apartments that shared the courtyard. Then, when Lucy was beginning to feel slightly dizzy from staring at the speeding footage, the two fake cops appeared.

"Stop!" she ordered.

Sid hit the remote, and everything slowed down. They all leaned forward, studying the image. "It's their backs," complained Rachel.

"They have to come out," said Bill, and Sid hit FOR-WARD once again, until the two men reappeared, exiting the apartment entryway. He hit STOP, and they could see blurry images of their faces.

"I'm not sure," said Lucy, "but they look a lot like . . ."

"Those friends of Elizabeth's. We met them at the birthday party," added Bill. "What are their names?"

Sid hit REWIND and played the footage again, and a third time.

"Adil and Malik," said Lucy. "I think that's them, but why? What were they looking for?"

"Adil and Malik," repeated Bill. "What the hell?"

Chapter Twelve

What on earth were Adil and Malik doing, breaking into their apartment? And what were they looking for? Lucy remembered how their supplies of kitchen staples had been dumped out, as well as Rachel's creams and bath salts, all clear indications they were definitely searching for something. But what? And why? It was all very strange, very puzzling. "They seemed like such nice boys," she said, thinking aloud.

"What did you say?" demanded Bill. They were walking along the narrow sidewalks to the rue Saint-Antoine with Ted and Pam, on their way to meet Richard Mason at his favorite seafood place. It was a chance for the journalists to talk shop and for the others to enjoy *les fruits de mer.*

"I said Adil and Malik seemed like such nice boys, so well mannered," said Lucy.

"Yeah, well, I don't think breaking and entering and tossing somebody else's place is exactly good manners," said Bill. "The cops left the apartment just as they found it."

"Rachel said they didn't seem to find whatever they were looking for," said Lucy as they turned the corner and encountered an amazing display of fish and shellfish, arranged on a mountain of ice contained in a metal counter, right on the sidewalk outside the restaurant, complete with a waterfall, which provided a cooling backdrop for the fresh seafood.

"It smells like home," said Lucy, momentarily transported to the fish pier in Tinker's Cove.

"They've got every sort of fish you could imagine," said Ted. "Look at that red one. I've never seen it before. What is it?"

"Orange roughy?" said Lucy, taking a guess. "Red snapper?"

Pam, however, wasn't quite as taken with the display as the others. "Are we supposed to eat seafood that's been sitting out here on the street all day?" she asked. "It doesn't seem very sanitary to me."

"After eating *tête de veau*, I think my system can handle just about anything," said Bill, causing them to laugh.

"Fantastic, isn't it?" asked Richard, joining the group. "I reserved a table, so let's go on in. It's my treat," he announced. "Order whatever you want."

Richard was known at the restaurant, where he dined often, and was warmly welcomed. The group was immediately seated at a big table by the window and provided with an enormous platter containing all sorts of shellfish: several kinds of oysters, pink crayfish, blue crabs, and enormous shrimp, all artistically arranged and punctuated with lemon slices and bowls of vinaigrette.

"No cocktail sauce?" asked Bill.

"You mean that red stuff? What is it? Horseradish, lemon juice, and ketchup?" asked Richard. "They don't do that here. They think it interferes with the natural flavor of the shellfish."

"I think they're right," said Lucy, raising her chin and tipping a firm and juicy oyster into her mouth. "Delicious!"

"That's a Cancale, from Brittany," said Richard.

"I can see why you like living in France," said Pam, biting into a large and plump shrimp.

"Oh, come on, Richard," said Ted. "Aren't you tempted to come back to the good old USA? Don't you get tired of the French attitude? Don't you miss steak and cheeseburgers and . . ."

Pam finished for him. "Chocolate milk shakes!"

Richard laughed. "Sometimes I do miss home, like when I have to pay five euros for a very small Coke. And there is an American grocery store. It's actually not too far from your apartment, over on the rue Saint-Paul. I could get peanut butter and Duncan Hines brownie mix, if I wanted." He chose an oyster, holding it in his hand. "I've gone by it often enough, but I've never been tempted to go in. Not when there are beauties like this to savor," he said, slurping the oyster out of its shell.

"But as a journalist, isn't it hard operating in another culture?" asked Lucy. "Our friend Bob, he's a lawyer. He's really struggling with the French justice system."

"It wasn't easy at first. I'm not pretending it was. But I've been here for more than twenty years, and I've got the hang of things." He paused to crack open a crab claw and extracted a chunk of meat, which he popped into his mouth. "I was quite the ambitious young man, and I didn't have a job waiting for me, like you, Ted, at a family-owned newspaper. And the community news thing, it wasn't for me. I've always been interested in the big picture, not whether the board of selectmen is going to support the new school."

"Hey," protested Ted, "that's important stuff. Schools, taxes, police and fire, all the stuff that makes a town work."

"I'm not saying it's not important. I'm just saying it's not important to me. I'm more interested in what the IMF is going to do about the Greek debt, and whether the French are going to step up and play a role in Africa, or if they're going to let the Chinese take over."

"The Chinese are in Africa?" asked Lucy.

Richard laughed. "Big-time. I did a three-part story for the *Times,* front-page stuff, but Americans don't really care what goes on in the rest of the world. You're all focused on the price of dump stickers. . . ."

"Going up," said Ted.

"They are?" asked Bill. "I suppose that means contractors' waste fees are going up, too."

"Oh, yeah," said Ted. "Double."

"Oh, nuts," said Bill.

"See what I mean?" demanded Richard with a self-satisfied smirk.

After they demolished the mountain of shellfish, which was merely a first course, they proceeded to their second courses of various savory fish dishes, followed by green salads, desserts, and, finally, cheese. It wasn't until they were sipping their coffee that Richard asked if there was any progress toward regaining their passports.

"Now that Chef Larry's dead, the investigation is heating up," said Ted. "I'm hoping they will wrap it up soon and let us go."

"The oddest thing happened," said Lucy. "Ted told you how the apartment was searched, absolutely destroyed, and we thought it was the police. Well, it wasn't the police at all. The police finally came today. The concierge apologized and showed us video. They have a security camera, and it turns out the searchers look an awful lot like two guys who work with my daughter at the Cavendish Hotel."

"We can't be sure," said Bill. "The images are fuzzy, but we thought we recognized them from a party at Elizabeth's place. Adil and Malik, that's their names." He took a sip of coffee. "If it really is them."

"There's a lot of unrest in the Arab community right now, overflow from the Arab Spring," said Richard. "Are they Syrian?"

"Egyptian," said Lucy. "But they're not first generation. Their parents emigrated when King Farouk was thrown out."

"Everybody seems to be getting a turn in Egypt," said Richard, leaning back in his chair. "First it was the army, then Morsi and the Muslim Brotherhood, but the mob got rid of them. Believe it or not, there's even a royalist group that wants to put Farouk's son—his name's Fouad—back on the throne. They hate Morsi, they hate the Muslim Brotherhood, and they want to bring back the monarchy. I wrote a story about it."

"We read your story," said Lucy. "And these boys are in that group. They told me all about it. But in your story you said that Fouad himself isn't too interested in claiming the throne."

Richard chuckled. "That's right, and who can blame him? Right now the Egyptians are more interested in demonstrating and overthrowing governments than in keeping them. Fouad leads a quiet life in Switzerland. And he's getting on in years. He's not a young man."

"And I imagine he must have bad memories of his family's expulsion and exile," said Pam.

"I don't know about that. He was just a baby at the time. The prime mover behind the group is Khalid Sadek. His father was Farouk's closest advisor. He's trying to pressure Fouad emotionally . . . you know, 'Restore your family's honor,' that sort of thing. But he's also raising money, hoping to tempt Fouad with a big pile of cash," said Richard.

"Well, this is all very interesting," said Bill, "but it doesn't explain why two young men, certainly French now but of Egyptian heritage, would ransack our apartment, does it?"

"No," agreed Richard. "It's usually drugs. They steal stuff to sell to get money for drugs." He paused. "Maybe they were acting on orders from Sadek, stealing stuff that he could sell for cash to finance the movement."

"You interviewed this Sadek fellow, right?" asked Ted. "Do you think he'd do something like that? Encourage two young men to steal for him?"

"I wouldn't put it past him," said Richard. "I did get the impression that he runs a tight ship. He's very authoritarian," said Richard.

"It's a moot point, anyway," said Lucy. "Nothing's missing. They didn't steal anything."

"Well, that is odd," said Richard, signaling for the check. "I suppose you could chalk it up to youthful high jinks."

Bill and Ted both reached for their wallets, but Richard insisted on paying the entire bill, saying he'd invited them and it was his treat. "My pleasure," he said as they thanked him effusively for what they all knew was a very expensive dinner.

When they got back to the apartment, Bill announced that a big meal always made him sleepy, and got busy shooing the others off to their rooms and unfolding the sofa bed, wasting no time climbing in and settling down for the night. Soon he was snoring away. Lucy, however, felt far too full to attempt sleep and headed down the long hall to the bathroom, planning to have a nice long soak.

The tatty old bathroom was her favorite room in the apartment, and not only because of the previous day's romantic interlude. She loved the big old-fashioned tub and the cracked tiles and the colorful glass panels in the door. In her opinion, the heated towel bar was an invention second only to bagged salad in improving the quality of life. But even the relaxing bath wasn't enough to make her sleepy, so she decided to call Elizabeth. It was only a little after ten, and she was sure Elizabeth would be awake. It was Saturday night, after all. She hoped Sylvie had turned up and Elizabeth wasn't worrying about her.

"No, she hasn't come home, but I'm not worried," Elizabeth insisted in reply to her mother's concerned inquiry. "She's done this before. She isn't scheduled to work this weekend, so she's probably out on the town. I'm not her mother, and she doesn't tell me where she goes or who she goes with."

"But don't you think it's funny she didn't say good-bye to us?" asked Lucy. "It was kind of rude, and she seems so polite."

"I've told you, Mom. Sylvie is very self-centered. She doesn't think about other people. Like whether or not I enjoy sleeping on a futon and being wakened by some stranger tramping through at five a.m. Frankly, I'm glad she's not home. I hope she stays out, because maybe then I'll get a good night's sleep before I have to go to work tomorrow morning."

"Well, if you're not worried . . ."

"I'm not, and you don't need to worry, either."

"I won't," promised Lucy. "Listen, have you seen Adil and Malik lately?"

"No. We've been working different shifts, I guess. Why do you ask?"

Lucy yawned. She was growing tired. "Well, you know how we thought the police had searched our apartment? It wasn't the police. It was Adil and Malik. They were caught on video."

"That's crazy. It couldn't be them," said Elizabeth.

"It really did look like them."

"Well, appearances can be deceiving," insisted Elizabeth. "I know them, and I'm sure they would never do anything like that. Why would they?"

"You're probably right," said Lucy, too tired to argue. She yawned again. "I'm going to head to bed."

"*Bonne nuit. Dors bien,*" said Elizabeth.

"You, too, sweetie. Good night and sleep well."

Next morning they all slept later than usual, and at breakfast Sue advised them to eat lightly because Madame Defarge had invited them to Sunday lunch, her way of apologizing for letting the intruders search the apartment and to thank Bill and Sid for building the closet. "And dress nicely," advised Sue. "Sunday lunch is a formal affair in France."

At one o'clock they gathered in the courtyard and knocked on the concierge's door. She welcomed them warmly and promptly served aperitifs, whiskey for the men and champagne cocktails for the ladies, along with delicious homemade cheese treats. Once everyone was supplied with a drink, she disappeared into her tiny kitchen. Gounod, her little dog, absented himself after the introductions and curled up in his basket, aware, no doubt, that he would be rewarded with the leftovers.

"These are delicious," enthused Lucy. "What are they?"

"*Galettes au fromage,*" replied Sue. "And I bet we'll have some sort of soup for starters, then a roast chicken with vegetables, salad, strawberry tart for dessert, cheese, and coffee. I hope you're hungry."

"Not terribly," admitted Lucy.

"And it will all be served on her best china and crystal," added Sue.

"That's a lot of dishes to wash," said Rachel. "We ought to offer to clean up for her."

"Don't you dare," hissed Sue. "It would be considered an insult, and she would be offended."

"That's fine with me," said Pam, sipping her cocktail. "I'd probably break the Limoges, anyway."

The luncheon was almost exactly as Sue had predicted, and it was a leisurely affair, but Lucy found it surprisingly enjoyable. It was pleasant to take time over a meal and to savor each course. Somewhat surprisingly, Madame encouraged them to discuss each dish, and the conversation became quite lively as they shared favorite recipes and family traditions.

"What's the best way to make an omelet?" asked Rachel, confessing that hers always stuck to the pan.

"You must use . . . I don't know the English . . . *la beurre*," advised Madame.

"Butter," said Sue.

"But-tare," she repeated, trying out the word. "Not only in the pan, but you put some in with the eggs, too."

"*Vraiment?*" Sue, who watched calories with the concentration of a robin chasing a worm, was doubtful.

"*Oui, absolument,*" insisted Madame. "And I always beat the eggs with *une fourchette.*"

"A fork? Not a whisk?" asked Sue, her eyebrows rising in surprise. "What about the pan? Le Creuset?"

Now it was Madame's turn to be surprised. "*Non, non, non.* Only copper. It distributes the heat evenly."

"I guess that's the problem," admitted Rachel. "I've been using an old Teflon pan."

"Not Teflon!" protested Pam. "You're poisoning your-self!"

"It's too late for me, then," admitted Rachel. "Most of the Teflon is worn off."

"What is this Teflon?" asked Madame, and they all laughed.

"It's a nonstick coating on pots," explained Lucy.

"Ah, you Americans." Madame shook her head and clucked her tongue. "In France, but-tare is the nonstick coating."

Lucy couldn't remember enjoying a meal more, not even Richard's seafood feast the night before. Then there had been more than a hint of pretension in the lavish presentation, and she'd felt guilty about the exorbitant cost. But at Madame's table the food was not only an exhibition of their hostess's culinary skill but also a genuine expression of her regard for them. But when it was over, after consuming two huge meals in two days, Lucy felt rather sluggish.

"Want to catch a movie?" asked Ted. "Pam and I are meeting Richard at the cinema."

"What's the movie?" asked Bill.

"Dunno. But Richard says it's a must-see," said Pam.

"Then I guess you must," joked Lucy, who was beginning to wonder about Ted's infatuation with his old friend and about whether Pam was growing a bit tired of it. These days it was always "Richard says this . . ." and "Richard says that . . . ," as if Richard was the ultimate authority on everything under the sun. "I think I'd like to get some exercise, maybe walk along the quais."

"Sounds good," agreed Bill, turning to Sue and Sid. "Want to come?"

"No, thanks. We're going to a concert with Bob and Rachel over at the Sainte-Chappelle."

"How lovely. Have a good time," said Lucy, taking

Bill's hand and strolling off with him. "Where shall we walk? The Île Saint-Louis?"

"There's a Berthillon ice cream shop there," he said.

"How can you even think of ice cream after that huge meal?"

"I can always find a little room for ice cream," he said. "And portions are small here."

"I'll have a lick," said Lucy. "Just a taste."

He laughed as they joined other couples and families promenading along the river. It was a lovely spring afternoon, the trees were leafing out, and the river water lapped gently against the stone embankment. Here and there lovers were sitting on benches, wrapped in each other's arms.

Perhaps inspired by all the public displays of *amour,* Bill chose passion fruit ice cream, and it was so delicious that Lucy had more than one taste. They were heading home beneath a ravishing pink sky when Lucy's cell phone rang.

As soon as she heard her daughter's voice, Lucy knew something was wrong. "Mom," wailed Elizabeth. "I can't believe I said all those bad things. I should have done something. . . ."

"What's happened?" asked Lucy.

"It's Sylvie," sobbed Elizabeth.

"She had an accident?"

"No, she's dead! Murdered."

"Are you sure?"

"The cops are here. . . . Will you come?"

Bill took the phone. "As fast as we can, baby," he promised. "As fast as we can."

Chapter Thirteen

A taxi was letting off a passenger just a short distance down the street, so they ran and were able to catch the driver's attention before he drove off. Bill gave him Elizabeth's address, while Lucy checked her smartphone for any information about the discovery of Sylvie's body. At home, she knew the Twitterverse would have plenty to say, as no police activity went unobserved, especially the discovery of a body. In no time at all photos would be posted on Facebook, videos would appear on YouTube, and the mainstream media would be quick to pick up the story. Here in France, however, discretion ruled, and there was little information beyond a brief official press release from the *brigade criminelle* announcing that the body of a female had been discovered on the quai de Grenelle earlier that day and police were investigating.

When the taxi pulled up in front of Elizabeth's building, Lucy was out before the car had fully stopped, leaving Bill to pay the driver. He joined Lucy at the doorway, where she was frantically punching at the security keypad. Finally, the door opened, but they were confronted by a uniformed flic, who was blocking their way. *"Désolé,"* he said, firmly shaking his head. He went on to offer a lengthy explanation, but all Lucy understood was the word *interdit,* which meant they were not going to be allowed in.

"Nous sommes les parents de Mademoiselle Stone," responded Lucy, and after checking via two-way radio with a supervisor, the flic stepped aside with a nod.

They hurried up the stairs, all four flights, and arrived at Elizabeth's apartment completely out of breath, finding the door open and Elizabeth seated on the futon, looking very small and pale, between a couple of plainclothes cops.

"Mom! Dad!" exclaimed Elizabeth, sounding greatly relieved. "I'm so glad you're here."

The cops moved to the other side of the room, allowing Lucy and Bill to embrace their daughter and reassure themselves that she was all right. Lucy's first reaction was that the French police were wonderfully polite. Then she realized they were watching and noting everything they did.

"Madame, monsieur," began one of the detectives, who had a sad, sympathetic face, with bags under his eyes, which, she figured, served him well in his chosen line of work. "This is a very sad event for your daughter, and we are most sympathetic. Let me assure you we do not consider Elizabeth a suspect, but we believe she may have important information that will be most helpful in this investigation." He spoke English with a pronounced accent, saying "ahn-for-mah-see-on" for "information," but Lucy wasn't about to quibble. She was deeply grateful that he spoke English at all. "My name is Guillaume Girard, Commissaire Girard."

"We understand," said Bill. "Elizabeth will be happy to cooperate."

"And so will we," said Lucy. "This is terrible. I assume Sylvie's death was not an accident?"

"*Pas du tout,*" he said, with a doleful shake of his head.

Just then a couple of crime-scene investigators, wearing white jumpsuits and toting cases of equipment, arrived and were directed to Sylvie's bedroom. Lucy and Bill were asked to seat themselves at the round table, which took up most of the small room, and Girard continued his interrogation of Elizabeth.

Lucy and Bill listened as Elizabeth explained Sylvie's disappearance at the café in the flea market, becoming uneasy as Girard pressed Elizabeth for details.

"You were not concerned about your friend's absence?" he asked, furrowing his creased forehead.

"No," replied Elizabeth. "She had done this sort of thing before, left me when we went out together if an attractive man came along. She came and went. She didn't share the details of her life with me. There were a lot of men. She would bring them here. It made me uncomfortable."

"Did she seem upset, tense, in the last few days?"

"No." Elizabeth shook her head. "If anything, she was nicer than usual. I was surprised when she offered to bring my mother and her friends to the flea market. It wasn't at all typical."

"Do you think she had some reason for going to the market, other than being a good hostess?" asked Girard. "Could the trip have been a cover for something else?"

"Like what?" asked Elizabeth. "Drugs?"

Girard was right on it. "Did she use?"

"A little pot. She said it helped her relax. That's all."

"Where did she get it?"

"I don't know," said Elizabeth. "I'm not interested in that stuff."

"I see," said Girard, sounding skeptical. He turned to

Lucy and Bill. "Your daughter cannot stay here tonight. We must conduct a thorough search of the apartment, and there is also the matter of her emotional well-being. She should not be alone. Can she stay with you?"

"Of course," said Lucy, thinking of the second sofa in the living room at the apartment. "Can she take a few things? Clothes and a toothbrush?"

"*Bien sûr,*" agreed Girard. "And before you go, you must all give me your contact information."

Bill took care of that while Lucy helped Elizabeth gather a few necessities from the ugly 1930s sideboard trimmed with crudely carved wood, where she kept her clothes, tossing them into a duffel bag.

"How long will she need to stay away?" asked Lucy when Elizabeth went into the bathroom to get her toothbrush and other toiletries. Lucy took advantage of this opportunity to question the detective and also asked for one of his cards, for future reference.

"I do not know, madame," said Girard, stepping close and presenting her with his card. "You must keep an eye on your daughter, take special care of her. What happened to Sylvie was not pretty." He lowered his voice to a whisper. "She was tortured. . . ."

Lucy gasped.

"And then she was killed execution-style. A very professional job."

"Ohmigod." Lucy felt the floor shifting beneath her feet. "What was that girl involved in?"

"That, madame, is what we must discover."

All three were silent in the taxi they took to the apartment, each thinking their separate thoughts. Lucy kept remembering Sylvie as she last saw her, with her blond hair cut in a chic bob, her porcelain skin, those delicately arched eyebrows, and that bemused smile, and struggled to understand why anyone would want to hurt, much less kill, such a beautiful young woman. She held her daughter's hand tightly, troubled by Girard's warning, but Elizabeth pulled it away in a gesture of stubborn independence. Lucy knew she had to tell her the truth about Sylvie's death, but decided to wait until morning, until after she'd had a good night's sleep. If her daughter could sleep, which Lucy doubted. She knew that Elizabeth took after her and was a light sleeper, unlike Bill, who could sleep through a tornado.

When they arrived at the apartment, the friends were gathered around the kitchen island, sipping herbal tea and recounting their evening activities.

"Chamomile tea?" offered Pam. "I also have Sleepy-time, which I brought from home."

"Sleepytime would be great," said Lucy. "Elizabeth's staying with us for a few nights. Her roommate . . ."

"Sylvie?" prompted Sue. "What's she getting up to?"

"Sylvie had an accident," began Bill, intending to break the news as gently as possible.

"She was murdered," Elizabeth announced abruptly. "The police said I can't stay in my apartment."

There was a long silence, finally broken by Ted. "Another homicide?"

"So it seems," said Lucy.

"That does it. We're never going home," said Bob, shaking his head. "Being involved in one murder is bad enough, but two . . . ? This is a legal nightmare."

"Is that all you can say?" demanded Rachel. "This isn't about us. Two people are dead, two people we knew and liked. Two friends. Two young friends. It's tragic."

"I can't believe it's happening," said Sue.

"That's a normal reaction," said Rachel. "It's going to take time to process. It takes time for the reality of death to really sink in."

"And they say America is violent," offered Sid.

"Isn't France supposed to have a much lower murder rate than the U.S.?" demanded Ted.

"That's what I've heard," said Pam.

"Something's going on," said Sue, "and somehow we're involved."

If you only knew the half of it, thought Lucy, cradling the cup of hot tea in both hands and inhaling the grassy, herbal scent. She was convinced they had stumbled into something very big and very bad, and she was afraid they weren't going to escape unscathed.

Maybe it was the tea, or maybe it was some sort of subconscious effort by her brain to delay processing Sylvie's death, but Lucy slept soundly right through the night and woke in the morning, surprised to find she felt refreshed and optimistic. She had known Chef Larry only in a casual way, she realized, which made it almost impossible to investigate his murder. But Sylvie, on the other hand, was her daughter's roommate, and Lucy had much better access to information about her. Elizabeth maintained that Sylvie had been very private, but Lucy suspected her daughter knew more about her roommate than she realized. This time she had a real opportunity to get to the bottom of things, and she was determined to take advantage of it. Her primary motive was to protect her daughter. She knew she wouldn't feel that Elizabeth was safe until whoever had killed Sylvie was caught and jailed, but she was also convinced that the only way she would ever see Tinker's Cove again was if she solved both murders. She had a hunch the two deaths were connected, perhaps even committed by the same killer. The police didn't seem to be making much headway, and they wouldn't get their passports back until the matter was resolved.

Now all that remained was deciding on a plan of action. She yawned and stretched and got out of bed and, tiptoeing past her sleeping husband and daughter, went into the kitchen to start the coffeepot. She had just come back from the bathroom and was pouring herself a cup when Elizabeth joined her.

"You're up early," said Lucy.

"I've got to be at work by eight," said Elizabeth.

"Oh, no," said Lucy. "No work for you today."

"Don't be silly, Mom," snapped Elizabeth. "I've got to go. I think that whatever happened to Sylvie—"

"What happened to Sylvie was dreadful," said Lucy. "You need to know what Girard told me. She wasn't attacked by some random rapist or something. She was grabbed and tortured and killed execution-style. They think she was involved in something that got her in trouble, probably drugs."

"Duh," replied Elizabeth sarcastically. "And I'm pretty sure that it's happening at the hotel."

Lucy thought her daughter was on to something. The Cavendish had gold-plated faucets in the marble bathrooms and Yves Delorme linens on the beds. The upper crust gathered in the tastefully decorated dining rooms to enjoy delicious food, excellent service, and distinguished company. But the hotel also employed a small army of workers who didn't earn very much and were expected to serve people who had more money than they knew what to do with. No wonder there was a thriving black market operation, and now, she suspected, a drug operation. The more she thought about it, the more it seemed that a hotel like the Cavendish, with staff and guests coming and going, not to mention a constant stream of deliveries, would be an excellent cover for illegal activities.

"I don't want you—" began Lucy.

Elizabeth cut her off. "And I'm not going to be able to figure out what's going on unless I'm there."

Lucy didn't like the idea, but she knew that Elizabeth was right.

"I don't want you to put yourself in danger," she said, this time finishing her sentence. "You're going to have to be very careful," warned Lucy. "And you better watch out for Adil and Malik. I'm pretty sure they're involved somehow."

"I'm not going to trust anybody," said Elizabeth, surprising her mother by actually agreeing with her. "Getting Sylvie's killer behind bars is the only way I'll ever feel safe."

If only there was some way she could be there, helping Elizabeth, thought Lucy, and then she realized that there was. "Okay, but you have to stay in constant contact with me. You can text, okay?"

"Yeah," agreed Elizabeth, with a relieved sigh. "I'll feel better if I know you're keeping tabs on me."

"That's a first," said Lucy, causing Elizabeth to grin.

"I'd like to get into her locker," continued Lucy. "But I have a feeling the cops have already sealed it."

"Probably," agreed Elizabeth, "but she used to keep a black duffel bag of stuff under the reception counter, way in the back. I don't think anybody knows about that but me."

"We have to find out what's in that bag," said Lucy, and Elizabeth nodded.

It took some convincing, but in the end Bill finally agreed to let Elizabeth go to work, as long as either he or Lucy accompanied her to and from, and she promised to text them regularly throughout the day. Lucy took the morning shift, leaving with Elizabeth and taking the

Métro to the hotel. Finding the lobby sparsely populated at this early hour, Lucy decided to stick around for a while, hoping she'd have an opportunity to check out that black bag belonging to Sylvie that Elizabeth had mentioned.

Elizabeth had to change into her Cavendish uniform in the locker room, and Lucy waited anxiously, sitting on one of the luxurious velvet sofas, for her to reappear and take her usual place at the concierge's desk. Moments later, after taking a phone call, Elizabeth moved over to the reception desk, apparently filling in for the deceased Sylvie and joining a similarly young and attractive colleague. When the other worker took a break, she signaled her mother and reached under the reception desk, passing her the duffel bag that had belonged to Sylvie.

Lucy tucked it under her arm and made her way to the delicately perfumed ladies' room, where she installed herself in one of the roomy cubicles, each one of which was equipped not only with a toilet but also with a private sink and a makeup table with a stool and large mirror. She sat right down, eagerly unzipped the bag, and pulled out the contents. These were the sorts of things any working girl might keep on hand at her job, including a couple of packs of panty hose, a cosmetic bag, tampons, and cigarettes. There was also, more surprisingly, a French sex manual and some items that Lucy suspected—but she wasn't absolutely sure—were sex toys. One clue was the fact that they were wrapped in a very skimpy black lace teddy.

Living in New England was a curse, thought Lucy, thinking that at her age she ought to be a bit more sophisticated. She was an experienced woman, a mother of four, after all, and she shouldn't feel squeamish about the things consenting adults did. But in her world, she admitted to herself as she stuffed the sex aids back into the bag, you wore thick flannel to bed, and lots of it.

There was also a special compartment in the duffel that, Lucy knew, was designed to keep sweaty workout gear separate from the bag's other contents. Lucy was just about to open it when her smartphone buzzed. It was Elizabeth, sounding rather frantic.

"It's Sylvie's parents. They're coming from Chartres. They have to identify the body." She paused. "They want me to meet them at the station."

"Not a problem," said Lucy, sensing an opportunity. "Your dad and I can meet them."

"They're taking the train. It arrives at Montparnasse station at nine-oh-two."

Lucy glanced at her watch. "That's in fifteen minutes!"

"You've got to hurry," said Elizabeth. "Are you going to give them the duffel bag?"

Lucy hesitated. The bag would absolutely have to go to Sylvie's parents eventually, but perhaps not just yet. A collection of sleazy sex toys wasn't exactly the sort of thing you wanted to present to the grieving parents of a young woman.

"Oh, I don't want to cart it around Paris," said Lucy, hedging.

Elizabeth's interest was piqued. "What's in it?"

"Just tampons and cigarettes and gym gear."

"Oh," said Elizabeth, sounding disappointed.

"And a few sex toys," said Lucy.

"Why am I not surprised?" asked Elizabeth with a sigh, ending the call.

Lucy made a quick stop at the reception desk and handed over the bag, then called Bill as she hurried out of the hotel and into a cab. He agreed to meet her at

Montparnasse station, and true to his word, she found him waiting for her at the main entrance. They had only minutes to spare before the train from Chartres was due to arrive.

Even though she'd never met them, Lucy had no trouble identifying Monsieur and Madame Seydoux when they debarked from the train; they wore their grief as plainly as their practical tan raincoats and sensible shoes. Monsieur Seydoux was tall, and his gray hair was cut military-style. He held himself stiffly, as if he feared he might explode if he relaxed. Madame was much shorter and rounder, her hair dyed strawberry blond, and she held on tightly to her husband's arm. Lucy noticed she'd tucked a black and beige scarf into the neckline of her coat. It seemed that Frenchwomen had an appropriate scarf for every occasion, including a trip to the morgue.

"Nous sommes les parents d'Elizabeth Stone, la *camarade de chambre* de votre fille," said Lucy, who had checked her dictionary for the term for *roommate* and had practiced the sentence. "Je m'appelle Lucy, et mon mari est Bill."

Monsieur and Madame stared at them, clearly wondering what on earth they were doing here at the station, meeting them.

"Pas de police? Pas d'autorités?" Monsieur asked, puzzled.

"Non," responded Lucy. "Nous voudrions vous aider," she added, hoping she was saying they wished to be of service.

Monsieur responded with a barrage of French, which Lucy did not understand, and she decided to admit defeat. "Do you speak English?" she asked.

"A leetle," said Monsieur.

The conversation continued in a mixture of French

and English, with many stops and starts, as Lucy and Bill led the Seydouxes to the taxi rank, where Monsieur gave the driver the address of the morgue. The driver emitted a sympathetic sigh before shifting into drive and diving into the constant stream of traffic.

Lucy and Bill accompanied them inside, waiting on a bench in the hallway as the couple went through a heavily scarred metal door. They were gone a good three-quarters of an hour, most of which, Lucy suspected, was devoted to the endless red tape the French were so fond of, before they emerged. Both looked as if they'd been sucked dry by vampires. Their faces were white, and Monsieur had to support Madame, who seemed ready to collapse. Bill jumped up to help, taking her other arm, and between them they were able to lead her out of the building and into a nearby café, where Lucy ordered *café* for everyone and double brandies for the Seydouxes.

Lucy didn't know what to say, even without a language barrier. They sat at the table in the nearly empty café, two sets of parents separated by a gulf deeper and wider than the Atlantic Ocean. The Stones' daughter was alive, busy at work building her future, and the Seydouxes' daughter was laid out in the morgue, her life over.

Madame finally spoke when she had finished her coffee and had had a sip or two of brandy. "Où est votre fille?" she asked.

"At the Cavendish. Elle travaille aujourd'hui," replied Lucy, explaining that Elizabeth was at work. "Voulez-vous parler avec elle?"

Receiving a nod, Bill asked the counterman to call a taxi for them, and when it arrived, they all squeezed in for the trip to the hotel. When they arrived, the handsome Serge was on duty in the lobby, and he hurried over to express, in the most elegant manner conceivable, his condolences to the Seydouxes. Lucy and Bill left them to it and went to the concierge's desk, telling Elizabeth that Madame wanted to speak to her.

"How are they doing?" asked Elizabeth.

"About like you'd expect," said Lucy.

"Sylvie complained about them all the time," said Elizabeth. "They were so proper, so conservative, and cheap, too. I don't remember her saying a single nice thing about them."

"Don't tell them that," said Lucy.

"Of course not," said Elizabeth. "I was just thinking how ironic it is, that's all. I was wondering, what if it was the other way round? What if it was one of the parents who died? Would Sylvie be as upset as they are about losing her?"

"Probably," said Bill. "You know what they say: You don't appreciate what you have until it's gone."

"Maybe you'll appreciate us now," said Lucy, partly serious and partly attempting to lighten the moment. "Go on. Tell them how much you liked Sylvie and how much you'll miss her."

Much to Lucy's surprise, Elizabeth grabbed her hands tightly and squeezed. "I do, Mom. I really do appreciate you and Dad. You're the best."

Lucy and Bill watched as their daughter joined the group and exchanged *bisous* with Monsieur and Madame Seydoux, then walked to the side of the lobby, where they sat down on a sofa. "So much for my plan to question Sylvie's parents," said Lucy. "Even if I could speak French well, I wouldn't have been able to do it. They seem so shattered and vulnerable."

"I doubt they'd have much to say," said Bill. "They probably don't have any idea what their daughter was up to here in Paris."

Lucy thought of Sylvie's black bag and nodded. "I bet you're right."

Then the group broke up. Serge strode across the lobby in the direction of the elevators, and Elizabeth approached with the Seydouxes.

"They want me to thank you for your help today," said Elizabeth. "Now they're going back to Chartres. They have a little shop there by the train station, and they can't leave it unattended. They also have to plan for the funeral, and they'll let us know when it will be."

Lucy and Bill exchanged hugs and *bisous* with the Seydouxes and waved them off to the train station in their taxi. When it was gone, Lucy fell into Bill's arms.

"I'm exhausted," she said. "Imagine how they must feel."

"I hope I never have to find out," said Bill.

Chapter Fourteen

Leaving Elizabeth at the hotel, Lucy and Bill decided to grab a quick lunch at a café, where they discussed their plans for the afternoon. Bill was tired and wanted to go back to the apartment, where he hoped to enjoy a little downtime and finish reading Hemingway's *A Moveable Feast*. That left Lucy with time to kill until it was time to accompany Elizabeth back to the group's apartment for the night. She wanted to stay close to the Cavendish, in case Elizabeth needed her, so she decided to do some shopping in the nearby *grands magasins* Printemps and Galeries Lafayette.

Lucy enjoyed browsing through the huge department stores, but prices were high and her only purchase was a striped Breton-style shirt for her grandson, Patrick. Throughout the afternoon she contacted Elizabeth regularly and got prompt replies. **Okay?** she'd text, waiting anxiously until she received Elizabeth's response, a smiley face. At a quarter to six she was back in the Cavendish lobby, waiting for Elizabeth to get off work. Seeing her enter, Elizabeth beckoned her over to the reception desk.

"The police called, Mom, and said they're through with the apartment and I can go back."

Lucy didn't think this was a good idea. "Are you sure you want to do that?"

"I think I do. Commissaire Girard is going to meet me there, just to make sure everything's all right. I have to do a walk-through with him and sign some papers because the police took some things from the apartment." She paused. "I think he must be satisfied that it's safe."

Lucy didn't like this one bit. "You're sure you don't want me to come? Someone should stay with you."

"I'm sure. I'm a big girl now, and when Girard leaves, I'll put the chain across the door and I won't open it for anybody. Okay?"

"What if you have to go out? Do you have food?"

"Yes, Mom. There's soup in the fridge."

"Soup for supper?"

"I had a big lunch. I often have soup at night."

Lucy couldn't let go. "Listen, if you feel the least bit nervous or anything at any time, give us a call. Your dad and I can be there in a few minutes."

"Will do," promised Elizabeth. "Now relax. Everything will be fine."

Lucy knew she had no choice but to let her daughter go home, but she couldn't help worrying about her safety. She was reminded of those nights when Elizabeth was in high school and was going out with friends. The danger then in Tinker's Cove was underage drinking and driving, and Lucy always used to tell Elizabeth she could call for a ride home, at any hour of the night, if she found herself in a risky situation. Back then Elizabeth had to deal only with peer pressure from kids, not quite the same as the threat posed by the professional criminals who, the police believed, had tortured and killed Sylvie.

It was rush hour in the Métro, and Lucy's attention

was focused on getting safely through the stampeding crowds of commuters without being trampled underfoot or losing her bag to a pickpocket. She was tired and was looking forward to relaxing with a glass of wine and some lively conversation when she got home, but her friends were not in a convivial mood.

"We're just back from the lawyers," said Rachel. "I'm afraid they weren't much help."

"Useless, utterly useless," fumed Bob. "They said we should be patient and have faith in the French justice system. That's it."

"I wonder how much they're charging Norah," said Sue.

"Oh, plenty, you can be sure of that," said Bob.

"Better Norah than us," said Sid. "She can afford it."

"The office was very luxurious," said Rachel, "and in a very nice neighborhood. Gucci, Hermès, that sort of thing."

"Absolutely rotten with little dogs," added Bob, practically snarling.

"Bob stepped in some pooh," said Rachel.

"In the lawyer's office?" Lucy couldn't believe it.

"No. In the street," said Rachel.

"Dog doo, red tape, it's all the same merde," said Bill.

"I think there's nothing for it but to drown our troubles," said Lucy.

Sue was never one to refuse a tipple. "Open a bottle, Sid, will you?"

He was just pouring when Pam and Ted arrived, along with Richard. "I must have heard that cork pop," said Ted, making a joke.

Nobody laughed, but Sid offered to open another bottle. "We've got plenty, and there's more at the Monoprix."

"Do I sense a mood of gloom?" asked Pam. "What's going on?"

"The lawyers weren't very helpful, and Bob stepped in dog doo," said Sue.

"*Quelle catastrophe,*" said Pam. "I heard a woman say that into her cell phone."

"Sounds about right," said Bob, drinking deeply from his glass of *vin rouge.*

"Ted told me about your daughter's roommate," said Richard, speaking to Lucy. "I'm very sorry."

"It's very upsetting. I'm so worried about her," replied Lucy, touched by his concern. "I'm afraid she's in danger. Two deaths, and the police don't seem to be making any progress."

"Do you think they're connected?" asked Richard.

"They must be, don't you think? It can't be a coincidence that two people we know were murdered, but I can't figure out what any of it has to do with us. We're innocent, but I think we must have unwittingly stumbled onto something."

"Lucy's right," said Bob. "The authorities seem to think we're involved, that, at the very least, we know something. That's why they're detaining us. It's so frustrating."

"My fear is that the bad guys also think we know something," said Bill.

"We know nothing," said Sid in a fake German accent.

"I think you're right to worry," said Richard as Sid refilled his glass. "There's a lot more going on underground in Paris, and I'm not talking about the sewers and the catacombs. It's easy to make a wrong step. . . ."

"You can say that again," said Bob. The wine seemed to be taking effect, brightening his spirits.

"I'm serious," said Richard. "The French are in a

very uncomfortable situation right now because the Arab or Muslim population, whatever you want to call them, is booming. France has always been popular with émigrés—think of all the Russians and Poles who've come here through the years—but the Arabs are different. They want to preserve their culture, and they're not interested in assimilating. They're mostly interested in getting back to where they came from.

"There are all these factions, all these groups of disaffected people, who are here because they had to flee their homelands. They don't love France. They hate the West. The irony is that they enjoy freedom and safety here, but they don't approve of a culture that celebrates pleasure, especially sex. They see one of those sexy billboards advertising bras in the Métro—well, they don't even let their women out of the house unless they're covered head to toe—and they conclude France is deeply corrupt."

"And then there's the wine, which is a big part of French culture," said Sid, uncorking another bottle.

"Right," agreed Richard. "They don't drink alcohol."

"Now, that's what I call a sin, refusing to drink wine in France," said Sue.

"So true," agreed Richard, smiling. "But what I'm trying to get to is the fact that terrorists are a dime a dozen here. There's more plots afoot than you can imagine. Every week it seems the antiterrorism brigade uncovers another scheme to blow up the Eiffel Tower or to assassinate some government official. They even have plots against other terrorist groups. It's crazy."

"It sounds like the Wild West," said Rachel.

"It is," said Richard, "and if you're smart, you'll keep your heads down." There were a few chuckles, and Richard continued, "Be careful, watch your step, and don't go looking for trouble. That's my advice."

"Good advice, anytime," said Bill, giving Lucy a look.

After they had consumed several bottles of wine, it was generally agreed that it was too much trouble to cook dinner, so they decided to go to Loulou's bistro on the corner. They enjoyed a leisurely meal—service was never fast there—and it was after eleven when they finally left. They were walking down the narrow cobbled street, lit by lanterns that hung from the buildings, when Lucy got a call from Elizabeth.

"What's up?" asked Lucy, falling a step or two behind the group.

"I'm so scared."

Lucy could hear the fear in her daughter's voice, and her stomach did a somersault. "What's wrong?"

Bill heard her anxious tone and left the group, joining her on the sidewalk to listen to the call.

"Adil and Malik tried to break in."

"Are you okay?" Bill demanded after seizing the smartphone and holding it so they could both listen.

"Yeah. Just scared. It was weird. I was in my pajamas and I had a mask on my face and there was a knock on the door. I looked through the peephole and saw Adil and Malik in the hallway, and because of what you told me, I decided I'd better ignore them. Besides, I didn't want them to see me like that, and I, well, I just didn't want to deal with anyone, so I pretended I wasn't home. Like you do when the Mormons ring the doorbell."

"You did the right thing," said Lucy.

"But they weren't Mormons. They picked the lock! I heard these scratches, and I'm standing there, wondering what's going on, and the door opened. I couldn't believe it. They must have picked the lock."

"Did they get in?" demanded Bill.

"No. I'd put the chain across, so it only opened a few

inches. I heard them swearing, and then they left. I heard them going down the stairs."

"You didn't believe me, but I was right about them," said Lucy in an "I told you so" voice. "They did search our apartment, here, pretending to be police. The concierge showed us a security video. I was sure it was them."

"If I hadn't seen it, I wouldn't have believed it." Elizabeth paused. "Do you think they killed Sylvie?"

"I guess it's possible. I don't know. They seemed like such nice guys," said Lucy.

"That's what they always say about these nuts," added Bill.

"What if I hadn't put the chain across, Mom? What do you think they would have done?"

Lucy didn't want to think about it. "You can't stay there alone," said Lucy.

"I'm on my way," said Bill.

They spent the rest of the night in Elizabeth's apartment, where Bill and Lucy shared the opened futon in the salon. Elizabeth took the bed in Sylvie's room, fastidiously wrapping herself in an extra blanket and sleeping atop the covers. Nobody slept very well.

In the morning, after drinking a couple of cups of strong coffee, Lucy came to a decision. "You have to call Girard and tell him what happened, and I think we have to tell Lapointe what's been going on, too," she said.

Bill nodded in agreement. "I'll call and make an appointment," he said.

"I have to go to work," said Elizabeth, prompting the same reaction from both parents.

"Call in sick," they said in unison.

"I can't," she protested.

"Oh, yes, you can," said Lucy.

"You're not going anywhere alone until this is cleared up," said Bill. "And that's final."

In the past, such an ultimatum would have been like a red flag to a bull, but this time Elizabeth didn't put up any protest at all. In fact, thought Lucy, she seemed relieved to have the matter taken out of her hands. She dutifully called Girard, but her call went to phone mail, so she left a message describing the attempted break-in. Bill had more luck with Lapointe, who agreed to see them at ten o'clock at the quai des Orfèvres.

Lapointe wasn't the least bit surprised to see them; he seemed to regard their decision to meet with him as inevitable, part of the immutable course of events in any investigation. "You have something to tell me?" he said with a mournful sigh.

"Last night two men tried to break into my daughter's apartment," said Bill. "She was able to identify them as colleagues from the Cavendish Hotel."

"Their names?" inquired Lapointe with a raised eyebrow.

"Adil Sadek and Malik Mehanna," said Elizabeth. "They work at the Cavendish Hotel, where I work."

"You say they tried to break in? They were not successful?"

Lucy jumped right in. "Fortunately, she had fastened the security chain."

"But the locks?" asked Lapointe.

"They were locked, but they opened them somehow. I heard scratching sounds."

"And why did you not open the door when they knocked? They did knock?"

"They knocked," said Elizabeth. "But I was not presentable."

"Ah," he sighed, giving Elizabeth an appreciative once-over. "*Déshabillée.*"

Lucy didn't think Lapointe was taking the attempted break-in very seriously. "You know what happened to my daughter's roommate? Sylvie Seydoux? She was murdered. Her body was found in the Seine."

"Ah," said Lapointe. "I did not make the connection." He paused. "Your daughter made a wise decision, I think."

"No thanks to you or your department," snapped Bill. "Do you guys talk to each other? Do you share information? Look for connections?"

Lucy thought it was time to intervene, before Bill completely lost his temper. "And those two men also broke into our apartment, where we're staying with our friends. It was all caught on a security camera. They told the concierge they were police, and she let them in. She was in a hurry to get to the market." Lucy paused. "We think it's all connected to the Cavendish in some way. Chef Larry and Sylvie both had ties to the hotel."

"What is this break-in? Why was I not informed?"

Lucy was quick with an answer. "I told the *proc,* Madame Hadamard," she said, thinking that Bill was on to something. The *proc* was supposed to be supervising the investigation into Chef Larry's death, but she wasn't sharing information with Lapointe, the chief investigator in the case. Meanwhile, Lapointe wasn't communicating with Girard, who was investigating Sylvie's death. The situation was all too familiar to her from home, where public safety officials seemed more interested in defending their turf and only grudgingly cooperated with each other.

True to form, Lapointe was quick on the defense.

"There is more to this than you comprehend. All is not as it seems," he said. "I assure you we will no doubt get to the bottom of all this. Meanwhile, mademoiselle, for your safety and your parents' peace of mind, I would advise you to take a leave of absence for the next week or two." Elizabeth began a mild protest, but he shook his head. "No, mademoiselle, it will not be a problem. Your employer will certainly understand that you need time to grieve the loss of your friend and to recover your equilibrium." He paused, tenting his hands. "In fact, I will put in a word for you."

It was obvious that the interview was over, but Lucy still had something to say, although it was not something she wanted to say in front of Bill and Elizabeth. As she put on her coat, she reached into the pocket and found the apartment key, which she tucked beneath her on the chair, leaving it behind. They were about to leave the building when she pretended to discover the loss.

"I'll go," offered Bill.

"No, no," she said a bit too quickly. "It was my mistake. I'll go. Why don't you wait for me in that café?"

"Okay," he said somewhat dubiously.

"I'll only be a minute," she promised, heading for the stairs.

When she returned to Lapointe's office she found him with his elbows propped on the desk, dangling the enormous key from its silk cord, clearly waiting for her to return. "Madame, you have forgotten your key."

"I left it on purpose," she said. "I wanted to speak to you alone."

His eyebrows shot up. *"Vraiment?"*

"Oui."

"You have something to confess, madame?"

"I did a foolish thing," she began. "I went to the hospital after Chef Larry was attacked. The guard left his post for a moment, and I slipped into his room. I was looking for some clue to the attack."

"Did you find this clue?"

"I think I did. He was conscious, and he asked me to deliver a message for him. He wanted me to tell Serge at the Cavendish Hotel to visit him."

"And did you do that?"

"Indirectly. I went to the hotel, and my daughter introduced me to Serge d'Amboise. He's an assistant manager. I didn't want to admit to him that I'd broken the rules and gone into Larry's room, so I just told him that Chef Larry was no longer unconscious and was recovering." She took a deep breath. "Also, as I told you before, the two boys who broke into our apartment, they also work at the hotel. Their names are Adil Sadek and Malik Mehanna."

"Ah, yes, I will look into this connection," said Lapointe.

"I just wanted to get this off my chest. I know I behaved very foolishly."

"Indeed," said Lapointe. "This is very serious, interfering with an investigation."

"I am most sincerely sorry," said Lucy, once again imagining the dark, dank cell that most probably awaited her.

"No matter," said Lapointe with a wave of his hand. "Go to your husband and daughter, and do not involve yourself anymore with this matter. Today it is *bœuf bourguignon* at the café on the quai, and I can recommend it. And the house wine is not bad, either. *Allez.*"

"*Merci,*" said Lucy, somewhat shocked and definitely puzzled. She would never in a million years understand these French people.

Chapter Fifteen

As she made her way to the café, Lucy decided that perhaps France really wasn't so bad, after all. No one in America would expect an employer to grant a worker time off for equilibrium recovery, but it was apparently the norm here in France. And there was no eating breakfast on the run or eating lunch at your desk, either. You never saw anyone carrying around an enormous cardboard container of coffee and a doughnut, as you did in the States, and snacking was out of the question. Instead, the entire country paused at noon for a three-course sit-down lunch with wine. And nobody rushed through that meal, either. She thought of the gentlemen she and Bill had sat next to a week or so ago, when Bill ordered that dish of *tête de veau*. They were obviously businessmen of some sort, but they were in no hurry to get back to work. Not only were they the two founding members of the clean-plate club, but they had each polished off a generous carafe of wine, too, and had even lingered afterward for coffee and brandy. In America, she thought, that sort of thing was a relic of the past, resurrected for the twenty-first-century audience's amazement in the TV show *Mad Men*.

It was a bit early for lunch, so Bill and Elizabeth were

able to get a table by the window in the café, where they were studying menus.

"Get the *bœuf bourguignon,*" suggested Lucy when she joined them. "It comes highly recommended."

"Okay," said Bill, always agreeable when it came to food.

"Not me," said Elizabeth. "I will have a *salade niçoise.*"

The waiter came with water and bread and took their orders, returning quickly with their wine.

"When in France," said Lucy, allowing Bill to fill her glass. Elizabeth declined, which worried Lucy. "You aren't thinking of going back to work, are you?" she asked.

"Not today, Mom, but I'm definitely going tomorrow."

"What's the rush?" asked Bill.

"Lapointe said you should take a leave of absence for a week or two, for your own safety," said Lucy.

"He didn't say that at all, Mom. He said I should take time to recover my equilibrium, and I don't need that. I am *équilibrée.* No problem. I didn't like Sylvie, and I'm not going to pretend I'm broken up about her death."

There was a pause in the conversation while the waiter delivered their dishes, but as soon as he was gone, Lucy spoke up, leaning across the table for emphasis. "Look, for your safety, I think you should stay with us. I don't think you should be alone. And I definitely think the farther you stay from the Cavendish, the better."

Elizabeth speared a piece of tuna and chewed it thoughtfully. "Look, I know you're concerned about me, but I can take care of myself. The last thing I want to do is hang around with your weird friends." Elizabeth caught herself and apologized. "Sorry, Mom."

Then she continued, "I've finally got a place to myself, and I can't wait to claim it. I've been thinking that if I work just a little overtime, I can afford the rent all by myself and I won't need to get a roommate." She poked at the salad with her fork. "I'm just not cut out for sharing, I guess. I really want my own place."

Lucy caught Bill's eye, prompting him to deliver a fatherly ultimatum and getting a slight shrug in return, and scowled back at him. It was always like this. He came on tough at first, but then he'd cave, unable to deny his children anything, no matter how misguided.

"I think you're making a big mistake," said Lucy, "but you're all grown up, and I suppose you can take care of yourself. You'd better be extra careful, though." She popped a tiny white onion into her mouth. "So what are your plans for the apartment? We're happy to help, you know. We've got plenty of time on our hands. Do you want to paint?"

"That's a great idea," said Elizabeth, pleased that her mother had changed her tune. "But first things first. I have to pack up Sylvie's stuff."

"I can help you with that," offered Lucy, sensing an opportunity to investigate.

"I'll go to BHV and pick up some paint chips," said Bill. "What colors were you thinking of?"

"Something neutral," said Elizabeth, grinning. "Anything would be better than that green!"

Lucy felt uneasy when she and Elizabeth returned to the apartment, but she had to admit Elizabeth had a point. The place was tiny, really too small for two people to share. It had been built, she guessed, in the early 1900s as cheap housing for workers leaving the farms and coming to the city to work. An entire family, or perhaps even two, had probably once squeezed into the three small rooms, sharing a toilet on the landing.

As time passed, some improvements had been made, and a miniscule bathroom had been installed when the kitchen was remodeled, sometime in the 1950s. The previous tenant was an old lady who had moved in with her husband many years ago and had remained after his death. Sylvie had moved in when the old lady died, but she hadn't made any changes apart from the addition of the cheap futon in the salon. The bulky oversize furniture, the mossy green walls, and the busy rug with its faded pattern of roses had all remained in place, along with some ugly green and black mod curtains, which had probably been hung in the swinging sixties.

"A coat of paint will make a big difference," said Lucy, looking around. "A light color will make the rooms look much bigger."

"I don't know how much I can do. I have to check with the landlord," said Elizabeth.

"Just getting rid of the curtains and this horror of a rug would be a start," said Lucy. "What's the bedroom like?"

"About like the salon," said Elizabeth. "Dark and crowded."

Elizabeth was right, thought Lucy, taking a good look at the huge armoire and the double bed with its ornate carved headboard and footboard. The bed was covered with a leopard-print duvet. Pulling it back revealed red satin sheets.

"Oh, my," gasped Lucy. "The cops must have loved these."

"I don't think they searched very thoroughly," said Elizabeth. "They certainly didn't disturb anything."

Lucy remembered a series of flashes, indicating the crime-scene investigators had taken photographs, but she had to agree that Sylvie's room was quite neat and tidy. It must be the policy of the French police to leave things as they found them, she thought, recalling that they had done the same when they searched the friends' apartment. And Girard had told Elizabeth the police had no further need to examine the apartment, and he'd given her the okay to return.

"Maybe we should get rid of these bedclothes," suggested Lucy. "How can we pack them up for her parents?"

"Just fold them up and put them all in that hamper," said Elizabeth, pointing to a wicker trunk in the corner. "If there's one thing I know about French people, it's that they keep track of their stuff. If the sheets are missing, there'll be hell to pay. They'll think I stole them."

"They stink of musky perfume," said Lucy, wrinkling her nose as she shook a pillow out of its red satin case. "I was thinking this decor might be ironic, kind of a joke, but this perfume tells a different story. But I still can't get a handle on it. She dressed so conservatively, she used very little makeup, and she had that simple little haircut." She paused. "I don't think she even wore perfume. I bet this scent came from the guys she, uh, entertained here."

"That's disgusting, Mom," said Elizabeth, opening the armoire and revealing only a few pieces of clothing. "*Regarde,*" she said. "The typical Frenchwoman's wardrobe. One black tailored jacket, one jean jacket, one pencil skirt, two pairs of black slacks, a white blouse, a black turtleneck, a gray cashmere sweater, a puffy down jacket, black pumps, a pair of Tod's driving shoes. *C'est tout.*"

"She was wearing jeans, boots, and a trench coat when she disappeared, right?" asked Lucy.

Elizabeth had pulled open the drawer at the bottom

of the armoire, revealing carefully folded lacy lingerie in a variety of colors, a neat stack of scarves, and rolled-up hosiery.

"This will all fit in her suitcase," said Elizabeth, hoisting the large roller bag that was stored on top of the armoire.

Lucy wandered over to the fireplace, which was closed off, and checked out the items arranged on the mantel, beneath a spotted old mirror. There was a half-empty bottle of Le Muguet cologne, which, after one sniff, Lucy knew was not the musky, overwhelming scent that permeated the bedding. There were also a few childhood books, including *Le Petit Prince*, several Babars, and the fables of La Fontaine, and a carved wooden box containing a few pieces of jewelry. *Good jewelry*, noted Lucy, examining cultured pearl earrings, a gold cross and chain, a simple gold bangle bracelet. Closing the box, she gathered it all up and added it to the linens in the wicker hamper.

"Are her parents coming?" asked Lucy. "Is there going to be a funeral?"

"I don't know. I haven't heard anything from them. The police may still have her body. I don't know how that works."

"Neither do I, but I'm sure her parents would like to get their daughter buried as soon as possible," said Lucy, sitting down on the bed. "Everything here speaks of a neat, organized girl, albeit with an interesting sex life, but she still had her Babar books. And that nice jewelry, probably gifts from her parents for graduations and first communion . . . but she was tortured and murdered. It doesn't make sense."

"Like girls who wear cashmere sweaters and pearl earrings shouldn't get killed?" asked Elizabeth.

"That's the hope," said Lucy. "Your Coach bag is a talisman that will protect you from evil."

"It would be one thing if she was mugged or raped. That sort of thing could happen to anyone. This was different. Her killers were after something," said Elizabeth. "And Adil and Malik know about it and want it. That's why they searched your place, and why they tried to get in here. I don't think they killed her, but I think they're involved somehow. But whatever it is, it doesn't seem to be here."

"It's kind of funny," said Lucy thoughtfully, watching as Elizabeth yanked the duvet off the bed and began folding it. "There's no checkbook, no bills, not even a savings account."

"She used a debit card for everything. Everybody does now," said Elizabeth, stuffing the bulky down-filled comforter into the wicker hamper. Lucy joined her, stripping off the red satin sheets, revealing a thick quilted mattress pad, which was somewhat stained.

"Ugh," said Elizabeth, wrinkling her nose at the sight. She added the pillows to the linens in the hamper, then flicked loose one of the elastic straps that held the mattress pad in place. It popped up, revealing a second pad made of memory foam. "I guess she liked her comfort," said Elizabeth, who was folding up the quilted pad.

"Most likely the mattress is worn out. This was cheaper than replacing it, I suppose," said Lucy, wondering how she was going to pack up the bulky thing. And, there was also the black duffel that Sylvie kept at work. What had Elizabeth done with it?

"We mustn't forget the duffel bag Sylvie stuffed under the reception desk," she said.

"Oh, right," said Elizabeth. "I shoved it under the bed when I saw what was inside." Her cheeks reddened.

"I see why you didn't want to give it to her parents the other day."

"Sylvie was a very interesting girl," said Lucy.

"You can say that again," agreed Elizabeth, pulling the bag out and plunking it on the naked bed. "But," she said, speaking slowly, "she didn't go to a gym. Frenchwomen despise exercise."

"So it isn't sneakers in that compartment for sweaty gear," said Lucy.

"I doubt it very much," said Elizabeth, reaching inside and pulling out a thick wad of euros stuffed into an envelope. "Ohmigod," she said, dropping the bills on the bed, as if they were too hot to handle.

"I guess we know what Adil and Malik were looking for," said Lucy, examining the bundle.

"How much is there?" asked Elizabeth.

"It's all five-hundred-euro notes," said Lucy, who was busy counting. When she was through, she'd counted a hundred bills, totaling fifty thousand euros.

"Where'd she get it?" Elizabeth wondered aloud. "She couldn't have made this much working at the hotel, not unless she was paid a lot more than I am."

"Frenchwomen are known for their thrift," said Lucy, earning a long look from her daughter.

"Not funny, Mom." Elizabeth gathered the bills into a neat stack and replaced them in the envelope. "I thought she was an enthusiastic volunteer, but do you think she was getting paid for sex? Could she have made this money doing tricks?"

"I'm not up on the current rates," said Lucy, "but I doubt it."

"What are we going to do?" asked Elizabeth.

"We're calling Girard," said Lucy, reaching for her phone.

The call went to voice mail, so Lucy left a message, saying only that she had found something of interest that belonged to Sylvie. She didn't know how messages were handled by the French police and was leery of giving too much information.

"I don't like this," she said to Elizabeth, who was holding the envelope of money. "I feel like we're in danger as long as we have this. I want to get rid of it."

"We could hide it."

"Not here," said Lucy. "It's too dangerous. What about the Cavendish? They must have a safe there."

"Too many people have access," said Elizabeth.

"There's a safe in the apartment," said Lucy. "It's like the ones they have in hotel rooms. You punch in a PIN code."

"Do you really want to be tortured for your PIN code?" demanded Elizabeth.

"Not really," admitted Lucy, thinking that it really wouldn't be necessary. Any idiot could guess her code, as it was the last four digits of her phone number. "We have to take it to the police."

"You're crazy. We can't carry fifty thousand euros on the Métro."

"Who's going to know?" asked Lucy.

"They're probably keeping watch on the apartment right now. They'll see us leave with a package."

"I have a big purse." It was true. Lucy was carrying a big catchall, with plenty of room for a camera, guidebook, and water bottle.

"They'll follow us. It's a couple of blocks to the Métro station, and this isn't a very good neighborhood."

"We could call a cab," suggested Lucy.

"I'm not leaving here," said Elizabeth, hugging the

envelope to her chest. "Try that cop again, okay?" Her face was ashen, and her lips seemed to have disappeared. "Please."

This time Girard answered his phone and promised to send a couple of officers to pick up the money. "Don't open the door to anyone, even if they're wearing a uniform," he said. "Make sure you see their IDs."

"I couldn't tell a real one from a fake one," said Lucy, trying not to panic. This was really getting out of hand.

"Give me a password," he said.

Lucy thought she'd stepped out of real life and into a film noir. "Breathless," she said.

"Interesting choice," said Girard. "Remain calm. They are on the way."

Lucy felt a huge sense of relief. This would all be over soon. The cops were on the way. They'd be here any minute. In fact, they might be here already, she thought, hearing a knock on the door.

Or not, she discovered, peering through the peephole and seeing a figure with a remarkably distorted face. She was puzzled at first, wondering if this was a person with a terrible injury, but she finally realized it was a man with a stocking over his face.

She was hitting REDIAL, calling Girard, when to her horror she saw the door open, restrained only by the security chain. She reached for the knob to pull it shut but was too late; the stocking man had inserted a pair of bolt cutters through the slim opening and had snapped the chain. It was only when the bolt cutters were withdrawn that Lucy saw her chance and pulled the door shut, yelling for Elizabeth.

Elizabeth took in the situation immediately and grabbed hold of the few inches of chain that remained, dangling from the door. She held on as tight as she could, and

Lucy hung on to the knob, but the assailant was strong and had the advantage of leverage. Peering through the peephole, Lucy saw he'd placed his foot on the wall, beside the door, and was using it to brace himself.

Lucy's hands were sweating. She felt the knob slipping from her grip in what she feared was a deadly tug-of-war. Elizabeth was also straining to hang on to the short piece of chain, her body pressed against Lucy's.

"I can't hold it much longer," she whispered.

"Me, either," said Lucy, who suddenly remembered her high school physics class, something about equal and opposite forces. "At the count of three, let go," she whispered.

Elizabeth shook her head. "I'm scared."

"It's our only chance," said Lucy. "Trust me."

"Okay."

Lucy whispered the count. *"Un, deux, trois!"* They let go simultaneously, and the door flew open, sending the assailant flying across the small hallway at the same time they heard the *woo-wah* of a police siren approaching. The guy ran for the stairs, and Lucy pulled the door shut, her chest heaving.

Once they were safely inside, she and Elizabeth fell into each other's arms.

"That was good thinking, Mom," said Elizabeth.

"I got an A in physics," said Lucy, who was still breathing heavily.

"It's broken," said Elizabeth, who was examining the lock. "And the chain's cut. I can't lock the door. What am I going to do?"

It was suddenly quiet; the *woo-wah* had stopped, and they heard footsteps on the stairs. A moment later two uniformed flics were at the door.

"You're *breathless,* madame?" asked one, emphasizing the password. He was young and good-looking in a rakish way, and Lucy thought he looked a bit like the young Jean-Paul Belmondo.

"*Oui*," said Lucy, still panting from the exertion of holding the door shut. "Breathless."

Chapter Sixteen

The Jean-Paul Belmondo cop wasn't interested in talking to Lucy, but he and his shorter, darker partner were questioning Elizabeth closely, nodding along as she showed them the broken locks and the duffel bag that had concealed the cash-filled envelope. When she'd finished, he called headquarters and asked for Girard. After a somewhat lengthy conversation, which Lucy couldn't follow, he informed them that the apartment would be sealed as a crime scene and Elizabeth would have to move out temporarily.

"Not again," sighed Elizabeth.

"Do you have a place to go?" he asked, rubbing his cheek with his index finger.

Lucy thought his tone was rather too concerned; next thing he'd be offering to put Elizabeth up at his place. "Yes, she can stay with me and her father," said Lucy.

"D'accord," he replied with a professional nod.

"You must be very careful, mademoiselle," advised the partner.

"I will make sure she does not go anywhere alone," said Lucy, feeling like a nineteenth-century chaperone. "And you are taking the money?"

"*Oui, oui,* I have the papers right here," said the partner, producing some closely printed documents on very thin paper. "You must sign here, please."

So Lucy signed and handed over the envelope while Elizabeth, once again, packed a bag. Then a taxi was called, and Lucy and a rather sullen Elizabeth went back to the vacation apartment, where the friends were just sitting down to a simple dinner of pasta with cheese, salad, and bread.

"Comfort food. Just what we need," said Lucy, tucking in. Even Elizabeth, she noticed, had loaded up her plate and was eating as if she'd never heard of calories. There was nothing like a near brush with danger to perk up the appetite. "We've had quite an interesting afternoon," she said, going on to tell the group about discovering Sylvie's cache of cash. She'd just started to tell them about the attempted break-in when Richard arrived, bearing a box of assorted pastries.

"So Sylvie was a call girl," suggested Sue, who was arranging the colorful fruit tarts and the éclairs on a plate. "I've heard that can be very profitable, if you have the right clientele."

"And the Cavendish Hotel would certainly have plenty of the right clients," said Richard.

"But she would have to be terribly discreet, or she'd lose her job, wouldn't she?" asked Rachel.

"And how much could she earn that way?" asked Pam. "I mean, fifty thousand euros is a lot of, well, bonking, for lack of a better word."

"Bonking's fine with me," said Ted with a leer.

Elizabeth glanced at her mother and rolled her eyes, sending the message that this was just the sort of thing she couldn't stand about her parents' friends.

"I mean, what does a first-class bonk cost?"

Sue was directing the question to Richard, who put

up his hands and shook his head. "Why are you asking me?"

"You're a reporter, that's why. I thought you guys have inquiring minds," she answered, placing the platter of pastries on the table. "Coffee will be ready in a minute."

Elizabeth was helping herself to a plump chocolate-covered éclair filled with mocha cream. "I don't think Sylvie was a first-class professional bonker, not from the guys I saw her bring to the apartment. I think she was an amateur," she said, taking a big bite. "An enthusiastic amateur."

"Well, we know there was a black market ring operating at the hotel. Maybe she was involved with that," suggested Bill, choosing a mille-feuille topped with a strawberry.

"She would have to be the mastermind to have that much money," said Richard, "and pretty young girls aren't usually at the top of the criminal food chain."

Lucy thought he was right about that. Her experience as a reporter had taught her that attractive young women were usually the victims of crime, subject to abduction, rape, beatings, and worse.

"She was no mastermind," said Elizabeth, reaching for a second éclair.

"She was obviously holding the money for somebody," said Bob, speaking with authority as he dug into a strawberry tart with his fork. "And it seems obvious that Adil and Malik were looking for it. I suppose they must have had trouble breaking in to the girls' apartment, so they thought they'd try our place, on the off chance the money had been hidden here."

"I guess whoever they're allied with is getting a bit desperate," said Lucy, who had chosen an éclair and was scraping her plate with her dessert fork to get every last bit of cream filling. "That guy this afternoon seemed like a pro, with a stocking mask and bolt cutters." A horrible thought occurred to her. "Maybe he was the one who killed Sylvie."

Silence fell at the table as the group members began to realize the terrible danger Lucy and Elizabeth had been in.

"Just imagine . . ." began Rachel, only to be interrupted by her husband.

"Sylvie was probably holding the money for somebody, and they sent that guy to get it back. Money laundering is big business, and it's endemic. It's everywhere. Even respectable banks do it. The Swiss have made a specialty of it," said Bob.

"He's right," agreed Richard. "Paris is full of Arab factions, all busy raising money for weapons and equipment. Just look at Syria, for example, and Iraq, and of course, there's Egypt. And now that France has started aggressively hunting down Muslim radicals in former colonies like Mali, there's been a real upsurge in resistance. And that's on top of the more established groups, like Al-Qaeda and the Muslim Brotherhood."

Elizabeth was leaning back in her chair with her hand on her stomach and a blissful expression on her face. "Boy, that was good," she said. "I guess I needed carbs."

"You do, after a scare like you had," said Pam, who took nutrition seriously. "It's the aftereffect of all that adrenaline. Your body thinks you ran a marathon, and wants to replace all those nutrients you burned."

"This is so weird," said Elizabeth. "I can't believe I lived with Sylvie for six months and knew so little about her."

"She must have been very secretive," said Sue.

"I think she was really a nice girl who got in over her head," said Rachel.

"Perhaps *nice* isn't the right word," said Pam. "It seems she was a little too wild to be nice, but I do think she was basically a good person. I don't think she would have done anything she believed was evil."

Lucy wondered if Pam was drawing on her own experience here. She knew she'd been a bit of a wild thing before she met Ted and settled down.

"*Believe* being the operative word here," said Richard. "None of these terrorists think they're evil. They think they're fighting the good fight, jihad."

"Yup," added Bob. "They think that if they die, they're going straight to heaven and they'll be awarded a whole bunch of virgins."

"Talk about misogynistic," said Sue. "All those veils and blankets the women have to wear. So unchic."

"Not Sylvie," said Elizabeth. "She didn't care about issues. She only cared about Sylvie."

"That will always get you in trouble," said Sue, carefully cutting a raspberry tart in half and taking one piece for herself and giving the other to Sid, adding it to the half-eaten éclair that was already on his plate.

"Madame, you are too kind," said Sid, licking his lips.

When Sid said the word *madame*, Lucy had a fleeting image of Madame Seydoux, Sylvie's mother. Mothers and daughters had a unique knowledge of each other, she thought, even when they didn't seem very close. There was something about a mother-daughter bond. Maybe it was nothing more than shared genes, but it was there. She'd seen it operate in even the most destructive relationships; nobody knew better how to hurt the other than a mother or a daughter. She amended the thought. Except, perhaps, sisters. Lucy didn't have a sister herself, but she'd seen the dynamic at work in her own family, among her daughters.

"Did Sylvie have any sisters?" she asked hopefully.

"As far as I know, she was an only child," said Elizabeth.

"Then I think we should take a little trip to Chartres tomorrow, to express our condolences to Madame Seydoux."

"Well," admitted Elizabeth, "I have been wanting to see the cathedral."

When the train arrived at Chartres the next morning, Lucy and Elizabeth didn't have to ask for directions to the cathedral. It was immediately visible, dominating the town from the top of a hill. Worshippers and sightseers alike had to make the climb if they wanted to gain entry to the church, and Lucy thought it was an apt metaphor for the Christian's path to salvation. A path that was guaranteed to involve considerable pain and sacrifice, but first, she wanted to visit Sylvie's parents and get rid of the heavy basket of fruit she'd brought from Paris as an expression of sympathy.

It was easy enough to find their *tabac*. It was in a prime location next to the train station, and the sign above the door identified the proprietor as M. Émile Seydoux. The modest little shop, which sold candy and gum, phone cards, papers and magazines, as well as cigarettes, must be a real cash cow, thought Lucy. The sign, however, was quite old-fashioned, with fading paint, and Lucy suspected it was a reference to a previous M. Seydoux, perhaps the founder of the business. Another sign, this one handwritten in shaky ballpoint pen and taped over a printed placard announcing, "OUVERT DE 6H00 À 22H00," read simply, FERMÉ.

"What now?" Elizabeth wondered aloud. "The shop's closed."

"I bet they live upstairs," said Lucy, pointing to windows above the storefront that were covered with spotless lace curtains. "I think that must be the door," she said, pointing to a simple wooden door beside the shop windows that was painted blue.

An old-fashioned bell pull was next to the door, and she gave it a good tug, producing a distant chime. A few moments later Madame Seydoux opened the door. Lucy was shocked at her appearance. Her hair was uncombed, and she was wearing a very worn and faded housedress, the sort of wrapper Lucy's grandmother used to wear when she tidied the house before dressing for the day.

"*Quoi?*" she demanded.

Lucy's French wasn't up to lengthy explanations, so she simply held out the fruit basket while Elizabeth expressed their condolences in French.

Madame took the basket with a curt "*Merci*" and was about to shut the door when Lucy spoke up.

"Elizabeth, did you tell her about the money?"

That caught Madame's attention; it seemed she did understand some English. "Money?" she asked, letting the door swing on its hinges.

"When we packed up your daughter's things, we found some money hidden in a duffel bag she kept at work," said Elizabeth, speaking in French.

"Sylvie was a very good girl, very thrifty," said Madame, taking a crumpled tissue from her pocket and wiping her eyes. "Where is this bag? Did you bring the money?"

"It was quite a lot," said Lucy. "We gave it to the police."

Madame was very distressed to hear this. "*Non, non,*" she said, shaking her head. "*La police? Pourquoi?*" Then she launched into a long tirade involving finger shaking and a few words that Lucy understood, mainly "*les im-*

pôts" and "*les officiels du gouvernement.*" Eventually, Madame ran out of steam, placing her hands on her hips and demanding to know how much money they had found.

"Cinquante mille euros," said Elizabeth, getting an incredulous look from Madame.

"Pas possible," said Madame, correcting Elizabeth. "C'est cinq mille, n'est-ce pas?"

"Non, madame," insisted Elizabeth. "Not five thousand. I know my numbers. It was *cinquante mille,* fifty thousand. Not five thousand, or *cinq mille.*"

Madame seemed to sway a bit on her feet, and Lucy took her arm and guided her to the stairs beyond, where she sat down heavily. "*C'est incroyable,*" she said.

"Ask her if she thinks Sylvie was keeping the money for someone," Lucy instructed Elizabeth, who obliged. While she and Madame Seydoux were talking, Lucy looked around the hallway, which was spotlessly clean. The stairs were covered with a thick striped carpet, and the banisters and railing were polished to a high sheen. A few pictures hung on the gray-painted walls. One especially large one was a photo of a handful of French legionnaires arranged in front of a pyramid.

"*Pardon, madame,*" apologized Lucy, interrupting. "Was Monsieur in Egypt?"

Madame looked at the photo, and her expression softened, as if she were remembering a younger, handsomer Monsieur Seydoux. "*Non,*" she said, shattering Lucy's assumption. Madame pointed to the picture. "My father. Sylvie took an old photo," she said, describing the snapshot's size with her fingers. "I don't know the word," she continued, pointing to the crisp new print. "For my *anniversaire.*" Then, regaining her energy, she stood up, her arms wrapped around the fruit basket. *"Merci, merci beaucoup,"* she said, making it clear it was time for them to leave.

"What did I miss?" asked Lucy as they followed the winding road up to the cathedral. "I gather the legionnaire was her father, and Sylvie had an old photo restored as a birthday present."

"That's right," said Elizabeth. "She said she didn't believe Sylvie had that much money, but she was really upset that we gave it to the police, although she finally admitted that we didn't have any choice. It was kind of weird. At first she thought the money should have gone to her and Monsieur, but when she realized it was really fifty thousand, she backed off, like she knew it was tainted in some way."

"Did she think Sylvie was killed because of the money?" asked Lucy, breathing hard as she pounded her way up the cobblestones.

"She didn't say that, but I got the feeling that she didn't want to be involved. She said the money must have belonged to the previous tenant, the old lady. She mentioned how those old folks who'd been through the war saved every penny. They were fearful that hard times would return."

"Did you tell her the envelope had the Cavendish logo?" asked Lucy.

"She said maybe the old lady worked in the hotel, too. I left it at that. I didn't tell her that it was the new logo, that they switched from green to gold about the time I started working in Paris."

"I wonder what Papa did in Egypt," mused Lucy as they reached the plaza in front of the cathedral, where there were also a few shops and a restaurant. "Maybe there's a link to Adil and Malik and Les Amis du Roi."

"Or their parents, maybe even their grandparents,"

said Elizabeth as they paused to admire the cathedral before attempting the steps leading to the cathedral doors. "That picture was taken years ago."

"But if the grandfather was involved with King Farouk," Lucy said, speculating, "there might be some sort of personal tie. I mean, it must be important to Madame Seydoux, or Sylvie wouldn't have made the enlargement for her. It has some significance."

Together they gazed at the enormous building, with its elaborate carvings around the doors, its flying buttresses, and its mismatched spires, one plain and the other elaborately carved, reaching heavenward.

"I'm sick of Sylvie and her complicated life," declared Elizabeth, referring to her guidebook. "The cathedral was built in the twelfth century. That's the eleven hundreds. However did they do it without modern machinery?" She paused. "The stained glass is original. It was stored during World War II to protect it from the bombings."

Lucy decided that Elizabeth had a point. Here she was, at one of the most famous cultural achievements in the world, and her mind was in the gutter, mired in a sordid tale of sex and murder. It was time to put that aside, she resolved, determined to stay focused on the moment.

She followed Elizabeth through the door, inhaling the familiar church scent of old stone and dust, and wandered through the aisles. The famous labyrinth on the floor was covered by chairs, but a sign stated that it was cleared once a month, so those interested in this ancient spiritual exercise could follow the twists and turns marked by the tiles, praying as they paced the same path pilgrims had followed for centuries.

Neither Lucy nor Elizabeth believed the tale about the

Virgin's camisole, which was supposedly preserved as a sacred relic in the church. "It would have had to be eleven hundred years old when the church was built," said Elizabeth. "It's hard to believe a poor woman's shift would have been preserved for that long."

"I sure hope nobody tries to save my underwear after I'm gone," said Lucy, thinking of her rather tired collection of cotton high-cuts and stretched-out bras. "I don't even want them to look. Just throw it all away."

"Believe me, Mom, nobody's going to want your underwear," said Elizabeth, pausing before a series of stone carvings depicting scenes from everyday medieval life.

"These are charming," said Lucy, captivated. "They're like photographs from long, long ago."

Leaving the church, they explored the quaint town, wandering through narrow streets, past ancient houses with steep tiled roofs that tilted this way and that. All the windows were carefully screened, many with lace curtains, and Lucy wished she could glimpse the interiors. Eventually, they found themselves at a park along a river, and they sat for a while, resting and enjoying the peaceful atmosphere, so different from Paris.

"I wish we could have walked the labyrinth," said Lucy, watching a couple of ducks paddling by.

"Really?" Elizabeth was surprised. "I've never thought of you as being religious."

"I go to church every Christmas, and sometimes at Easter, and I never miss a funeral," said Lucy, defending herself. "I know quite a few hymns by heart."

"But do you pray?" asked Elizabeth.

"Only as a last resort," admitted Lucy. "I thought it was worth trying the labyrinth, since nothing else has worked. I thought I might get some insight, some answers."

"Well, we have to walk back, so you can meditate as we go."

Lucy's stomach growled, reminding her it was past noon. "I have a feeling I'll be meditating on lunch," she said. "Crepes or *panini,* that is the question."

Chapter Seventeen

"What did you think of Sylvie's mother?" asked Lucy when they were back on the train to Paris.

"Pretty typical Frenchwoman," replied Elizabeth. "I read somewhere that if you want to marry an accountant, you should marry a Frenchwoman." She paused. "I bet Madame is the one who actually runs the *tabac*. There's a long history of women entrepreneurs in France."

"But women got the vote here only in . . . when?"

"Something like nineteen forty-four, I think," said Elizabeth. "I imagine the theory was that they didn't need it, because they were in charge of everything, anyway."

"It's a love-hate thing, isn't it?" mused Lucy. "They glorify women at the same time they tear them down."

"They punish them if they're powerful," said Elizabeth. "There were really terrible attacks on Madame de Pompadour, for example, and Marie Antoinette. They printed up these awful pamphlets full of lies and insults. And there's Marianne, the symbol of France. She's always bare-breasted, a national sex symbol."

"And Renoir," added Lucy. "He painted all those

beautiful nudes, but they say he treated his models very badly."

"You know, I'm glad I'm not a Frenchwoman," said Elizabeth. "They're supposed to be fortunate to have this wonderful government that provides child care and health care and everything, but there's so much pressure on them to be perfect. They're supposed to always be in control, always do things beautifully, always look beautiful. Their children are expected to be perfectly behaved, and if their husbands have mistresses, they're not supposed to mind. It's completely unrealistic. It would make me crazy."

"You know what really gets my goat?" said Lucy. "It's all these articles for American tourists advising us on how we can look French. Like there's something wrong with being American. Don't wear sneakers, don't wear T-shirts, dress up, and don't forget to wear a scarf. I mean, what is '*Liberté, Égalité, Fraternité*' supposed to mean?"

Elizabeth smiled, checking out her mother's orange plaid coat, Mom jeans, and running shoes, to which she'd added a blue scarf, as if it would fool any French person.

"It's a slogan," replied Elizabeth. "Like 'liberty and justice for all.' Something we say but don't necessarily do."

Lucy fell quiet, thinking about being American and being French, and how the two seemed very different but perhaps weren't. Of course you liked your country best. It was what you knew, what you were taught in school. America was the greatest, unless you were French or Chinese or Indian, in which case she supposed France, China, or India was best. Though there were some countries where even the most fervent patriot had to admit things weren't so great, like Afghanistan or Syria or seemingly most of the countries in Africa. In those cases, people tended to identify with their tribe or sect, believing it was superior to the others.

"There must be some connection between Sylvie, and Adil and Malik because of Egypt, don't you think?" she asked Elizabeth, suddenly breaking the silence. "There was that photo of her grandfather in Egypt."

"Yeah, that photo with the pyramid," mused Elizabeth.

"Yeah. Maybe Sylvie was holding the money for them. Maybe she was doing a favor for them, for old times' sake."

"This is Sylvie we're talking about, remember? She was not the least bit sentimental," said Elizabeth.

"I know, but just bear with me for a minute. Adil's and Malik's parents, maybe grandparents, left Egypt with King Farouk when there was a revolution or something. We know Adil and Malik are part of that royalist faction that's trying to put Farouk's son back in charge. At that party they were talking about how awful things are in Egypt."

"Okay, I can see that Adil and Malik might be involved in something like that, but Sylvie?"

"Some of Farouk's followers came to France. That means the French government accommodated them. And if Sylvie's grandfather was a legionnaire, he may have been involved. He might even have been part of the evacuation, maybe developed some sort of connection. A love affair or a friendship. I'm talking a couple of generations back, but these ties endure, especially if you're in an alien culture. Then the kids are part of the same circle. You know what I mean. When you were a kid, you played with my friends' kids, right?"

Elizabeth smiled. "But Richie Goodman and Tim Stillings haven't tried to break into my apartment," she said.

"And they certainly wouldn't ever harm you," said Lucy, her mind a confusing whirl of possible motives. "They would protect you."

"So it's some other faction, some rival faction, that killed Sylvie," said Elizabeth.

"Unless," said Lucy, thinking out loud, "unless her grandfather did something against their families."

"A love affair, that would do it," said Elizabeth. "They're all crazy about honor."

"Then it could be a revenge killing," said Lucy.

"Well, I'm glad we've cleared this up," said Elizabeth as the train glided into the Montparnasse station.

"Clear as mud," said Lucy, remembering Richard's assertion that the Arab Spring had created a huge power vacuum as dictatorships were toppled in some countries and civil war broke out in others. He'd said there were numerous factions, including Al-Qaeda and the Muslim Brotherhood, busy raising money in Paris. These groups didn't go door-to-door, begging for donations. They went into the much more profitable drug trade or the black market. It was possible that Chef Larry and Sylvie had run afoul of somebody's scheme, but whose?

They were making their way through the crowded Montparnasse train station to the Métro platform, which was busy with jostling commuters and noisy from the arriving trains and occasional loudspeaker announcements, when Elizabeth suddenly exclaimed, "Merde!"

"What is it?" asked Lucy.

"Oh, just one more reason why I hate France," fumed Elizabeth. "The transit workers are having yet another slowdown. They just announced it. They're *désolés,* of course, which is one word I've really come to despise. They're not the least bit sorry, much less seriously grieved at all. They're pleased as punch to cause a lot of trouble for everybody."

"They must have their reasons," said Lucy.

"Oh, sure. Maybe they can have only twenty-nine instead of thirty sick days a year, or they won't be able to retire until they're fifty instead of forty-five, or their vacations have been cut back from six weeks to five."

"I'm sure you're exaggerating," said Lucy.

"Not as much as you'd think," growled Elizabeth as they descended the steps to a very crowded Métro platform.

They slowly wove their way through the throng, Elizabeth in the lead, to the far rear of the platform. As they went, Lucy noticed that very few people seemed the least bit upset, unlike Elizabeth. They seemed to accept that this was the way things were. *Normal. C'est normal.* The workers had every right to take action if their livelihood was threatened. So different, she thought, from the United States, where the least inconvenience was greeted with outrage.

It was very crowded at the rear end of the platform, though not as crowded as the middle, and Lucy leaned against the tunnel wall, resting her back. She could feel the vibration produced by an approaching train, which slid smoothly into the station, already full of people. She wanted to wait for the next train, but Elizabeth shook her head.

"It's now or never, believe me. It will only get worse."

Together they joined the crowd squeezing into the car and just made it, the doors sliding shut behind them. Lucy had never been in such a tight situation before. She could barely breathe because of the number of people packed into the car. She looked at the faces of the people around her, none of which showed any signs of discomfort or anger. They were blank. And the people carefully avoided eye contact, if not actual physical contact, with their fellow passengers.

Although their expressions were identical, Lucy was struck by the diversity of the crowd. Old and young, male and female, Asian, Middle Eastern, black and white, they were all there, crammed together in the speeding train. And if a terrorist were to attack the train, the attack would kill not only the hated Westerners, but many of the terrorists' own people, as well. That was how it was in the 9/11 attacks, how it would be in any cosmopolitan city. It all seemed so crazy.

As the train proceeded toward the center of Paris, there was a slight release of the pressure at the stations, when some people struggled through the crowd and got off, and before others got on. It was during the pauses at the stations that Lucy and Elizabeth were able to worm their way into the interior of the car and eventually were able to hang on to a pole, which made it easier for them to keep their balance, so they weren't constantly banging into their neighbors when the train swerved as it sped through the underground tunnel. Lucy counted down the stations to Châtelet, where they would change to another line: Saint-Sulpice, Saint-Germain-des-Prés, Saint-Michel, Cité, and finally Châtelet. At their stop the struggle to exit caused them to pop onto the platform, where they had to fight their way against the press of people intent on getting on the train.

Châtelet was a major junction point, and even more crowded than Montparnasse had been, and Lucy and Elizabeth found themselves buffeted from every direction as they made their way to the platform for the number 1 line, which would take them to Bastille, near the place des Vosges. At one point Elizabeth was knocked backward into her mother, who saved her from falling by grabbing her arms. It was then that Lucy realized Elizabeth's shoulder bag was missing.

"Your bag!" she exclaimed. "Didn't you have a bag?"

Elizabeth patted her chest, discovering her shoulder bag was indeed gone. "Pickpockets!" she wailed. "Bastards! I hate Paris! I want to go home!"

Battered and exhausted, Lucy could see her point. "Were you carrying anything valuable?"

"No, just stuff. I've learned to keep my money and ID and credit cards in a pouch I tuck into my waistband. I don't keep any cash in my bag, but, damn it, that thief got my new Chanel mascara!"

"How did it happen? I never saw anything suspicious."

"In that crowd anything could happen. They use knives and cut the strap. I should've been more careful."

It was difficult to carry on a conversation in the noisy station, and Lucy was at the end of her rope. The station was so crowded, she felt the beginning of a panic attack and decided she had to get away from all the people and get some air as quickly as possible. "Let's get a taxi," she said, grabbing Elizabeth's hand and pulling her toward the exit.

Once they were on the street, however, Elizabeth delivered some bad news. "I'm pretty sure the taxi drivers will be protesting in sympathy with the transit workers."

"No taxis?"

"Probably not. It's back in the Métro, or else we'll have to walk."

"Well, I'm not going back," declared Lucy. "The exercise will do us good."

Mother and daughter decided to take a break in a café, where they had glasses of lemonade and used the facilities before beginning the long trek to the Marais. There was plenty to see in the streets, where they observed *grand-mères* walking along with their adorable grandchildren, couples holding hands, funny little Smart cars, and always the beautifully decorated shop windows. In addition to the pedestrians, the sidewalks were filled with café tables and chairs, and the displays of fruits, vegetables, and flowers that spilled from the stores. Before long Lucy found herself in familiar territory and paused at one shop to buy a bunch of bright yellow daffodils. She buried her nose in the petals as they continued on their way, inhaling the musky, spring-like scent.

"Pretty," said Elizabeth. "I missed the changing seasons when I was in Florida."

"Well, spring's rather disappointing in Maine, but fall is pretty spectacular," said Lucy. "What with the leaves turning colors and apple picking and the pumpkin festival."

Tinker's Cove was one of a number of Maine towns that held pumpkin festivals in October in hopes of extending the tourist season. All sorts of pumpkin-themed events were planned, including giant pumpkin-growing contests, bake-offs, pumpkin boat regattas and even pumpkin tosses, all accompanied by large amounts of locally brewed pumpkin beer. The pumpkin toss, in which contestants vied to catapult a pumpkin the greatest distance, was quite controversial since some residents feared damage from pumpkins landing on their property.

"I can't say I miss the pumpkin fest," said Elizabeth.

Lucy thought this might be a good time to pose a question she'd wanted to ask for quite some time. "Do you miss Chris Kennedy?" she asked, referring to the young man Elizabeth had been dating in Florida.

"I knew this was coming," said Elizabeth, her cheeks dimpling.

"You have to give me points for waiting this long," claimed Lucy, examining the flowers.

"You've been quite restrained," admitted Elizabeth. "Especially since you're so fond of Chris yourself."

"He's a nice fellow," said Lucy, "but you haven't mentioned him lately."

"I haven't heard from him lately," said Elizabeth.

Lucy didn't think this was a good sign. "Really?" She plucked a leaf that had turned brown from the bouquet. "Do you think he's met somebody else?"

"No. Well, maybe. It's hard to know. He joined the Secret Service." Elizabeth paused. "He's in some training program, and it's all very hush-hush."

"He's going to be protecting the president?" asked Lucy, somewhat dismayed. "That's very dangerous. He could get killed."

"It's been a lifelong dream of his," said Elizabeth. "They do a lot more than protect the president, you know. They're actually part of the Treasury Department, and they investigate currency violations, stuff like that."

"I had no idea," admitted Lucy as they crossed the rue Saint-Antoine to cut through the Hôtel de Sully courtyard to the place des Vosges. The grand mansion was a favorite with architecture buffs, but Lucy couldn't care less. She saw it simply as a shortcut to the apartment. "But even if this program is very demanding, he must have some time off. Enough for a quick call. Or a text."

"I don't really know, Mom. He could have gone straight from training into some undercover mission."

Lucy couldn't understand her daughter's attitude. She had thought they were a perfect couple and had been hopefully expecting an engagement announcement. "Aren't you concerned?"

"What can I do?" asked Elizabeth as they ducked through the porch separating the courtyard from the formal garden, where little brown sparrows fluttered constantly from the ivy-covered walls, pecking at the bread crumbs people left for them. "We were just dating. It was very casual. We agreed our careers had to come first."

Lucy felt off balance as she took the steps down to the arcade that ran on all four sides of the place des Vosges, unsure whether it was the unevenly worn stone steps or Elizabeth's startling statement. "Your careers come first?" she asked, incredulous. "Before love and marriage?"

"Uh, yeah, Mom."

There were benches in the park in the middle of the square, and Lucy sat down on one. "Once I met your father, nothing else mattered," she said. "He was everything to me. All I wanted was to get married and start a family."

"Times have changed," said Elizabeth, sitting beside her. "I don't want to have to depend on a man, financially or emotionally."

Now that she thought about it, Lucy realized that very few of her friends' children had married. Her son, Toby, had married Molly quite young, but he was the exception. Sue's daughter Sidra was also married, but Tim Stillings, Richie Goodman, and Eddie Culpepper were showing no signs of settling down.

"I don't know if I ever want to get married," continued Elizabeth.

Lucy thought she might be having a heart attack. "Really?"

"Yeah, Mom. Look at you. It's taken you years and years to get to Paris, lots longer than it took me."

"But you don't even like it here," said Lucy.

"Yeah, but I found out early. Imagine if I'd spent my whole life dreaming of Paris, and then, when I got here, I'd be so disappointed."

Lucy wasn't convinced. "I was married by the time I

was your age, and was expecting a baby. Trust me, I think you might be disappointed if you get to be my age and you're all alone, no husband, no kids, no grand-kids, nothing but a cat for company."

"Meow!" said Elizabeth, hopping up and grasping Lucy's hands, pulling her to her feet. "C'mon. I bet Sue's cooked up something great for dinner, and I'm hungry."

"Meow, too," said Lucy.

Chapter Eighteen

There were no mouthwatering scents in the air when Lucy and Elizabeth got back to the apartment, and no dinner preparations were under way. Instead, everyone was clustered around Ted, who was pressing one of the expensive fillet of beef steaks intended for dinner to his eye.

"What happened?" asked Lucy.

By way of reply, Ted removed the steak, revealing a very black and swollen eye.

"Oh my!" she exclaimed. "Who did that?"

"Some *types,* tough guys," said Pam in a rather unsympathetic voice. "He was out with Richard, playing investigative reporter. They went to a *banlieue* where they had no business being."

"You mean one of the immigrant neighborhoods?" asked Elizabeth in a worried tone.

"Slum is more like it," said Pam. "Crowded, dirty, and filled with unemployed youth who have nothing better to do than beat up nosy Americans."

"Really, I don't see any reason to leave the center of town," said Sue. "I mean, when you visit New York, you don't go to the Bronx, do you?"

"I do. To see the zoo," said Lucy, "and the botanical garden."

"Not me. I stay as close to Bloomingdale's as possible," declared Sue.

"That's true enough," grumbled Sid.

"Ith wath rethearth," said Ted, speaking with a very swollen split lip.

"Research?" asked Lucy. "For what? The *Pennysaver?*" Lucy doubted that folks in Tinker's Cove were interested in the plight of immigrants in France. They didn't even seem interested in America's immigration problem.

"It was Richard's idea, a way to break into the big time," said Pam. "He was going to share the byline with him. . . ."

"Foh ma rethumay," said Ted.

"I think your résumé should include a trip to the emergency room," said Sid.

"That would be an interesting story," said Rachel. "Now that we have Obamacare, you could write about your experiences with the French universal health-care system."

"Nuh," said Ted, shaking his head.

"He hasn't heard good things about French medicine," said Pam.

"Rithard thayth—" began Ted, only to be cut off by Pam.

"Richard says. Richard says. I'm getting pretty sick of what Richard thinks!" she exclaimed. "If Richard's so terrific, how come he isn't helping us get our passports, huh?"

"He'th tryink," said Ted.

"I don't think so," said Pam, abruptly marching off to her room and shutting the door firmly behind her.

"Well, there is another couch, buddy," said Bill, slapping Ted on the back.

"But Elizabeth needs it," protested Lucy, with a nod to her daughter, who was busy with her smartphone. "She can't go back to the apartment."

"She can sleep with Pam," said Rachel, who was always ready with Plan B. "I'm sure she wouldn't mind sharing with Elizabeth."

"I'm thleeping with Pam," insisted Ted, encountering some skepticism from his friends.

"Maybe not, buddy," said Bill.

"Might be wiser to give Pam some space," said Bob.

"She seems pretty angry," said Sid.

"And jealous of all the time you've been spending with Richard," said Rachel. "She feels neglected."

"I don't blame her," said Bill, giving Lucy a meaningful glance.

She knew what he meant, thinking guiltily of her efforts to solve the murders. She knew only too well that he didn't appreciate her tendency to investigate crimes that sometimes put her in compromising situations.

"I don't go looking for trouble. It seems to find me," she said. "Take today. Elizabeth's bag was stolen in the Métro."

"You don't think it's connected to the murders, do you?" asked Sue.

Lucy seized on the idea. "I didn't, but now that you mention it . . ."

"No, Mom," said Elizabeth. "It was just a pickpocket. Happens all the time."

"The Louvre is papered with notices warning about them," said Rachel.

"A handy cover for somebody who's after something he thinks you've got," said Lucy. "I think we should call Girard."

"No need." Elizabeth was consulting her smartphone. "He just texted me. It's okay for me to go back to my apartment. The lock's been fixed, and they're done checking for fingerprints."

"No way!" declared Lucy. "You're staying right here with us, where it's safe."

"Safe? Are you crazy? Look at him!" Elizabeth pointed to Ted. "And this place was tossed, too. It's not safe here. It's not safe anywhere, but in my own place. . . ." She paused, obviously rephrasing her thoughts. "I really just want to be by myself."

"And how are you going to get there tonight?" asked Lucy. "The Métro's impossible due to the slowdown."

"I got a ride from a friend."

"How?" demanded Lucy. "When?"

"Just now, on my phone," replied Elizabeth in a "How dumb can you be?" tone of voice.

Bill got right to the heart of the matter. "Who? Who's giving you this ride?"

"Really?" Elizabeth cocked her eyebrow. "I don't think it's any of your business."

From outside, they heard a couple of quick beeps.

"He's here," she said, dashing for the door. "Bye."

Bill was right after her, rushing out the door and following her down the stairs. When he came back, he shrugged. "It was a guy from work. Serge something. He seems nice enough. He has a motorcycle."

"Oh, no!" moaned Lucy. "You didn't let her go, did you?"

"What could I do?" He paused. "Like I said, he seems nice. He even had a helmet for her to wear."

"So that makes it all right?"

"Not really," sighed Bill. "But we can't lock her up like Rapunzel, can we?"

"I wish we could," said Lucy.

"Daughters," muttered Sid, adding a sympathetic nod. "Well, life goes on. We've got to eat. . . ."

"Eathy for you," groused Ted.

"We'll pick up some soup for you," said Sue. "I guess I'll grab another fillet steak and some bread and salad at the Monoprix. Okay with you all?"

"Sure. I'll go with you," offered Rachel.

Lucy was tired and wanted some time to herself, so she went into the living room and turned on the TV, watching the news report of the Métro slowdown and trying to follow the weather report. There was definitely rain in the Pyrenees, but that was all she understood, unable to translate the Celsius temperature into Fahrenheit. There was a simple formula. She'd learned it once but couldn't remember it now, when the knowledge would actually be useful. Life was like that, she thought.

When Sue and Rachel returned, they arranged a buffet on the kitchen island and encouraged everyone to help themselves. Lucy took a piece of steak and a bit of salad and retreated to her spot on the sofa. She wanted to be alone with her worries about Elizabeth and her irrational anger toward Bill. She knew she was being unreasonable. There wasn't anything he could have done differently, but at least he could worry along with her. Instead, he was sitting with the others at the big table, where the wine was flowing along with the jokes, most of which were at Ted's expense. Ted was taking it good-naturedly, however, now that Pam had returned and was sitting by his side.

Eventually, even Lucy gave up and joined the others for coffee and dessert, little tubs of packaged chocolate mousse that was surprisingly delicious.

"I'm really going to miss the Monoprix when I get

back home," declared Sue. "Everything's so good . . . the bread, the cheese. Even the butter is more buttery somehow."

"That's if we ever get home," said Bob. "I'll call Air France tomorrow and see what we have to do to change our flight."

"And I'll check in with Sidra," offered Sue, "and see what Norah wants to do about our accommodations."

"Try for the Cavendish," said Pam.

"I wouldn't advise it," said Lucy, licking the last bits of chocolate off her spoon. "I'm beginning to think the Cavendish is a cover for crime."

"Like Bertram's Hotel in the Agatha Christie book?" asked Rachel.

"Exactly," said Lucy.

"But even Miss Marple appreciated the service at Bertram's," said Rachel.

"I could use some five-star pampering," said Pam.

"I'll see what I can do," promised Sue.

After dinner, when the dishes were finally all washed and put away, Lucy retreated to the old-fashioned bathroom for a long restorative soak in the huge tub. Her feet and legs were tired from so much walking, and she was emotionally drained. It had been a very long day, beginning with the trip to Chartres and the meeting with Madame Seydoux. Lucy tried to put herself in Madame's shoes, but no matter how hard she tried, she could not understand Madame's strange reaction to her daughter's death. It was all too easy for Lucy to imagine the horror of losing one of her children. She lived with that fear constantly. Whenever she read of a young person killed in a car accident or a missing college coed, she knew in her heart that there was no immunity from tragedy, which could strike unexpectedly at any time. She and Bill had done their best to raise sensible, careful kids who didn't engage in risky behaviors, but as Elizabeth had demonstrated that very evening, much of their advice had gone in one ear and out the other.

Madame Seydoux clearly mourned her daughter: she'd been quite tearful when Lucy and Elizabeth expressed their condolences. But when they told her about the money Sylvie had hidden, her attitude had changed. That bothered Lucy, who found it unseemly. Kids benefitted financially, sometimes, when their parents died, but it was unusual for a parent to inherit money from a child. Maybe that was it. Maybe there had been a communication gap. Maybe what she was taking for greed was something else. Incredulity. Surprise. Shock. Maybe even the suspicion that Sylvie had been involved in something illegal and that was why she was killed. Now, that was something Lucy could understand, she decided, reluctantly pulling herself out of the steamy bathwater and reaching for a towel.

The apartment was quiet when she made her way down the long hall to the living room, where Bill had pulled out the sleeper sofa and was already sound asleep. She pulled back the covers and slipped in beside him, nestling her back against his chest. He stirred and wrapped his arm around her, pulling her closer.

It was cozy in bed, and Lucy was tired. She didn't think she'd have any trouble falling asleep, but she did. The problem, she decided, was her aching legs, a reaction to all that walking. So she got up and tiptoed down the long hall to the bathroom, where she took a couple of ibuprofen.

That should do it, she thought, slipping back between the sheets. This time, when she nestled against Bill, he groaned and flipped over, turning his back to her. Unfazed, she nuzzled against him, slipping her arm around his waist, and closed her eyes. When she had trouble sleeping, she had a trick of picturing the waves rolling in over the rocky shore at Tinker's Cove. With each breath she took, she imagined the foamy water spreading over the speckled pebbles, and as she exhaled, she pictured the seawater withdrawing in the timeless rhythm of the sea. Tonight, however, other images kept intruding on her visual mantra: the blood that pooled on the floor beneath Chef Larry, the euros pouring out of the envelope onto Sylvie's bedding, the tidal wave of commuters in the Métro station, and the roar of the motorcycle that carried Elizabeth off into the night.

Checking the time on her phone, she saw it wasn't all that late, not even eleven. Elizabeth was probably still awake. It wasn't too late to call and make sure she was okay. Lucy slipped out of bed once again, taking the phone with her into the kitchen, where she made the call.

Perhaps she was wrong, she decided, as the call went straight to voice mail. Elizabeth had turned her phone off, as she was probably having an early night. It was completely understandable, thought Lucy. Her daughter was probably tired after all that walking, too. Or maybe she'd just forgotten to charge it. Kids were like that.

Lucy opened the fridge, intending to have a glass of milk, but the container was almost empty, with only enough for Bill and the others who took milk with their morning coffee. She personally didn't see the point of diluting coffee with milk, but she wasn't about to deprive anyone of their favorite morning beverage. She shut the refrigerator door, wishing there was some way she could reassure herself that Elizabeth was safe, but the Métro slowdown meant she'd have to walk. On the other hand, she realized, she wasn't going to get to sleep anytime soon. A stroll in the night air might be just what she needed, and if it took her clear across town to Elizabeth's apartment, so much the better.

Since they didn't have a room of their own with an armoire, Lucy and Bill had stashed their suitcases in their bathroom, which made it easy for Lucy to throw on some clothes without disturbing anyone. Before she knew it, she was down the stairs and in the moonlit courtyard, where she spied several bicycles neatly stored in a rack.

Considering the French fondness for locks of all kinds, she expected the bikes to be secured, but when she took a closer look, she found no restraints of any kind. Weird, but lucky for her, she decided, rolling one of the bikes across the cobblestoned courtyard and out to the street. She was just borrowing it. She'd put it back exactly where she found it.

It was great fun riding through the empty streets of Paris—well, not exactly empty, but the traffic was much lighter than during the day. The sidewalks were broad, and she tried to stay on them as much as possible, carefully avoiding the few pedestrians she encountered. The Métro slowdown had done her a favor, she decided, guessing that most people were staying home.

As she zipped through the dark streets, feeling free and rather giddy, she almost forgot the purpose of her midnight excursion. A speeding police car with flashing blue lights was a stark reminder, and she bent lower over the handlebars and pedaled harder, with new determination.

Finally arriving at Elizabeth's street, she looked up at the dormer windows of her daughter's apartment and found them glowing with light. *Good.* Elizabeth was awake. She rang the buzzer but, receiving no reply, grew anxious. She rang again. This time Elizabeth's voice came over the intercom.

"*Oui?*"

"It's Mom," said Lucy. "I just wanted to make sure you're okay."

There was a long pause. "I am. I'm fine."

Lucy didn't think Elizabeth sounded fine. She imagined a guy with a two-day beard and a shaved head holding a knife to her daughter's throat. "Are you sure?"

"I'm sure, Mom. Everything's fine. Go home."

"I'm not going until I see you," said Lucy. "Buzz me in."

"No, Mom. That's crazy."

"Let me in, or I'll call the cops," said Lucy.

"You are stark, raving mad," said Elizabeth.

"After all that's happened, I don't think I'm crazy to worry about you. I'm not kidding. I've got Girard's number right here."

There was a long sound of static, which Lucy thought was a sigh, and then the buzzer sounded. She yanked the bike through the door and stowed it on a rack with others, then started the climb up to Elizabeth's attic apartment. When she reached the top floor, she found Elizabeth's door open. Elizabeth was leaning against the jamb, her hair mussed and she was wearing a silky kimono. Her cheeks were flushed, and her lips were very plump and red.

"You've seen me," said Elizabeth. "Now please go home."

"You're with a man!" exclaimed Lucy, genuinely shocked.

"And what if I am?" demanded Elizabeth. "I'm a big girl now."

"Who is it?" demanded Lucy.

"It's none of your business, Mom. Now, go on home."

Lucy's mind was reeling. She was embarrassed, horrified, appalled. She felt the floor tilting this way and that beneath her. "I just wanted to make sure you're okay," she said, speaking in a very small voice.

Elizabeth was laughing. "Never better, Mom. Trust me."

"Okay," said Lucy, heading down the stairs. Halfway down the first flight she turned. "Is it that Serge?" she asked, but Elizabeth was gone and the door was closed.

Chapter Nineteen

When Lucy got back to the apartment, Bill was still sound asleep. She snuggled in beside him, but even though her body was tired, her mind was racing. She knew the usual advice for insomnia was to get out of bed and do something until you felt tired, but perhaps riding a bicycle through nighttime Paris wasn't quite what the advice columnists meant, especially if it meant finding yourself in an excruciatingly embarrassing situation. She tried to tell herself that Elizabeth was a grown woman, capable of managing her own love affairs, but she didn't quite believe it.

In her heart, she realized with a shock, she distrusted all Frenchmen. It seemed to her that they were egotistical, self-absorbed, cared way much too much about fashion, and were much too casual about sex. They didn't respect women, at least not in the way she expected. Of course, she admitted, her experience was limited pretty much to Bill and the example set by her father. But why couldn't Elizabeth settle down with a man like Bill? He was dependable, he drank beer, he liked sports, and he didn't care what he wore as long as it was clean and comfortable. Like her dad, he never cried, and she liked that about him.

She thought about Chris Kennedy and wished things had worked out differently. He was a nice guy, and he'd certainly seemed stuck on Elizabeth, but that was apparently all over. She wondered if Elizabeth hadn't encouraged him enough. The days when a girl could play hard to get were long past. Now that men were all so afraid of commitment, she had to help him along. She couldn't throw herself at him, of course. It had to be subtle, and Elizabeth wasn't subtle. Maybe that was the problem. Or maybe Elizabeth was right, and he really was focused on his career right now.

It had been so much simpler for her. She and Bill met in college and started going steady. They got engaged during senior year and were married the week after graduation. She'd never had a career, really, just a series of jobs until she got pregnant with Toby. Then they'd moved to Tinker's Cove, and her focus was on their growing family. She enjoyed her part-time job at the *Pennysaver* newspaper, but it was hardly what you'd call a career. Phyllis, the receptionist at the paper, always said they were really volunteers, because the pay was so low, and Lucy was lucky if her check covered a week's worth of groceries and a tank of gas.

Sometimes she wondered if she'd made a mistake by missing out on a career, but she didn't think so. She was happy with her life, and she wanted Elizabeth to be happy, too, and she didn't think having casual sex with every Frenchman who came along was the way to achieve that. Especially now, when you couldn't tell the good guys from the terrorists and criminals. What did Elizabeth really know about Serge? What if he turned out to be one of those monsters who preyed on women, a French version of Ted Bundy?

Her thoughts kept going round and round, until

eventually she heard the birds chirping in the vines that covered the building and Bill woke up.

"Damn birds," he muttered, burying his head in her neck. "Just like home."

"I wish," sighed Lucy. "I wish we were home."

She debated with herself whether to tell Bill about her midnight adventure and finally decided he didn't need to know. He'd be furious with her, for one thing, and she wasn't sure how he'd react to the idea of his daughter having an active sex life. But it was Elizabeth herself who broke the news, calling her father on his cell phone and catching him when Lucy was busy in the bathroom.

"What were you doing running all over Paris last night?" he demanded, confronting Lucy as she poured herself a cup of coffee. For once, they were alone in the kitchen.

"I was worried about Elizabeth. I called, and she didn't answer, so I borrowed one of those bikes downstairs and went over to her apartment."

"She says you woke her up, and she's worried that you're freaking out."

"Woke her up? That's funny," said Lucy.

Bill furrowed his eyebrows. "What do you mean?"

Lucy would never have said it if Elizabeth hadn't put her in the awkward position of having to defend herself. "She was entertaining a male caller," said Lucy, regretting the words the moment she said them.

"My little girl?" demanded Bill. "Are you sure?"

"She's a woman, Bill," said Lucy. "And I'm quite sure."

"Who was it?"

"Putting two and two together, since she left here on a motorcycle with Serge, I imagine it was him."

"That bastard," growled Bill.

"You said he seemed nice. He made her wear a helmet," said Lucy, throwing her husband's words back at him.

"That was before I knew he was screwing my daughter."

"Look, I'm glad to know she survived the night," said Lucy. "I don't trust anybody anymore."

"Neither do I," said Bill. "I'm going to have a word with this guy, make sure he knows that he'd better treat my daughter right, or he'll have me to deal with."

"I don't think that's a good idea, Bill," said Lucy, but it was too late. Bill was already on his way out the door.

She put her coffee down and ran after him, grabbing her coat and handbag as she went and catching up to him as he rounded the corner and headed for the Métro station. The slowdown was over, and the trains were running on schedule today, delivering them to the boulevard Haussmann in record time, which Lucy found ironic. If only the Métro workers had continued their protest today, she wouldn't be in this situation, terrified her husband was going to get in a fight and end up in one of those dreadful French prisons.

"Please, Bill, we can't meddle in Elizabeth's love life," she protested as the doorman in his splendid green Cavendish uniform trimmed with gold braid held the door wide open and Bill marched into the lobby, looking very much like a man with a mission.

Elizabeth was seated at her desk and spotted them; she hopped to her feet and met them in the middle of the enormous lobby. "What are you doing here?" she demanded.

"I want a word with that Serge fellow," said Bill.

"You can't do that," she protested.

"Why not?"

"Well, because . . . ," Elizabeth began, hesitating. "Because he's not here."

"Funny, isn't that him right over there?" asked Bill.

He was high on testosterone, thought Lucy. That was the only explanation. She reached for his arm, trying to restrain him, but he brushed her off and strode across the plush carpet, planting himself in front of Serge. "I understand you've been seeing my daughter," he said. His voice was even, but Lucy noticed Bill was clenching and unclenching his fist, itching to punch Serge in the face. She hurried after him, trailed by Elizabeth.

Serge didn't seem the least bit intimidated, however. "Yes, I have," he said in a respectful tone, taking Elizabeth's hand. "Elizabeth is a lovely woman, and I have great respect for her and her family."

"Well," said Bill, somewhat deflated, "that's good."

"I would never do anything to hurt Elizabeth," continued Serge, gazing at her fondly.

It occurred to Lucy that he truly was ridiculously handsome, and the French accent didn't hurt, either. More importantly, he did seem to care for Elizabeth. Perhaps he was even in love with her.

"Of course not," said Bill. "That's exactly what I wanted to hear."

"You understand why we're concerned," said Lucy. "After what happened to Sylvie . . ."

"Absolutely," agreed Serge with a solemn nod.

"And Chef Larry," continued Lucy. "I've heard rumors he was involved in something dodgy here at the hotel, and since you work here, too, naturally we were . . ."

"It is understandable that you would be concerned. Rest assured, we are conducting our own investigation here at the hotel," said Serge. "We are cooperating with the police and expect the matter to be resolved, perhaps as soon as today."

Lucy could hardly believe it, wondering if this meant the police were finally wrapping up the investigation of the murders. Maybe this awful nightmare was coming to an end. "Really?"

"I am hopeful," said Serge, leaning close to Lucy and Bill. "I don't know the details, but we have all been told to watch for a certain man, an American. If he comes, we are to call the police *immédiatement.*"

"I just got his photo," said Elizabeth, "but I haven't had a chance to look at it."

"Maybe your parents know him," suggested Serge.

"I doubt it very much," said Lucy, thinking it was ridiculous for Serge to think all Americans in Paris must be acquainted with each other. "We hardly know anyone in Paris."

Reaching the ornate boulle desk that served as the concierge's post, Elizabeth picked up an interoffice manila envelope and brought it over to the group. Getting a nod from Serge, she returned to her post at the concierge's desk, where a guest was waiting for her.

Lucy unwrapped the little string fastener and pulled out a grainy photo, shocked to discover she recognized the man captured by the security camera.

"That's Richard Mason!" she exclaimed.

"It sure is," said Bill, shaking his head. "There must be some mistake."

"*Impossible,*" said Serge. "The investigation has been very thorough."

"I can't believe it," insisted Lucy. "He's such a nice guy." She paused. "Ted's going to be devastated. Imagine. His best friend is involved in the black market."

"Not merely involved," said Serge. "He is the—what you call it?—brains of the operation."

Hearing this, Lucy felt dizzy and felt as if her legs

were going to give way. Bill caught her by the elbow, and she leaned unsteadily against him. Taking in the situation, Serge was quick to act.

"Perhaps you would like some refreshment? I can arrange for complimentary service in our Marquis de Lafayette Café."

"That would be great," said Bill. "We didn't have any breakfast."

"It is better to hear bad news on a full stomach," said Serge, leading the way down a lushly carpeted hallway, past the discreetly labeled restrooms, to a sun-filled restaurant overlooking a walled garden. He had a quick word with the maître d', and they were seated on upholstered chairs at a linen-covered table beside one of the several French windows and provided with menus.

Acting on Serge's murmured instructions, a waiter immediately brought Lucy a glass of orange juice, which she sipped gratefully. The sugar gave her a boost, and she began to feel better.

"I guess I'll go for the American breakfast," said Bill, scanning the international array of offerings, which included a Japanese breakfast of miso soup, steamed rice, a soft-boiled egg and pickles, as well as a *petit déjeuner pour le chien* of steak tartare, Badoit water, and a genuine Milk-Bone biscuit.

"They'll even feed your dog, for a hefty price," he said, trying to distract Lucy, who was, in fact, rallying and was beginning to take in the luxurious surroundings: the gleaming silver and porcelain, the potted orchids, the pleasant background music.

A waiter arrived with a silver pot of coffee for each of them, and they gave their orders. Bill stuck with the American of two fried eggs with bacon and home fries, and Lucy chose the classic continental, with croissants and brioches. Soon they were tucking into the delicious food, enjoying every bite, although Lucy's enjoyment was tempered with guilt.

"The rich are different," said Bill, wiping his lips with the enormous linen napkin. "They eat better food."

"But not much of it," said Lucy, with a glance at the very thin ladies seated at the next table. Their teased and tangerine-colored hair was the most substantial part of their stick-figure bodies.

A waiter appeared at the table and inquired if their breakfasts had been satisfactory, and Bill asked for the check, just in case he'd misunderstood Serge's invitation. He hadn't, and the request was dismissed with a smile.

"We do hope you'll come again," said the maître d' as they departed, the plush carpet giving them the feeling that they were walking on clouds.

"That was lovely," said Lucy as they emerged onto the busy boulevard Haussmann, where hurrying Parisians on their way to work were dodging the cleaners spraying the sidewalk with water and the gardeners tending the potted plants outside the grand hotels. "I can see how Richard was tempted. The good life can be addicting."

"Let's amble on down and take a look at the Palais Garnier," suggested Bill. "I could use some gentle exercise, if you feel up to it."

"I am fully recovered, and I could use a little distraction," said Lucy, taking his arm and strolling along, enjoying the passing parade. "She looks like a secretary, don't you think?" said Lucy, with a nod at a simply dressed girl absorbed in checking her cell phone.

"Top executive," said Bill, checking out a tall man in a beautifully tailored striped suit, carrying a very thin, very expensive briefcase.

"Janitor?" guessed Lucy, referring to a disheveled fellow whose plaid shirttails were flapping.

"No, too young. I bet he's a techie," said Bill.

Lucy chuckled, then stopped abruptly and grabbed Bill's arm. "Speak of the devil, that's Richard."

"You're right," said Bill, spotting the journalist striding along on the opposite side of the boulevard, wearing a messenger bag and involved in a cell phone conversation. "Do you think he's headed for the Cavendish?"

"Let's find out," said Lucy, turning around and heading in the opposite direction.

"What if he spots us?" cautioned Bill.

"What if he does? He doesn't know that we know about his illegal activities."

"I feel crummy about this," said Bill. "He's headed for a trap, and he was nice to us. Remember that seafood dinner?"

"Which we now know he paid for with ill-gotten gains," said Lucy. "Even in Paris I don't think journalists make a lot of money."

As Richard neared the Cavendish Hotel, he suddenly dashed across the street, taking advantage of a break in the traffic. Lucy and Bill had nowhere to go and couldn't avoid an encounter, even if they'd wanted to, which Lucy certainly did not.

"Richard!" she exclaimed. "You're out and about bright and early."

"Lucy, Bill! I could say the same to you. I thought vacationers like yourselves would want to sleep in."

"Not in Paris," said Lucy. "There's too much to see."

"Have you time for a quick coffee?" he asked, glancing at a nearby café, where a handful of diners were seated at the outside tables, sipping coffee and perusing their morning papers.

Bill started to make an excuse, but Lucy seized on the invitation. "We're on vacation, so we've got plenty of time," she said. "We're flaneurs today."

"That's the best way to experience Paris," said Richard. "Forget about *Fodor's* list of must-sees and just relax and experience it."

The three seated themselves at one of the tiny round tables, and they were soon provided with tiny cups of espresso coffee. Richard downed his in one gulp, but Lucy and Bill sipped at theirs. Richard was a charming conversationalist, and they passed a pleasant quarter hour, during which Lucy found it increasingly difficult to believe Serge's accusation. How could this wonderful, generous man be involved in crime? She had to know.

"I've heard strange rumors about you, Richard," she said, getting a sharp kick in the ankle from Bill. "That you have a second career."

Richard seemed taken aback and blinked a few times before pasting a smile on his face. "Paris is full of rumors," he said. "I do pick up a little extra here and there. I have to. Paris is expensive, and a journalist's salary, well, it doesn't begin to cover the rent."

"But you don't do anything illegal, do you?" asked Bill, offering him a way out.

Richard tilted his head this way and that, grinning slyly. "I guess it depends what you think is illegal," said Richard. "Sometimes I do skate on thin ice, if you know what I mean, but I'd never hurt anyone. That's my red line, and I don't cross it. A bit here, a bit there, sure, but only from those who won't miss it. Big companies who rip off their customers and have lots of insurance, they factor a certain amount of loss into their budgets, right?"

"I suppose they do," said Lucy. "But sometimes people do get hurt, like Chef Larry."

Richard's genial manner was gone, replaced with a stone face. "Chef Larry got himself killed, and that's the truth."

Something in his tone struck Lucy, prompting a memory. "You were at the hospital the day he died," she said, but Richard was already on his feet, making a show of checking his watch.

"Thanks for the coffee," he said. "I'm afraid I have to dash. I'm running late."

"Didn't Richard invite us for coffee?" asked Bill, signaling the waiter for the check.

"Yeah," said Lucy. "What of it?"

"Well, he should have paid for the coffees, right?"

"Oh, I have a feeling he's going to pay a hefty price," said Lucy, watching as Richard gave a nod to the doorman and entered the Cavendish Hotel.

A few moments later the *woo-wah* of sirens was heard, and a small fleet of tiny police cars with flashing blue lights swarmed down the boulevard, braking in front of the hotel. The flics dashed in, and moments later Richard emerged, handcuffed, and was stuffed into the back of a van. A few passersby stopped to watch, but the excitement was almost over before it began, and the police cars vanished as quickly as they had come.

"I wouldn't want to be in his shoes," said Bill, counting out euros and putting them on the table.

They were preparing to leave—Lucy was slipping the strap of her handbag over her head—when they noticed a harassed-looking Malik practically collapsing onto a café chair and lighting a cigarette with shaking hands.

This was her chance, she thought. She'd never have another opportunity to question him. "Malik, are you okay?" she asked, approaching his table.

Malik's shoulders jumped. He was clearly startled, but he relaxed a bit upon recognizing Bill and Lucy. "Monsieur and Madame Stone," he said, hopping to his feet. *"Enchanté."*

"We were just leaving," said Bill. "I guess you had some excitement at the hotel."

"You saw? The flics, they arrested a man." He took a long drag on his cigarette, clearly upset.

"But it was nothing to do with you, right?" asked Lucy.

"Not this time, but you never know, not when you are *un étranger,* like me. They see brown skin, and it means you're not French, so you're guilty."

"Come on, Malik," said Lucy. "It's time to come clean. We know you and Adil searched our apartment, and you tried to break into Elizabeth's place, too. What were you looking for?"

"Never!" he exclaimed, his dark eyes darting nervously from one to the other.

"There's a video. You're on tape," said Bill.

"The police questioned us," he said, surprising Lucy. "But we had alibis. We were with Adil's grandfather. He told them so." It was obvious he was reciting an agreed upon story, and realizing he didn't sound very convincing, he added, "And the video images were not clear." He paused, and this time his voice had the ring of truth. "But it was not so good at work. We were put on probation."

Lucy's emotions were in turmoil. On one hand, she felt guilty about getting the boys in trouble, but on the other, she was positive they had tossed the apartment. Even worse, they'd tried to break into Elizabeth's place. "Look, I think you and Adil are good guys, but you're involved in something dangerous," she said. "I know Sylvie had a lot of money. . . ."

He was suddenly on it, like a drug-sniffing dog scenting a stash of coke. "You found it?"

"In her room. We gave it to the police."

He sat down hard, his head in his hands. "I'm so screwed."

"Whose money was it?" asked Lucy.

"Adil's grandfather's, well, not his, exactly. It's for the royalists, to restore the monarchy in Egypt. They are raising lots of money, and he asked us to hold it, to hide it for the group. His father was King Farouk's advisor. He remembers the king giving him chocolates." Malik shrugged. "A fat, old, rich man gave a little boy a piece of candy all those years ago, and he doesn't forget. He does all sorts of illegal stuff and makes his grandson get involved, and me, the friend of his grandson, I cannot betray them. It is a matter of honor. I have to help, and so I will end up in jail."

"You could go to the police, tell them what you know in exchange for immunity," said Lucy.

"You're a French citizen, right?" asked Bill. "You have rights."

Malik laughed, scoffing at Bill's naïveté. "I'm a legal citizen. I have a French passport, *oui*. But there's lots of things they can charge me with, and that's before they even get to the money. I don't get treated the same, because I'm not white and not Catholic."

"Most French people aren't religious," said Lucy, confused.

"*C'est vrai.* They don't go to church on Sunday, and they don't even believe in their white God with the long beard, but the babies are all christened, the marriages are in church, and the funerals are very traditional. You'll see, if you go tomorrow. Sylvie will be buried at the Cimetière Montparnasse. The priest will be there in his robes, and his words will promise eternal life and salvation. For that *putain*."

Lucy was shocked at his vehemence, at the venom in his tone, as he spit out the word *putain*, calling the woman she thought was his friend a whore. "Tell me you had nothing to do with her death," she said, practically pleading.

"Me? No. I had nothing to do with it." He stared at his hands, large hands. "I don't think the police will believe me. I think I will, like in your gangster movies, take the fall."

"Son, you need a lawyer," said Bill.

Malik grimaced. "They'll give me a lawyer, a lawyer who will make sure I'm the one who gets locked up."

"Look, is there some way we can help?" asked Bill.

"*Les Américains* always want to help. It's not World War II," said Malik, standing up. "I have to get back to work. I'm on thin ice as it is. Au revoir."

"Au revoir," repeated Lucy, wondering if she really ever would see Malik again.

"That was weird," said Bill, taking Lucy by the arm and resuming their stroll. "Do you think we should tell Lapointe?"

"No," said Lucy, hoping she wasn't making a mistake, but unwilling to betray Malik. She knew he had lied to her, but she couldn't help feeling protective of this young man who was in such a difficult situation. Poor Malik was caught between two cultures, neither of which was exactly warm and fuzzy. She only hoped she wouldn't regret her decision. "You're not a rat, see," she said, imitating James Cagney. "And neither am I, see?"

Feeling a bit at loose ends, they continued on to the Palais Garnier, where they took the tour and Lucy gazed for a long time at the Chagall mural on the ceiling, which depicted colorful abstract figures swirling in an endless dance. Slightly dizzy, she let Bill lead her to a bistro for lunch, where they finished off a bottle of *vin rouge*. Slightly giddy, they spent the afternoon on a *bateau-mouche,* cruising the Seine.

When the boat docked, they knew they'd put it off as long as they could and now they were going to have to tell Ted about his friend Richard. They stopped at a café for a quick brandy and, thus fortified, climbed the stairs to the apartment with heavy hearts.

But when they entered, they found the group members were all in high spirits.

"Guess what?" demanded Bob, who was practically giddy with excitement. "We got our passports!"

Lucy's and Bill's eyes met. "Really? You've got our passports?"

"Right here," said Bob, handing them over with a flourish. "We can make our flight on Sunday. We're going home!"

"That's great," said Lucy, running her fingers over the smooth leatherette booklet with the gold seal of the United States of America. Such a little thing, maybe four by six inches, she thought, and you handed it over at immigration checkpoints as if it were an airplane ticket. But it had the power to open national borders when you had it; without it you were really and truly stuck. She opened it and glanced at the unflattering photo, checking that she had the correct document, then closed it and tucked it in the zip pocket of her purse to keep it safe.

"A toast!" suggested Ted, raising his glass. "*Vive l'Amérique!*"

"*Vive l'Amérique!*" she repeated, accepting a glass of champagne and joining the others in the toast. This was not the time, she decided, to deliver bad news. And if she had suspicions about Adil and Malik, if she wasn't entirely convinced of their innocence, it didn't matter. For once, she was willing to admit that she didn't understand what was going on and it would be better to leave matters in the capable hands of the police. She was going home!

Chapter Twenty

Sid had just popped the cork on the second bottle of champagne when Ted commented that he'd been trying to reach Richard ever since they got the good news, but all his calls had gone to voice mail.

"That's unusual for him, isn't it?" said Pam, accepting a refill. "Maybe he forgot to charge his phone."

"Not Richard. He always stays connected. He doesn't want to miss a story. I think ink runs in his veins. He's a real old-fashioned reporter."

Lucy's and Bill's eyes met, Bill gave her a nod, and Lucy took the plunge. "I'm afraid I've got bad news, Ted. Richard was arrested this morning at the Cavendish."

Suddenly everyone was silent. It was as if the champagne had gone flat.

Finally, Ted spoke. "That's impossible."

"We were there. We saw the police take him away in handcuffs," said Lucy. "I'm sorry."

"But why?" asked Pam.

"The hotel did an internal investigation into the black market ring and discovered that Richard was running it," said Bill.

There was a long stunned silence as the group processed the news.

Finally, Sue spoke. "So he was partners with Chef Larry?" she asked.

"Something like that," said Lucy.

"Come to think of it, he never seemed short of cash," said Pam.

"That seafood dinner must've cost a thousand euros, easy," said Ted.

"He didn't even blink at the bill," said Pam. "I feel so guilty. I ate the lobster and the shrimp as if I was entitled to it, and it was all paid for with dirty money."

"Richard was a generous host," said Bill, "when he was spending other people's money."

"He was certainly a smooth operator," said Sue. "I had no idea that he even knew Chef Larry. They sure had me fooled. I really thought we were getting all that champagne and wine at legitimate wholesale prices."

"Stop it!" yelled Ted in a quavering voice. His face was red, and his hands were trembling. "Richard's my friend, and he's in trouble."

"Sorry," murmured Bill.

"I'm out of here," declared Ted, heading for the door, with Pam dashing after him.

"He needs some time," said Rachel. "This is like a death. He has to come to terms with it. He has to work through a lot of disturbing information. The fact that Richard wasn't honest with him makes even their friendship suspect. Imagine the sense of betrayal."

"Does he stick with Richard or turn against him?" mused Bill.

"That's the question," said Bob. "I see families grappling with it all the time in my legal practice when a beloved family member runs afoul of the law. The ones who do the best are the ones who decide to love the sinner but hate the sin."

"But the sinner committed the sin," said Lucy.

"We're all flawed," said Rachel in a gentle voice. "We have to accept that and forgive those who make mistakes. Nobody's perfect."

"Easy to say but hard to do," said Sid.

Forgiveness became even harder the next morning, when the lead story in the *International New York Times* broke the news that one of the paper's own reporters had been arrested and charged with the murder of Laurence Bruneau, a noted chef and *pâtissier*. The motive, police charged, was a dispute resulting from the pair's involvement in a black market operation at several high-end hotels, including the Cavendish, an operation that stole liquor and expensive foods, such as truffles and caviar, and sold them through a phony wholesale company.

Ted read a paragraph or two, then tossed the paper on the floor. "Trash," he declared. "This isn't journalism. They're just reporting the prosecution's side of the story!"

"You never really know another person," said Lucy, but Ted was having none of it.

"Maybe you believe this stuff, but I'm sticking by my friend," said Ted, heading for his room and slamming the door behind him.

"Denial," whispered Rachel. "It's the first stage of grief."

"But not the last," said Lucy, wishing there was some way to prepare herself for the overwhelming sadness she knew she would feel at Sylvie's funeral, scheduled for later that morning. If only there was a product like sunblock for grief: if you plastered on SPF 50, the grief would bounce right off, instead of burning through your defenses and rekindling long-buried sorrows. Whenever she attended a funeral, Lucy found herself grieving once again for her parents, gone for years now, and dear friends who had met untimely deaths, and she prayed for the health and safety of those she loved.

Paris was a gray city, but nowhere was it grayer on this rainy Saturday than the Cimetière Montparnasse, where the narrow cobbled pathways were lined with bulky tombs and looming statuary, dotted with a few trees, their leaves dripping. According to Lucy's guide-book, a lot of famous people were buried there, including sexy rock star Serge Gainsbourg, and famous authors and lovers Simone de Beauvoir and Jean-Paul Sartre. Their tombs were marked with lipstick kisses and gifts of cigarettes, which Lucy felt was a desecration. She de-cided she preferred the spacious, neat, and grassy ceme-tery perched high on a hill overlooking the harbor in Tinker's Cove, where tributes were limited to geraniums planted on Memorial Day and tasteful baskets of ever-greens placed on graves at Christmas.

Lucy and Bill found the somber group gathered for Sylvie's burial and spotted Elizabeth among them, stand-ing with Serge and a number of other hotel employees. Malik and Adil were also there, she noticed, standing rather uneasily on the edge of the group, as if they were no longer accepted by the others. She raised a hand in a small wave, but neither responded, both apparently wrapped up in their own thoughts.

Lucy and Bill were not able to stand next to Elizabeth without jostling and disturbing other mourners, so they took places at the foot of the grave. Elizabeth pointedly avoided looking at them. She was hanging on to Serge's arm and gazing fixedly at the open grave, where Sylvie's rain-spattered coffin was balanced above the void. Lucy wondered what her daughter was thinking. *There but for the grace of God go I?* Or perhaps she was regretting that she hadn't been closer to Sylvie. Or maybe she was simply thinking about paint colors for the apartment.

Monsieur and Madame Seydoux were standing on the opposite side of the grave, accompanied by a nun, who was saying the rosary. It was impossible to know if they were receiving any comfort from the recitation. Their faces were grim, and they seemed terribly tired, defeated by this most cruel and unfair twist of fate. The priest had had the foresight to cover his skullcap with a clear plastic protector, and the sight of it, and the cheap plastic poncho covering his vestments, struck Lucy as wildly incongruous.

She was working hard to stifle a nervous giggle when he began to intone the words of the funeral service, and she tried to focus on the French words of the burial service, but she was distracted by a sudden flurry of movement. To her horror, she saw that Adil and Malik had suddenly sprung into action and had grabbed Elizabeth by the arms and were dragging her away from the gathered mourners and through the cemetery, toward a cobbled roadway, where a white van waited, its motor running.

"Stop! *Arrêtez!* Stop!" she screamed, taking off after them. This was her worst nightmare come true, and Lucy could hardly believe what she was seeing. She was struggling on the uneven paving, slipping on the wet stones in her leather pumps, weaving through the narrow spaces between the graves, her heart pounding. Bill overtook her, and Serge dashed ahead of him, gaining on the abductors. Elizabeth was screaming and struggling, trying to free herself, but her captors had almost reached the van when a whistle blew and it suddenly seemed that the cemetery was filled with black-clad commandos.

A shot was fired, and the sound startled Lucy. Her ankle bent under her, and she fell to the ground, banging her elbow painfully on a raised grave. Tears stung her eyes as she struggled to her feet, desperate to save Elizabeth, who was being shoved into the van. The rear door was slammed shut, and the engine roared as the wheels spun on the slimy stone paving, then lurched forward toward the gate. Adil and Malik took off in opposite directions, leaping over the graves as if they were hurdles. A sharp pain tore through her ankle, and Lucy grabbed a stone angel, bent sorrowfully over the grave of a child, for support.

Then there were more shots, and the van veered toward the stone wall, crashing against it. The commandos were everywhere, swarming through the cemetery in their bulletproof vests and helmets. Bill was beside her, supporting her, and they ran toward the van, only to be stopped by a commando armed with a nasty-looking machine gun. Lucy recognized him, with a shock, as the guy who had been following them, the guy she'd chewed out at the café. So the *proc* had been telling the truth, she realized. The group had actually been under police surveillance.

"That's our daughter," Lucy cried, watching as Elizabeth was helped from the rear of the van by another commando. A commando who was taking a rather extreme interest in Elizabeth, she thought, watching as he attempted to wrap his arm around her waist. Elizabeth shook him off, and Lucy could hear her daughter insisting that she was perfectly fine and didn't need any help, thank you. Then she suddenly lost her footing and was caught by the commando, who scooped her up in his arms and carried her to her parents. He set Elizabeth down on a raised grave, then raised his visor, and Lucy realized the man she thought was a French commando was actually Chris Kennedy.

But her attention was focused on Elizabeth. Lucy hugged her as tight as she could, and for once, Elizabeth didn't pull away. She let her mother smooth her damp curls away from her face, she let her father pat her on her shoulder, and she let Lucy wipe her face with a crumpled old tissue. Then she had enough.

"Okay," she demanded, glaring at Chris. "What the hell is going on?"

"What are you doing here?" asked Lucy.

"Who are you?" demanded Bill.

"Sorry, sir. I'm Secret Service agent Chris Kennedy, and I'm an old friend of Elizabeth's." He extended his hand, and Bill took it, giving it a firm shake.

"Secret Service?" asked Bill.

"Yes. I believe Elizabeth has a valuable coin in her possession, which, as a United States citizen, she is obliged to surrender."

"That's crazy," said Elizabeth.

Lucy's thoughts were beginning to sort themselves out. "Your good luck piece . . . ," prompted Lucy.

"That old thing?" Elizabeth slipped her hand into the waistband of her skirt and produced a slim leather purse, which she unzipped. "It's just some funny old coin," she said, pulling out a large, somewhat grimy coin. "I found it in the bathroom when I was cleaning. It was behind a loose tile. I don't think it's worth anything."

"It's a Double Eagle," said Chris. "They were taken out of circulation when the U.S. went off the gold standard, and it's illegal to have one."

"Weird," said Elizabeth, extending her hand with the coin, ready to give it to Chris.

But before he could take it, a gray-haired man in a pin-striped gray suit knocked into Elizabeth, snarling at her. "*Putain stupide!*" he hissed, lunging for the coin, only to be neatly blocked by Serge, who delivered a sharp jab to the man's windpipe, causing him to fall to the ground, gasping for air.

"Nicely done," said Chris approvingly, pulling the old guy to his feet. He remained defiant even as the handcuffs were applied, glaring evilly at Elizabeth.

"I know you," said Elizabeth. "You're Adil's grandfather. I worked with you at the hotel, setting up your meeting."

Lucy had a sudden flashback, recalling a worn pin-striped suit in that exact shade of gray and a head of thick silver hair. Sylvie had been bent over, moving the table in the restaurant the day they all went to the flea market. He'd brushed against her, making his way to the door. Her eyes had met his, and there'd been a moment of recognition, a flicker of fear. "You're the one. You killed her," said Lucy.

There was a cry, and Madame Seydoux threw herself on him, grabbing him by the neck. It took two commandos to pull her off him, but still she struggled as they held her by the arms, spitting at him.

"She deserved what she got. It was a pleasure to punish her," he snarled, glaring at Madame. "*Pas respectable, pas gentille, pas chaste.* Exactly what you'd expect from a mother like you."

Madame Seydoux collapsed in her husband's arms, wailing.

Sadek wasn't through, however, even though the commandos were hustling him away. He turned toward Elizabeth, stretching his neck out like a wrinkled old snapping turtle. "You are filth, just like her," he hissed before he was finally dragged away and loaded into a police van.

Elizabeth watched, waiting until the doors of the van were closed on Khalid Sadek and he was out of sight. "What a horrible, nasty old man," she said.

A shout, a yelp of pain, caught their attention, and their heads turned in time to see a flic twisting Adil's arm behind his back as he cuffed him and pushed him into the back of a police car, where Malik was already confined.

This time Lucy was the one who turned away. She no longer felt the least shred of sympathy for either young man.

"You had a close call," said Serge, with a nod at the coffin containing Sylvie's body. He slipped his arm around Elizabeth's waist, supporting her.

"Not that close," said Chris, bristling. "I was here, and I wasn't going to let anything bad happen to Elizabeth."

"You could've acted a little sooner," complained Elizabeth. "I was really scared."

"We had to wait long enough to get evidence," said Chris.

"So I was like a pawn? How far were you going to let them go?" demanded Elizabeth.

"Let's talk about it over dinner," suggested Chris.

Elizabeth did not seem inclined to accept his invitation, so Lucy intervened. "Good idea. We're all going to Le Grand Colbert tonight. Why don't you both join us? I bet you've got a lot to tell us, Chris."

"Only if Serge can come, too," said Elizabeth.

"Of course," said Lucy, who knew when it was time to cut her losses. "We'd be delighted if Serge would join us."

"I would be honored," said Serge, taking her hand and kissing it.

Looking over Serge's shoulder, Lucy got the clear impression that Chris was not delighted.

A *woo-wah* siren broke the silence, and the diminished group of mourners watched as the police cars left the cemetery, lights flashing. Then they gathered once again around the open grave and prepared to commit Sylvie's body to the earth, to eternity.

That evening the group gathered at a long table against the back wall of the bistro, where Sue informed them they had to have the chicken, because that was what Diane Keaton had in the movie *Something's Gotta Give,* when she jilted Keanu Reeves and admitted she really loved Jack Nicholson.

"I would've stuck with Keanu Reeves," said Sue, grinning wickedly at Elizabeth, who was seated with Serge on one side and Chris on the other. Serge looked very continental, wearing a silky black T-shirt beneath his suit jacket, while Chris was the all-American boy in a button-down oxford shirt and boxy blue blazer.

"Not me," said Lucy. "Keanu was a little too . . ."

"Young?" offered Rachel.

Lucy searched for the right word. "He was too nice. Jack was a bit of a diamond in the rough."

While the conversation was aimed at Elizabeth, she seemed oblivious and was thoroughly enjoying the attention of her two rival swains. Bill noticed, too, and decided to put an end to it.

"Okay, guys," he said. "I think we deserve an explanation." He gave Serge a nod. "Let's start with Chef Larry and the black market ring."

"D'accord," began Serge, scratching his chin. "It's pretty simple, really. Chef Laurence worked at the Cavendish. That's where he got his start as a sous-chef. He was eventually promoted and put in charge of the ordering process. That was part of his job, and he started padding the orders, keeping some for himself. That's how he made enough money to open his school and his shop. At some point Richard Mason found out about it. He was an investigative reporter, *non?*"

"I still can't believe Richard was involved," said Ted, shaking his head ruefully.

"Maybe not. It is for the court to decide. But the police believe that Richard demanded more and more of the profits, and Chef Laurence didn't like that. They had a fight of some sort, there were knives, and Richard stabbed Chef Laurence. Maybe true, maybe not, but *c'est dommage.* It looks like your friend will be going to jail for a while. *Les flics* say they have enough evidence about the stolen goods to get a conviction, even if they can't pin the stabbing on him. They do have witnesses who saw him at the hospital on the day of the general strike, just before Chef Larry was found dead. The flics believe Richard smothered Chef Laurence so he could not identify him as his attacker."

"It's hard to believe," said Pam, covering Ted's hand with her own and squeezing it. "Richard is an old and dear friend."

"People change," said Rachel. "In a different culture, it's easier to give in to temptation. He may have felt a certain sense of immunity, believing that nobody here knew him, unlike at home."

"You mean like Vegas?" asked Sid. "What happens in Vegas stays in Vegas?"

Sid's comment elicited a few chuckles, and spirits rose as the waiter arrived with a couple of bottles of wine. When everyone's glass had been filled and orders had been taken, Lucy turned to Chris.

"So tell us about the coin, the Golden Eagle."

"Actually, it's a Double Eagle. When the U.S. went off

the gold standard, everybody had to turn in their gold coins, but a few remained uncollected, mostly belonging to noncitizens. The Secret Service has been tracking them for years, and we knew that King Farouk had at least one, and probably more. When he was deposed, a few faithful followers left Egypt with him, and we think he gave this particular Double Eagle to his advisor, as a token of appreciation for his faithful service. The advisor was Khalid Sadek's father, and when he died, the coin came into his possession.

"There's always been a small faction desiring the reestablishment of the monarchy, but it wasn't until the recent events in Egypt, the end of the Mubarak regime and the continuing turmoil, that the royalist movement picked up steam. Sadek realized that the Double Eagle could be used to raise money to finance a coup that would put Prince Fouad back in power, but it wasn't the sort of thing you could take to a pawnshop. It would have to be a top secret deal. He couldn't risk the U.S. getting wind of it, so he entrusted the coin to his grandson, Adil, who hid it in Elizabeth and Sylvie's apartment while they sought a buyer. They had already entrusted Sylvie with funds they had raised from contributors, funds they wanted to hide from the tax authorities. Unfortunately for Adil, Elizabeth is a good housekeeper. . . ."

"That's news to me," muttered Lucy, getting a scowl from her daughter.

"And she found the coin when she was cleaning and kept it for good luck. It wasn't good luck for Adil, however, when he tried to retrieve the Double Eagle and found it was gone. That's when he and Malik searched your vacation apartment, desperate to find the coin. When it didn't turn up, Sadek seized Sylvie, demanding to know what she'd done with it. When she couldn't tell him, she was killed." Chris paused. "I suspect Sadek wanted to go after Elizabeth next. That's when Adil and Malik bought some time by attempting to search her apartment. When that didn't work out, he ordered them to nab her at the cemetery. Elizabeth was going to be next."

"That's so scary," said Elizabeth, struggling to come to grips with her close escape. "I had no idea it was worth anything. I thought it was one of those weird French coins, ecus or francs or something that went out when the euro came in."

"You weren't far wrong," said Chris, "except it's American instead of French."

"Didn't you look at it?" asked Bill.

"Not really. I thought it was sort of pretty, so I kept it. I just threw it in my coin purse. I thought it would be good luck," admitted Elizabeth. "Is it worth a lot?"

Chris nodded. "One was auctioned a few years ago. The Secret Service made a deal with the owner and got a percentage of the sale price, which was almost eight million dollars."

Stunned, Elizabeth collapsed against the banquette. "I had a coin worth eight million dollars?"

"*Sacré,*" breathed Serge.

"Probably more now," said Chris.

"I was carrying it around like a lucky penny," said Elizabeth.

"That would be something like eight billion lucky pennies," said Bob.

"More like one billion," said Serge, getting a few puzzled looks. "I went to Sciences Po," he said with an apologetic shrug.

"That's a *grande école, n'est-ce pas?* A top university. Very impressive," said Sue.

Chris wasn't about to let that pass. "Maybe the coin was good luck, after all," he said, taking Elizabeth's hand. "It brought us together again."

Elizabeth withdrew her hand and took a sip of wine. Her enigmatic little smile reminded Lucy of the *Mona Lisa,* which she'd seen in the Louvre, where it always attracted a crowd of admirers. "Maybe," said Elizabeth, swirling the wine in her glass and taking another sip. "Maybe."